GLASS
FAERIE

Also by Rachel Morgan

Writing as Rochelle Morgan

GLASS FAERIE

CREEPY HOLLOW, BOOK SEVEN

RACHEL MORGAN

PART I

CHAPTER ONE

In the dirty alley between Tygo's Diner and the abandoned library, the stench of rotting garbage provokes my gag reflex. I focus on breathing through my mouth as I remove the crumpled brown paper package from my messenger bag and hold it up. "You know the price, Slade." I wave the package at him. "Take it or leave it."

Slade raises an eyebrow. He breathes out a painfully long sigh before turning to the wad of notes in his hand. He flicks lazily through them, counting out the right amount. But instead of handing the money over, he leans one shoulder against the wall and watches me with a smirk. "You drive a hard bargain, Emerson Clarke."

"Stop being an idiot. The price is exactly the same as last time. Do you want it or not?"

"Course I want it. Lighten up, Em." He shrugs, his shoulder rubbing against the giant yellow X graffitied across the bricks. "Just trying to make this exchange more entertaining."

I shove the bag against his chest and remove the cash from his hand. "I don't need any more entertainment in my life."

"Hey, you seriously need to chill out," he calls after me as I turn away.

"Thanks for the advice." I don't bother to look over my shoulder at him as I stride away, my sneakers crunching against the damp, dirty ground. I'm almost at the end of the alley when the back door of Tygo's Diner swings open. I dodge out of the way to avoid being hit in the face. "Jeez, Marty."

"Oh, great, you're still here." He holds a trash bag out toward me. "You forgot this one."

I consider telling him my shift ended five minutes ago, but it isn't worth the argument. I press my lips together, push Slade's money into my jeans pocket, and take the bag. Marty lets the door slam shut without another word. Grumbling beneath my breath, I walk the few steps back toward the dumpster. Slade, still slouching at the other end of the alley, ignores me as I hold my breath, lift the dumpster lid, and heft the trash bag up and over the edge.

I'm about to lower the lid when I hear rustling from within the dumpster. *Just a rat*, I tell myself, knowing I should close the lid. But that part of my brain that always wants to know if the things I see and hear are actually real keeps my arm frozen in place. The scratching, rustling sound moves up the side of the dumpster. A scaly arm appears, clawing its way over the edge with blue talons and glowing yellow liquid dripping from—

I drop the lid and jump back, swearing out loud.

"Scared of something, Em?" Slade sniggers as he walks past me.

"No," I snap back. But as he rounds the corner and disappears, I swallow, my heart thudding way too fast. I peek around the side of the dumpster, looking for a half-squashed reptilian arm protruding from beneath the lid. But there's nothing there. "Overactive imagination," I mutter to myself as I hurry away, which is the same lie I always use.

I feel easier once I'm out on the main street. Hooking my thumb beneath the strap of my messenger bag, I slow my steps, no longer feeling as though I'm running from something. My fear evaporates as I remind myself that with Slade's money added to my savings, I finally have enough for a bus trip.

"Hey, Em!"

I swing around in the direction of the shout and find Val perched atop the wall surrounding Stanmeade Elementary School. "Hey." I wave at her as I change direction and cross the grassy area outside the school. I dump my bag on the ground, then run straight at the wall. My right foot strikes the bricks and launches me upward. With my palms flat on top of the wall, it's easy to pull my legs up.

"Nice one," Val says as I walk deftly along the top of the wall toward her.

"Thanks." I sit beside her and dust my hands on my jeans. "It's an easy wall, though. Not as high as some of the others we've tried."

"I know. Hey, check this out." She pushes her dark frizzy hair out of her face and holds her phone in front of me. "Latest Top Ten video from ParkourForLife."

Looking past the crack on Val's cellphone screen, I watch a guy leap from one building, somersault through the air, and land on the next building, followed by nine more spectacular moves. "Awesome," I murmur. "I'd love to be able to do all that."

"Totally," Val agrees. "I kinda feel like we'll have to go somewhere else to stretch our skills though. The urban playground here is just too limiting."

"The urban playground?" I repeat with a laugh.

"Yeah. People call it that, right?"

"Um …"

"Well, I call it that." She spreads her arms out, almost smacking me in the face with her elbow. "I present to you the Stanmeade urban playground. It's ugly, but it's where we started."

I shake my head, still smiling. "You got the ugly part right. And the limiting part. We know this place and its obstacles too well now."

"Yeah. Anyway, how was your shift?"

I shrug. "Slightly above average. I sold another one of Chelsea's homemade concoctions. Slade Murphy again."

"Again? Ooh, do tell. What secret recurring ailment is Slade Murphy suffering from? Anything super embarrassing we should warn his girlfriend about?"

"It was actually for his girlfriend. A contraceptive tea of some sort."

Val tilts her head back and laughs. "Well, let's hope that works."

"I guess it must be working, since this is the second pack I sold him. Anyway, that's not important." I pull my sleeves down to cover my thumbs. "What's important is that I've finally saved enough for another bus ride."

Val straightens. "To visit your mom?"

"Yes, obviously."

"Cool," she says, though her voice lacks enthusiasm.

"What?"

"It's just ..." She shifts a little. "Are you sure you want to do that? It really upset you last time you visited her."

I chew on my lower lip before answering. "I know, but I'm hoping it'll be different this time. She might be better. Besides, it'll be worth it to get out of this place for a little bit. I'm counting the days until I don't have to share a house with pain-in-the-ass people anymore."

"I hear ya," Val says, her curls bouncing as she nods. I know she doesn't entirely mean it, though. Our family situations are both tough, but in completely different ways. While I'm stuck with an aunt who hates me and a prima donna cousin, Val has four younger siblings her mom expects her to help take care of. And I know Val loves them, despite all her complaining. So in a few months' time when we're finally done with school, I have a feeling I'll be leaving on my own.

"Hey! Get off there!" We look over our shoulders into the school yard where Mrs. Pringleton is shaking her bony finger at us.

"But we're not doing anything wrong," Val shouts back.

Her gnarled hands form fists, and the pink birthmarks across one side of her face turn pinker. "I'm calling the police if you don't get off there in the next ten seconds!"

"Cool," Val says. "Tell Uncle Pete I say hi."

"Val." I nudge her arm while trying to keep from laughing. "Let's not give the old woman a heart attack, okay? We can climb right back up once she leaves."

"Fiiiiine." Val shuffles her butt to the edge of the wall and jumps down. I follow a moment later. "I guess I should go home to the mini monsters anyway," she adds. "But I'm giving myself another five minutes of freedom first." She sits on the grass and crosses her legs.

"Fine by me." I remain standing but lean back against the wall and play with the edge of my sleeve. "You're probably already in trouble for being late, so what's an extra five minutes?"

"Exactly."

A car rumbles by, and on the other side of the road I notice a person who wasn't there a minute ago. A guy with an annoyingly familiar swagger to his step. "Wonderful," I mutter. "What's Dash doing back here?"

"Hmm?" Val looks up. "Oh. Probably going to the party."

"What party?"

She twists her head to the side and looks up at me. "You know, the one at the Mason farmhouse."

"I didn't know, actually. Is Jade's brother home again?"

"Yeah. Supposedly looking after Jade and the other Mason kid while their parents are away."

"And instead he's throwing another party," I say with a sigh.

"Yeah. Lucky for us lowly high-schoolers."

"Sure. If that's your thing." I look back across the road at Dash. As always, he's highlighted his honey-blond hair with streaks of bright green. All I can do is shake my head at the odd color combination. "His hair is so weird. I don't know how they let him get away with it at whatever preppy school he goes to."

"You don't know how they let him get away with amazing hair?" Val asks with a laugh.

"No, I mean the color."

She laughs harder and shakes her head. "I don't know what you could possibly find offensive about that boy's beautiful hair, but okay. I won't argue with you."

I look down at her with a frown. "Beautiful hair? Really?"

She shrugs. "What can I say? I find him attractive."

I groan and look up once more, and Dash chooses that moment to glance across the street, give us a charming grin, and wink. "Seriously?" I mutter. "Who the hell winks at people?"

"Dash, apparently, although probably only at you." Val smacks my ankle. "You know he loves to irritate you. Anyway, you should come to the party. If Dash came all the way home for it, you know it's gonna be good."

"Please. Dash is probably bored out of his mind at whatever uptight, snooty private school he goes to. No doubt he jumps at the chance to go to *any* party."

"So ... does that mean you'll come?"

I shake my head as I watch Dash continue on down the street. "Not my scene, Val. You know that."

"You know you can still come to parties even if you don't want to drink, right?"

"So I can stand there totally sober and watch the rest of you get hammered? No thanks."

"Or you could just have a *little* bit." She pats my sneaker. "You need to chill out more, Em."

I fold my arms across my chest. "Remember how my uncle died of alcohol poisoning? And how my mom tried to drown out her delusions by drinking? Yeah. I'm trying to avoid situations like that."

Val is quiet as she gets to her feet. "Come on, Em. You know that's never going to happen to you."

I blink away the memory of that scaly, glowing arm reaching out of the dumpster. "Okay, here's a reason for you: Dash is going to be at that party, and I don't feel like ruining my night."

"Okay, okay, I get it. You're not coming to the party." She loops an arm around my neck and hugs me. "Try to have a good evening anyway."

"Thanks. I'll see you tomorrow."

We head in different directions, Val walking around the back of the school to cut across the field, while I continue along the road. Long shadows stretch across the pavement, and the washed-out orangey brown haze of sunset fills the sky. I turn just after the post office—

—and see a figure in a silver hooded cloak standing in the middle of the road. In front of him or her is a man with pointed ears. The cloaked figure touches the man, and the man becomes a solid statue of gleaming, faceted crystal.

With a gasp, I duck back behind the building, my heart thundering. I press my back against the warm brick wall and slap both hands over my eyes. I count to ten while forcing myself to breathe slowly. "There's nothing there," I whisper to myself. I start counting again, and this time I keep going. I reach eighty before I'm brave enough to lower my hands from my face. Slowly, I peek around the edge of the building—and of course, there's no sign that a hooded figure and a person made of crystal were ever there. *Because they weren't*, I tell myself. I press my back against the wall once more. "You didn't see anything," I whisper. "There was nothing there. You didn't see anything strange. You are not losing your mind."

But as I hurry along the main road, choosing to take the longer route home, I can't help thinking of all the times weird things like this have happened. The unidentifiable creature sitting on the park swing one day. That man with the pointed ears who came to the diner one afternoon. And that time I looked in the bathroom mirror and for just a moment, my hair was blue. "I'm not losing my mind," I repeat quietly, almost desperately. This is probably related to something I saw on TV. Or something I read. My brain is processing something fictional and regurgitating it more vividly than I expected. This is what people mean when they talk about an overactive imagination, right? "Yeah, that must be it," I murmur, choosing the same explanation as always. "That must be it."

It must be *anything* except the obvious: that I'm turning out just like my mother.

I try to keep my gaze focused on the ground at my feet the rest of the way home, not wanting to see anything I shouldn't be seeing. It's a much longer journey than if I'd used the street I was supposed to use. The street the cloaked figure was on. It's dark by the time I reach our driveway, and I almost run up it and around the side of Chelsea's house. I'm never this eager to get home, but I've somehow convinced myself that I'll be safe once I get inside. I let myself in through the kitchen door and take a moment to breathe as the door clicks shut behind me.

A boiling pot containing something that smells like it could be pasta sits on the stove. Through the open door that leads to the garage salon, I hear Chelsea and Georgia chatting. My earlier fear begins to seem silly in comparison to the ordinariness around me.

I cross the kitchen without calling hello to Chelsea and Georgia. They won't particularly care that I'm home, and I don't particularly care to greet them. Instead, I head straight for my bedroom, removing the money from my pocket as I go. I force my door open, shoving it past yet another box of Chelsea's salon supplies that seems to have found its way into this room since this morning. I let my messenger bag slip off my shoulder and onto the bed, my focus now on counting out my commission from the money Slade paid me. The rest, of course, goes to dear Aunt Chelsea. She's the one who makes the weird herbal remedies.

I pull my ice cream tub of toiletries off the shelf above my bed and look inside it for the resealable plastic bag I keep my savings in. I'll count it all now and make sure I have enough, then buy a bus ticket tomorrow. I riffle through the various bottles, my fingers feeling for the crumpled plastic bag.

It's gone.

My stomach drops as I empty the tub's contents onto my bed, just to be sure. I spread everything out, but the little zipper bag definitely isn't there. My skin grows cold, then hot. That was months and *months* of savings, all so that I could visit Mom, and now it's *gone*?

My hands become fists as I storm out of the room and head straight for the salon. I find Georgia lounging in one of the chairs, staring at herself in the mirror as she combs her hand through her sleek blonde hair. On the opposite side of the room, Chelsea stocks the shelves with more of her homemade herbal products.

"Where's my money?" I demand.

Georgia jumps in fright and almost slips out of her chair, but Chelsea is still for a moment before turning to face me. "*Your* money, Emerson?" she says. "I think you mean *my* money."

"Excuse me?"

"You've been stealing from me for months."

"*Stealing* from—I have never stolen a single thing from you. I always give you exactly what you're due and only keep the percentage I'm allowed. You know that."

"Right." Chelsea crosses her arms and nods. "And then you go back to my bedroom afterwards and steal whatever you want. Money's been going missing from my purse for months now. At first I thought I was imagining it, that it must be my mistake, but then I started keeping track of exactly how much was there." She gives me a triumphant smile, as if she's done something wonderfully clever. "And you know what I discovered? Small amounts of money started to disappear every week or so. And look where I found it." She digs in her pocket and pulls out a plastic bag. *My* plastic bag.

"That is my hard-earned savings," I tell her, feeling a knot of nausea forming in my stomach. "That is not yours."

"Don't lie to me. I know how you girls spend money. As if it grows on trees and you have no responsibilities in the world. What I want to know is where is the rest of it?" She shakes the bag in the air between us. "Because you've taken way more than what's left here."

"I didn't steal from you!" I shout. I glance at Georgia, who's watching the two of us with a small smile. My anger increases a level as I point at her. "You want to know where your money's been going? *That's* where you should be looking."

"Don't you dare pin this on Georgia. She would never steal from me."

"Well it isn't me, so that doesn't leave anyone else, does it."

Chelsea lets out an incredulous laugh. "I cannot believe you, Emerson. After everything I've done for you. I work so hard to take care of both of you, and this is how you repay me? You steal from me and then you run all over town doing that useless parkour nonsense."

"Everything?" I repeat. "Did you say after *everything* you've done for me?" Normally I'd keep my mouth shut. I'd bite down my anger and let her try to convince herself how amazingly charitable she is. But not this time. Not when she's taken my one chance at visiting Mom. "You mean giving me Georgia's second-hand clothing, making me sleep in what is essentially your storeroom for *five years*, and using me as your live-in maid?"

"I gave you a home," she shouts. "You should be grateful for the roof over your head. What would have happened to you if there'd been no one to take you in after they locked your mother up? Your father sure as hell didn't want you. He seems to be covering all your mother's medical bills in that fancy faraway hospital, but is he interested in supporting you? Nope. I've never even met the man."

Chelsea's used this tack before to try to hurt me, but it never works. I couldn't care less about my father or the fact that he has no interest in me. I don't even know what he looks like. "Please," I say between clenched teeth. "Just give me back my money."

"You're not getting this money back, Emerson. End of story." Chelsea tucks the plastic bag back into her pocket and turns to her shelves of herbal garbage. Georgia pushes herself out of her chair and leaves the room. I stand there feeling sick, my body shaking, finally realizing that the hope I've been holding onto for months—the hope of finally visiting Mom again—is gone. And I can't even blame Chelsea for it. Not entirely. Not when someone else is responsible for this mess.

I stride out of the salon and head for Georgia's room. She's sitting on her bed with a magazine, smiling sweetly, knowingly.

"It was you," I say, taking a few steps into her room. "You told her where my money was."

She lowers the magazine. "What could you possibly need all that money for, Em? You know we need it to keep the household running. How could you be so selfish?"

"How could *you* be so selfish stealing from your own mother?"

"I *need* things," she says. "Things you don't need. Things you wouldn't understand, and Mom doesn't seem to understand either."

I glare at her for another few moments, my anger so intense I could *scream*. But it would do no good. I still have to get through another few months here, and so I clamp my mouth shut, turn around, and aim for the door.

But that's when I see it: Hanging from a knob on the wardrobe, the tag still attached to the hem, is a brand new dress. "*This* is the stuff you need?" I demand, grabbing the hanger, spinning around, and shaking the dress at her.

"Yes." She sits a little straighter, as if I've finally got her attention now that I'm threatening her clothing. "I have a boyfriend and a social life and a future. That kind of stuff doesn't come for free. You have to look good if you want to—"

I fling the dress at her, and she yelps as it hits the side of her head. "You bought a *dress*?" I yell. "I've been saving for almost a year so I could visit my mother, and you took that away from me for a *DRESS*?"

Something flashes across the room. Light and heat and the sound of a sizzle. It vanishes as Georgia falls back against the pillows with a scream.

Fear cracks through my anger, drenching me in goosebumps. I rush over to Georgia. "What's wrong? What happened?"

She shoves me away with one hand, the other covering her cheek. "What the hell did you do to me?" she gasps, her eyes wider than I've ever seen them.

"I didn't do—"

"You threw something at me! Like a firecracker or something. You freak, what is *wrong* with—"

"I didn't throw anything!"

"Get off her!" Chelsea's hands wrap around my shoulders and tug me backward.

In the quiet that follows, all I hear is my heavy breathing and Georgia's whimpering. She lowers her hand, revealing blood seeping from a shallow gash across her cheek. She glares at me with renewed hatred. "Oh, my poor baby," Chelsea gasps, grabbing a tissue from the box on the nightstand. She drops onto the bed beside Georgia and presses the tissue against her cheek before turning her scowl toward me. "I can't do this anymore, Em. You have never shown any gratitude for the sacrifices I've had to make for you. You've stolen from me, and now you've physically assaulted Georgia. The police can deal with you."

"The *police?*"

She stands and brushes past me. "You're not my problem anymore." I follow her into the kitchen where she picks up her phone from the table. When she taps a few numbers and brings the phone to her ear, I realize she isn't joking.

Fear dissolves my anger. "Chelsea, wait. I'm sorry. Georgia provoked me, but I shouldn't have lost my temper like that. It won't happen again. You don't have to bring the cops into this. Please." I feel sick having to beg her, having to plead with this woman who's made me scrub toilets, do Georgia's laundry, lie to the various men she's always stringing along, and then demand my gratitude for the privilege of doing all these things for her. But it's only for a few more months. Then I'll be eighteen, school will be done, and I can make a plan to get out of here. But if the police get involved, who knows where I'll end up.

"No," Chelsea says. "I can't believe you're making me do this, but I have no choice now. I have to protect my daughter."

"Chelsea, please. Protect her from what?" I step closer, clasping my hands together beneath my chin. "I swear I'll never—"

"You're going to end up as crazy as your mother," she snaps, "and I don't want you in this house when that happens."

I reel back as if she slapped me.

"Hello?" she says into the phone, turning away from me. "Yes, um, please can you send someone to—"

I bolt past her toward the back door.

"Hey, get back here!" she yells as I tug the door open and run.

But I don't go back. And I don't stop running.

CHAPTER TWO

I RACE ACROSS THE BACKYARD, SCALE THE NEIGHBOR'S fence, and easily vault the low wall on the other side of their garden. I have no plan other than to get as far away from home as possible before the cops show up. My sneakers slam pavements and my body launches across several more obstacles before I realize I'm heading for Val's house. I get about halfway there when I remember she won't be home. I'm not sure what time that party was supposed to start, but things generally get going pretty early around here. It's not like there's much else to do. Besides, Val's house is probably the first place Chelsea will send the cops.

I slow my steps and place my hands on my hips as I catch my breath. My heart is thrumming, my body almost vibrating. I force myself to take a long, slow breath. "What the hell are you doing?" I mutter to myself. Maybe I shouldn't have run. Maybe I should have stayed and explained myself. What's the worst that could have happened?

You're going to end up as crazy as your mother.

If the cops believe Chelsea—if someone performs some kind of medical test on me and her words turn out to be *true*—then the worst that could happen isn't a physical assault charge. It isn't juvy or community service or whatever the local law enforcement decides is a suitable punishment for me. No, the worst thing would be ending up in a facility just like my mother's. Locked away to keep me from hurting others. Drugged to keep me from seeing things that aren't there.

Basically, my worst nightmare would come true.

I find myself running again, this time toward Jade Mason's place on the outskirts of town. It's further away than I remember, and I'm breathless by the time I get there. I slow down near the bottom of the long driveway so I'm not a sweaty, panting mess when I reach the party.

Outside the Masons' house, I find people milling around beside a bonfire and others sitting on the porch. Music reaches my ears. Not seeing Val anywhere outside, I run up the porch steps and into the house.

"Yo, Em, you made it this time." Eric, the idiot who sits next to me in English class, nods at me from where he's leaning against the hallway wall with some of his friends. "Hey, did you bring any of that herbal stuff your aunt sells?" He makes a few thrusting motions with his pelvis while his friends laugh. "You know how it gets me—"

"Is Val here?" I ask.

"Yeah, that way." He jerks his head toward the living room at the other end of the hallway. "Want a drink first?"

I walk past him without answering, letting the howls and boos from his friends mingle with the thumping background music. In the dim, smoky living room, Dash is standing just inside the doorway, commanding an audience of several girls. His eyebrows twitch momentarily into a frown when he sees me, but it only lasts a moment. Then he shakes his head and smirks.

Ignoring him, I walk into the room and spot Val on a couch with a bunch of our classmates. She has a cup in each hand. "Val!" I hurry over to her.

"Hey, you came." She beams at me as she shuffles over and nods her head toward the open spot on the couch. "Come sit here."

"No, I'm—can I talk to you?"

She must hear the urgency in my voice—or perhaps see it on my face—because she pushes herself to her feet immediately. "Something wrong?" she asks, walking with me to the edge of the room. We stop beside a window. My body still feels like it's humming, so I shake my hands, roll my shoulders, and force myself to breathe out slowly. Val frowns. "Em, what is it?"

"Chelsea found my stash of money. She freaked out and accused me of stealing from her."

"What? No way. You would never *steal* from her."

"Of course I wouldn't. It was obviously Georgia, but there's no point in telling Chelsea that. She would never believe her little angel capable of stealing. And then ... I—I lost my temper, and Georgia and I were fighting, and I scratched her face." I can't tell Val it wasn't me. I can't tell her that something strange and inexplicable happened in that room. She'd probably look at me the same way Chelsea did in the kitchen. *You're going to end up as crazy as your mother.* "And then she said she can't deal with me anymore and called the cops."

"Seriously?" Val looks at me as if she may not have heard correctly. "Chelsea called the cops because you scratched Georgia? That's ridiculous."

"I know. But …" I look around. "Is your cousin here? Lexi? If I can talk to her, then she can explain to her dad what actually happened, and he can tell the other cops, and then they won't take me away."

"Take you away?" Val starts laughing. "Em, you need to chill. Uncle Pete isn't going to take this seriously. He knows you're not, like, an actual criminal. Maybe he'll make you pick up litter in the park or something, just to keep Chelsea happy, but he isn't going to *take you away.*"

Suddenly I wonder if I'm being as silly as Val seems to think. It was just a scratch, after all. Well, a bit more than a scratch, but hardly life-threatening. "You think?" I run a hand through my hair, not willing to relax just yet.

"Yeah, come on. This is a small town. We all know each other. People don't get locked up for something this stupid."

"I guess."

"What do you mean you *guess*?" She smiles and nudges me with one hand still grasping a cup. Cold liquid sloshes over the edge and splashes my arm. "Obviously I'm right about this. So just relax. Have fun. Get a drink."

I sigh, trying to breathe out my panic and not fully succeeding. "You remember that this kind of setting isn't exactly my idea of fun, right?"

"I know. But Jade's brother's friend Marcus is gonna be here soon, and I need backup. You know I get weird when I'm left alone with a hot guy. Please stay."

I don't exactly *want* to stay, but it's probably the best option. Chelsea wasn't joking about pressing charges—or attempting to, at least—but she'll probably calm down if I give her a bit of space for the night. "Yeah, okay."

"Yay." Val grins. "Here, have a drink." She holds one of her cups out toward me, then rolls her eyes at my raised eyebrow. "It's non-alcoholic, I promise. Gotta stay hydrated, remember? Alcoholic—" she lifts the other cup "—and non-alcoholic."

I hesitate, but I'm thirsty after working in the diner's kitchen all afternoon, taking the extra-long route home, and then running across town to get here. I realize it's been hours since I drank anything. "Thanks." I survey the room over the top of the cup as I take a gulp, expecting something sweet and fizzy. But the drink burns like fire all the way down my throat. I cough and splutter and shove the cup back toward Val.

"What's wrong?"

"Val, this is awful," I manage to say. "What's in it?"

With a confused expression, she takes the cup from me and sips. Then she raises the other cup, sniffs, and tastes it. "Hmm." Her frown deepens. "I guess they both have alcohol. I must have finished the soda already." She shrugs. "Oh well. At least you only had a little."

"Val!"

"What? I'm sorry. I didn't do it on purpose. And one sip isn't going to kill you."

I cough again, trying to rid my throat of the burning sensation. "It was a bit more than a sip," I mutter.

Val downs the remainder of one cup, then leaves it on the windowsill and grasps my hand. As she tugs me behind her, I hope we're headed back to the couch I found her on. Instead, she pulls me into the next room where too many people are squished together, nodding their heads in time to the beat and yelling to each other over the music.

Val leans into me and says, "Ooh, Marcus is here already. See him over there in the corner? And you can snuggle up to that guy he's with. Maybe we'll both end up with someone by the end of the night, and then we'll go double-dating and get married and live happily ever after."

I shake my head at Val's ridiculous daydreams. "Right, and then they'll cheat on us, and we'll both end up alone like our moms."

"Hey!" Val smacks my arm, but her smile jumps back into place as she pulls me across the room toward Marcus and his friend. The friend's name is Trent, and sure, he's not bad to look at, but I'm way too distracted to enjoy his company. I lean against the wall, playing with the hairband around my wrist and occasionally nodding so the three of them think I'm paying attention to their conversation. Instead, my thoughts are far away, flitting continuously between Chelsea's words—*you're going to end up as crazy as your mother*—the cloaked person I imagined on the street, and the unexplained gash across Georgia's cheek. Around and around my thoughts go, until nothing seems to make sense anymore.

I become aware that my body is still humming. Probably Val's awful drink. *That doesn't make sense*, my thoughts whisper at the back of my mind, but I've never drunk alcohol before, so how would I know? Maybe everyone starts to feel strange after one giant sip.

Val is looking at me, smiling and speaking, and I try to follow what she's saying, but I can't seem to focus anymore. Her words slip in one side of my head and out the other, and the room is somehow … *tilting* just the slightest. I look at the floor, but it seems normal. This feeling in my head isn't normal, though. This hazy semi-awareness. The sensation that I'm cocooned in something soft that dampens the *thump*, *thump*, *thump* of the music and the sound of Val's voice. Perhaps I should be concerned, but I can't find the part of me that cares. The part of me that wants to fall into this soft cocoon and sleep is taking over.

I remember the couch in the next room. "I'm just … gonna …" I point to the door and start moving toward it. I've never had to concentrate on walking upright, but it's strangely difficult right now. The floor keeps wanting to move up toward me.

The couch is packed with people. They wouldn't like it if I lay down on them, so I manage to maneuver my way out of the room and into the hallway. I drag my hand along the wall, keeping myself upright as I make my way to the front door. The air outside is cooler, fresher. I stand on the porch for a while, leaning against the railing and breathing in deeply until I notice the air isn't that fresh after all. It smells like smoke.

I need to get home. I need to walk and breathe and leave this weird haziness behind. I need to *sleep*. Everything will be clearer when I wake up in the morning.

The porch stairs are a challenge, but I manage to navigate them. I'm relieved to be on the grass and moving away from the house and the people, but the cotton-wool stuffiness in my brain seems to follow me.

"Hey, there you are." Val appears at my side. "Are you leaving already?"

"Whatareyou … doingoutside?" I pause, open my mouth wider, and focus intently on not slurring my next words. "You should be in there with your hot guy."

"Ugh, no, I just said the dumbest thing ever. Marcus looked at me like I was a kid. *So* embarrassing. I swear, I wish the earth had just split open and swallowed me whole."

"So what?" I mumble, my voice resonating oddly in my ears as I sway on the spot. "Then let the earth split open and swallow you whole."

A tremor rumbles beneath our feet. "What was that?" Val asks.

With a grinding screech, a jagged line zigzags across the garden, tearing the earth open. Terror shreds through some of the cotton wool in my head, making everything a little clearer. I smother a scream and stumble backward.

But Val slips at the edge of the crack and slides into it.

"Val!" I fall onto my knees and scramble closer. She's clinging to the edge, screaming. I can't see how deep the crack is, but suddenly it begins narrowing. As I grab onto Val's arms, dark earth closes in around her body. "Stop!" I gasp. "Stop, please stop! Help!" I give her arms a desperate tug, lose my grip on her, and fall backwards.

And darkness envelops everything.

CHAPTER THREE

WAKING UP IS LIKE CLAWING MY WAY THROUGH THICK, sticky mud while someone whacks my head repeatedly with a hammer. When I finally manage to unglue my eyelids and blink several times, I squint at my blurry bedroom, trying to remember how I got home and into bed.

Except this isn't my bedroom.

Alarm rushes through me, clearing the haze and causing my head to pound even more. Nausea crawls up my throat as recent events flood my brain. The blood on Georgia's face—Chelsea calling the cops—the party—an earthquake splitting the ground open and—*what the hell happened last night?* That last bit can't have been real. There must have been something weird in Val's drink.

My pulse thumps in my ears as I take in the unfamiliar

bedroom and its stylish furnishings. On the other side of the room, someone opens the door and walks in. "Oh, you're awake," he says. "Morning."

"*Dash?* Where am ... Did you *abduct* me? What the actual fu—"

"Whoa, hold on there, Miss Potty Mouth." He picks up a chair and moves it closer to the bed. "Mom's nearby. She doesn't appreciate language like that."

I gape at him. "This is your house?" I had no idea rooms this nice existed in the crummy little town of Stanmeade. "What the hell am I doing here?"

"Well," he says as he drops into the chair, "I had to rescue you from the mess you made."

"The mess I made?" I press my hands over my face so I don't have to look at him. The pounding ache behind my eyes intensifies and the nausea threatens to overwhelm me. "What was in that drink?" I mumble.

"Nothing sinister," he says lightly. "Faeries don't respond well to the alcohol humans manufacture, that's all. I guess you've managed to stay away from it until now, otherwise you'd be familiar with the hangover effects."

I lower my hands and push the duvet back. "You know what, Dash? You can make fun of me all you want. I don't care, especially considering 'faerie' is probably the weakest taunt you've ever come up with." I stand, my feet sinking into the plush carpet. "Just let me out of here so I can get home."

Dash rises. "That's going to be a little difficult."

I place my hands on my hips and give him my fiercest glare—which probably isn't that fierce, given my current state.

"You're not seriously going to try and stop me, are you?"

"No, I'm not going to stop you from doing anything. I just need to explain a few things first. Well, a lot of things, actually. So you should probably sit down."

"I don't think so." I push past him, glancing at the mirror over the dresser, and— "What the—" I gasp, almost tripping over my own feet. I grip the edge of the dresser and stare for several horrified moments at the strands of bright color mixed in with my dark brown hair.

"Em?"

"My hair is blue!" I screech. I swing around, regretting it immediately when the room keeps spinning despite the fact that I've come to a stop.

"Oh. Yeah. I forgot you couldn't see that before."

"*Why is my hair blue?*"

He sighs. "You were born that way."

My voice is slow and shaky as I say, "I was not born with blue hair."

"You were. You just haven't been able to see it until now. It's ... well, it's a faerie trait. You're a magical being, but your magic is kind of ... faulty. Sometimes it's there—like the first time you saw me when I was actually hidden by a glamour— but most of the time it isn't. Well," he adds with a frown, "until last night when it exploded all over everything. It hasn't disappeared since then, so I have a feeling it's here to stay now."

Silence fills the room for several seconds, until I become aware of the fact that my mouth is hanging open. "You're insane," I whisper.

"I'm not insane. I'm just not doing this part particularly well, it would seem. Which isn't entirely my fault, I'd like to point out, seeing as you're already strongly biased against me."

"My strong bias exists for excellent reasons!" I yell. "Which now include the fact that you *dyed parts of my hair blue*!"

He blinks. "You need to get past the hair thing. It doesn't come close to being the biggest revelation of the day."

"This is complete crap." I turn and head for the door—but he gets there first and blocks the way with his body.

"You need to hear me out, Em. You're going to be horribly confused if you don't let me explain everything."

I swivel around and head for the opposite side of the room, to the glass double doors through which I can make out a balcony. I don't particularly want to climb down the side of the building in my current state, but I'll do it if it's the only way out of this room. I tug the doors open, hurry outside, and freeze.

In the expansive garden below, which is washed in the pale light of dawn, the trees and rose bushes are glowing. Not due to artificial lighting, but as if the luminescence emanates from within the plants themselves. Blueish white roses, and luminous purple leaves. Silver water trickles over the rocks in the water feature at the garden's center, where two tiny creatures that look like winged horses are drinking.

"Get me out of here," I whisper. My hands rise to squeeze the sides of my face, as if this is a terrible dream I can force myself to wake from. "Take me back home."

Above the thudding of my pulse in my ears, I hear Dash's footsteps moving closer. "I can't. Aside from all the things I still have to explain, you also need to tell me exactly what you did last night."

"Take me back."

"Emerson, you can't hide from this. I know you didn't expect everything to change, but now it has, so—"

"Take me back!" I yell, grasping his T-shirt in both my hands and tugging him closer. "I want to wake up. In my own bedroom. Far away from you and your—"

"Fine!" He removes my fists from his clothing. "If you insist on being so difficult. If you insist on ignoring what's right in front of your eyes." He holds his hand up, palm facing the bedroom, and something pen-shaped flies through the air— *through the freaking air*—and into his grasp. The blood drains from my face as my brain rejects what I'm seeing. Pinpricks of light slide across my vision as Dash writes on the wall beside the balcony door. His hand encircles my wrist and tugs me forward into the wall—*into* the wall—and when everything vanishes into darkness, I'm so relieved because I know the nightmare is coming to an end. I know I'll wake up soon.

"Happy now?" Dash says.

The darkness melts away, and I'm standing on the road a few houses down from Chelsea's. The kid from next door rides down the driveway on his older brother's battered bicycle. "Morning, Em," he says as he rides past, lifting his hand to wave at me, then returning it swiftly to the handlebars as he wobbles.

I blink. Without looking back, I start walking. Quickly, almost at a run, as my brain works furiously to come up with a logical explanation for what just happened. This is some kind of super vivid dream. Or maybe it *was* a vivid dream, and I've just woken up—on the street? Barefoot? I falter and throw a glance over my shoulder, but Dash is nowhere to be seen. Obviously, because I was never with him. I've been *dreaming*. Flip, there must have been something seriously weird in Val's drink last night. Something more than just alcohol.

I come to a sudden halt as an image of Val tumbling into a crack in the earth flashes across my vision. "That never happened," I whisper to myself. "Val is fine." I press my hands over my face, breathing in slowly and pushing aside the single thought that keeps trying to force its way to the front of my mind: *I'm mentally ill, just like my mother.*

I shake my head and hurry up the driveway, feeling for my phone as I go. It isn't in any of my pockets, though. Did I leave it at the party last night? I push the back door open and walk into the kitchen.

"Emerson!"

I flinch and look up. Chelsea rises from the table and takes a few fumbling steps backward, knocking a box of cereal off the counter in the process. Val's Uncle Pete, his uniform buttons straining against the bulge of his stomach, gets to his feet. He keeps his wary gaze on me as Chelsea asks, "Where have you been?"

"Uh ..." That's a good question, actually. One I wish I knew the answer to. "I knew you were pissed off," I explain carefully, "and I didn't want to make things worse, so I stayed away. And I'm *so* sorry about fighting with Georgia. But you know we argue all the time." My gaze flits to Pete before returning to Chelsea. "It isn't something you need to get the cops involved for."

I expect her to shout at me like she did last night, but her grip on the counter tightens as she swallows and looks at Pete. His fingers twitch, his right hand clenching and unclenching. "What happened at the Masons' house last night, Emerson?"

"The—the Masons' house?"

"Don't pretend you know nothing," Chelsea says, a slight wobble evident in her voice. "We've heard all about it. We saw the video."

"What video? What are you talking about?"

Pete moves forward, places his cell phone on the table, and pushes it toward me. I take a step closer and look down at the grainy, shaky footage of a bonfire and people laughing. The fire moves out of view as the person holding the camera turns and almost bumps into Val. After a quick apology, Val walks away. More laughter, someone shouts, "Emerson's drunk," and then the camera follows Val. It gets close enough to pick up her voice as she says, "I swear, I wish the earth had just split open and swallowed me whole."

My blood chills. I watch myself swaying, eyes half-closed. "So what? Then let the earth split open and swallow you whole."

I know what's coming before I see it. Goosebumps race across my skin as the footage wobbles again, then focuses on the ground. The earth rips itself open in one grinding, shuddering zigzag. Val slips and disappears. I hear screams and shouting, and then the video cuts off.

My brain wants to reject what I've just seen, but it can't. *It happened*, I say silently to myself. *It actually happened.*

Chelsea begins swearing repeatedly beneath her breath, and for some reason, Dash's voice resonates in my head: *Mom's nearby. She doesn't appreciate language like that.*

"What the hell was that?" Pete asks, his voice a whisper now.

I open my mouth, but I can't come up with an answer.

"Holy heck, it's like having flipping *Carrie* living under my own roof," Chelsea wails. "You have to take her away, Pete. Please just get her out of here."

"Wait! I … I didn't do that. It must have been a co-incidence. An earthquake happened at the same time I was talking. You don't think I could actually *make* that happen, do you?" I'm trying to convince myself as much as them. "And what about Val? Did she—"

"You don't need to worry about Val," Pete says. "But you do need to come with me."

"Are you kidding? You—I mean—didn't you see what else was happening there? Illegal underage drinking? You should be dealing with *that*, not this weird earthquake coincidence."

"Don't try to change the subject, Em." Slowly, as if approaching a dangerous animal, Pete comes toward me. I take a quick step backwards, moving beyond his reach. He frowns and hesitates. "Em, please. We don't need to make this un-pleasant. We just want to get you somewhere safe so you don't hurt anyone."

"But I'm not going to hurt anyone, I swear."

Another two policemen move from the hallway into the kitchen, and I realize they must have been waiting there the whole time. They're backup. Because I'm supposedly too dangerous for one cop to handle. I shake my head, barely able to believe this is happening, as I inch further away from them.

A pause.

No one speaks.

Then all three policemen lunge toward me. Chelsea screams, chairs are knocked aside, and moments later I'm being dragged outside. Rough paving grazes my feet, and pain shoots through my shoulders as my arms are almost yanked from their sockets.

"LET GO!" I yell.

Their hands spring away from me so fast that the momentum swings the three men around and dumps them on the ground. "What the hell?" Pete groans. He pushes himself onto his knees and dives for my legs.

I jump backwards out of reach. "Get away from me!"

As if kicked with superhuman strength, Pete slides across the grass, through the door, and into the kitchen table. Chelsea shrieks again. At the sound of a crackle, I look down and see sparks—*sparks?*—whizzing around my hands. Icy terror drenches me.

"Time to go," a voice says behind me. Something grips my arm, and before I have time to tear myself away, I'm pulled into darkness, a silent scream on my lips.

CHAPTER
FOUR

THE DARKNESS EVAPORATES TO REVEAL DASH AT MY SIDE and a garden bathed in the golden glow of sunrise. The same garden I saw from the balcony minutes ago. I shove Dash away from me, drop onto my knees, and throw up on the grass.

"Lovely," he says when I'm done. "Thank goodness I didn't take you back inside the house."

"What happened to … to Val?" I gasp, trying to swallow down the urge to throw up again and failing.

When my retching finally ends, Dash says, "She's fine. One of my teammates got her out of the ground. She's already forgotten the whole thing."

"How could she have …" My words trail off as I look up and see one of those miniature winged horses soaring through the air behind Dash. I climb slowly to my feet and look around. The roses and leaves are still faintly glowing, but their luminescence is less obvious now with the sun's golden light filtering through the trees. The little horse lands in a shallow part of the rock pool and begins frolicking, tossing droplets of silver water about as it plays. Wherever the water lands, a silver mushroom pops up.

My brain keeps repeating the same message: I must be dreaming. This is *not possible*. I've gone off the deep end and entirely lost my mind. But I don't think my imagination is capable of coming up with this kind of fantastical detail. And everything seems so *real*. The fresh scent of flowers, the prickle of grass beneath my feet. The sour taste of puke in my mouth.

"Explain," I whisper. "Make this make sense."

Dash folds his arms over his chest. "Okay then. Once upon a time there lived a little girl whose name was—"

I cut him off with a glare. "Don't turn my life into some fairytale crap. Just give me the facts." Something bright flies from the tip of my tongue, and my immediate thought is that I must be so angry I'm actually spitting saliva. But no. It's a spark of light. The same kind that crackled around my hands after Pete was somehow thrown away from me. Fear slithers down my spine as I clamp my mouth shut.

"Okay, here are the bare-bone facts," Dash says. "Magic is real, and it exists in a realm that overlaps with the world you grew up in. Fae live on this side; humans and all the other non-magical creatures you recognize live on the other side. I'm a faerie, like you. I'm also a guardian, which means I'm trained to fight dark magic, dangerous fae, that sort of thing. The day you and I first met, I had an assignment on your side of the veil."

"The day you ruined everything," I murmur, remembering my mother wailing, covering her head with her hands, shouting about things that weren't real.

Dash looks annoyed that I've interrupted his story. "You have *got* to stop hating me for that. You know they would have taken her away anyway. Maybe not that day, but soon afterwards. She wasn't in her right mind—"

"Don't you dare talk about her."

"*Anyway*," he continues loudly, "nobody was supposed to see me, but you did. And with that color in your hair, I knew you were a faerie. But then it kind of flickered and was gone, and you couldn't see me anymore. It was as if everything magical about you was suddenly bottled up, inaccessible. Once we were done with the assignment, I mentioned you in my Guild report, and they—"

"Your Guild report?" I say with a snort. "You were like twelve. Does this Guild of yours breed child soldiers or something?"

"No. We're not soldiers, and by the time training is done, we're not children anymore. And I was thirteen, not twelve. I'd just begun my training. It was a group assignment, but we were all in different areas of the park, and I was the only one who had any interaction with you. So yes, I reported it afterwards. Faeries with dodgy magic who think they're human shouldn't be ignored."

"Oh, right, because I'm probably a danger to society or

something like that," I say with a roll of my eyes.

"Potentially, yes." Dash's tone is deadly serious, and an image of the ground ripping open comes immediately to mind. I wrap my arms around myself and look away. "I don't know if the Guild investigated you at all," Dash continues, "because it was none of my business. I got on with my training, and it was about six months later when you showed up near another one of my assignments. Then a few months later you were there again."

"I remember seeing you," I murmur. "I figured you must live somewhere near Stanmeade. I thought it was weird, since it's so far away from where I first saw you. In that park near where Mom and I used to live. But I was so mad at you that I didn't focus too much on it being a weird coincidence."

"Well, the Guild didn't think it was a coincidence. They thought something else might be going on. That maybe your weird on-off magic was causing problems, or attracting trouble-makers or something, and that's how I ended up with three assignments near you. But they couldn't find any connection, and someone on the Council said you should be left alone. That the Guild shouldn't interfere with you unless there was evidence that your magic really was breaking free and causing trouble. But the rest of the Council wanted someone to keep tabs on you, just in case. They complained about it being a waste of time and resources for a trained guardian to do it, though, so I volunteered." His mouth pulls up one side in a half-grin. "We were encouraged to take on extra projects outside of training. It looks good on the resume. Shows initiative or something."

I throw my hands up. "Wonderful. You're my flipping babysitter."

"Uh, I think detective might be a more accurate comparison."

"Stalker, maybe?"

"I mean, it was like this ongoing puzzle, trying to figure out what was wrong with you and how you ended up in that awful little human town."

"Perhaps mad scientist would be more fitting. Highly offensive mad scientist."

He folds his arms over his chest. "I think we should stop the comparisons. You clearly don't understand the importance of what I do."

"And you clearly think far too highly of yourself. But then, I've always known that, haven't I."

"I think, Emerson," he says with an annoying smirk, "that we should focus on the great many things you *haven't* always known."

His words bring home the seriousness of the situation. I try to tell myself yet again that I'm dreaming or high or drunk, but it's a weak lie I have no hope of believing. I shut my eyes and press my fingers against my temples. "So I'm not crazy after all," I murmur. "The strange things I've seen—creatures that shouldn't exist—they've actually been real."

"Yes. Well, unless you really are seeing things that aren't—"

"Wait. Wait, wait, wait." I open my eyes, step closer, and grasp his T-shirt as hope comes to life inside me. "Does this mean my mother was never crazy either? The voices, the hallucinations ... her mind didn't make them up? They were actually there? Because, I mean, if I have this ... *magic*—" it still sounds so odd to apply the word to myself "—then she must have it too."

"Actually," Dash says carefully, removing my fists from his T-shirt, "the Guild sent someone to Tranquil Hills to check on your mother after the third time you showed up near an assignment. They couldn't sense any magic in her."

"So ... she's ..."

"Yes. I'm sorry. She's always been sick."

I turn away, not wanting him to see the crushing disappointment. I remind myself not to be surprised, though. Of course it was too much to hope that Mom might actually be sane. That's the way life works, right? You hope for something, and then life kicks you in the face and laughs at you.

I clear my throat. "So it must have been my father then. The loser I don't know at all. He must have been—you know—like me."

"Well ..."

When Dash doesn't finish, I turn back to look at him. "Well what?"

He screws up his face, then says, "Please don't hit me."

Dread stirs in the pit of my stomach. "Why would I hit you?"

"Because ... Okay, look. You're not a halfling. We know that for sure. You're a faerie, and that means you must have had two faerie parents. So ... therefore ... the woman locked up in Tranquil Hills Psychiatric Hospital isn't your mother."

I stare at him, unable to speak. His words seem to echo

around my head. *Isn't your mother ... isn't your mother ... isn't your mother.*

"Silence?" Dash says eventually. "I guess that's better than screaming and hitting and telling me I must be—"

"Shut up."

How can Mom not be my mom? For some reason, this is harder to comprehend than anything else. She's my *mother*. She raised me. Everything was great until her crazy moments started becoming a little harder to hide. Everything went to hell soon after that, but before, when she was normal, life was good. It was just me and her against the world. We were a team.

I bend over, my hands pressing against my knees, and breathe deeply. "It can't be true," I manage to say past the nausea. "There must be some other explanation. Something you people have missed. I don't know what, but ... something."

"Emerson ..."

"I think I might be sick again."

Dash pats my back briefly. "Well, at least we're outside."

"What am I supposed to do?"

"There's a very effective tonic for nausea. We can go inside and get some."

"With my *life*, you idiot." I straighten. "Everything is completely screwed up. I'm a magical freak, my aunt wants to get me locked up somewhere far away, my mother is apparently not my mother, and—and these damn spark things won't get off me!" I shake my hands as flickers of light dance about them once more. "Not to mention there's video footage of the whole disaster at the Masons' farm. It's probably online already, and soon the entire world will know that I'm—"

"Hey, calm down. The world isn't going to know anything. Do you honestly think this is the first time we've dealt with something like this? Of course it isn't. We're not amateurs. Most people's memories of last night had been altered by this morning, although we missed a few who still need to be dealt with, including whoever took that phone to the cops. But that footage will have vanished within the next few hours, I can promise you that." He gives me a reassuring smile. "No one will remember that you were involved, and the top story on the news will be about the unexpected earthquake that ripped through Stanmeade." He tilts his head. "Speaking of which, can you tell me what actually happened? Why did the ground tear open like that?"

"*Why?*" I stare at him. "Because apparently I have magic that suddenly decided to—and I quote—explode all over everything. Those were your words, right?"

"Yes, but I thought I heard you say something before it happened, and that's not—"

He cuts himself off as he looks over my shoulder. I swivel around and see a young woman walking toward us. "Well," Dash mutters. "That was terrible timing."

"Oh, because our alone time is up now?" I return my gaze to him. "Boohoo. I'm devastated."

His eyes narrow slightly. "You should be. There's something very important we need to—"

"Dash, we gotta go," the woman says as she reaches us. "One of the Guild Councilors is waiting to see the girl."

I'd like to point out that 'the girl' has a name, but I'm more concerned by what this woman just said. "A Councilor? Why?"

"Because you're a faerie who's been living in the human world," Dash says as the woman bends down and writes on the grass with a pen, "and now that your magic has appeared, you have no idea how to use it. There are protocols in place for this kind of situation."

"Protocols?" That sounds far too clinical for my liking.

"Yes, of course. They'll put you into their special program for people like you. Other fae who, for whatever reason, grew up in the human world without knowing how to use their magic. They're mostly younger fae, but every now and then someone older turns up, like you. It'll be fun."

No it won't. It doesn't sound fun at all. I don't want to meet strange people and learn how to become a member of their stupid magic club. I want to get back to my real life and pretend none of this happened. Or perhaps hide in a corner and fall apart because Mom isn't even my—

Don't go there, I instruct myself. I don't fall apart in front of other people. Especially not Dash.

"Shall we get going then?" he asks, gesturing to the ground where a dark hole has appeared beside the kneeling woman. A dark hole not of earth or rock, but of ... *nothing*. My brain tells me I should be shocked, but I think I'm beyond that point now. Nothing seems impossible anymore.

"Em? Ready to go?"

Ready to go? Such a simple, ordinary question. The kind of thing Val might say when she arrives at my place before school. Or Chelsea might say to Georgia when they're on their way to the shops. Or Mom used to say, with her hand reaching out for mine, when we'd finished playing at the park in the afternoon and had to walk home.

Mom.

An image of her flashes before my eyes again. A little house, wild roses in the garden, number twenty-nine on the old wooden gate. Mom pruning the bushes, and a young version of me dancing around her and singing while our new puppy chases butterflies. Mom who isn't my Mom. My heart cracks a little. I shove the pain aside. *Later*, I tell myself. *Deal with that later. Fall apart later.*

I take a deep breath that sounds as shaky as I feel. "Yeah. Let's go. Just ... can you get me that anti-nausea tonic first?"

CHAPTER
FIVE

DASH RUNS INTO HIS HOUSE TO FETCH THE ANTI-NAUSEA tonic, leaving me alone with his guardian colleague who makes it clear with her long sighs and deep frowns that she's annoyed by this waste of time. The hole she opened in the ground closes up, and she stands there with her arms folded over her chest, staring past me.

Fortunately, Dash doesn't take long to return. He hands me a small bottle made of brown glass. It's suspiciously similar to the bottles Chelsea packages her herbal remedies in. I remove the lid and sniff the contents. "Jeez, Em, it isn't poisonous," Dash says. "Just drink it."

I'm feeling horrible enough that I'm willing to risk the possibility of Dash playing a trick on me, so I tip the little bottle back over my mouth. The liquid doesn't taste like anything, but I instantly begin to feel better.

"Great," says the woman who's been giving her face a good workout by switching between sickly sweet smiles for Dash and irritated frowns directed at me. "Can we get moving?"

"Yes. And let's open an upright doorway instead of one on the ground," Dash says. "It'll be easier for Em to walk into and out the other side, considering she doesn't have much experience with faerie paths." He removes a pen and starts writing in the air. "If I could just … get it to …"

"Dash, this is a waste of—"

"Ah, there we go. Easy peasy." He gives the woman a dazzling smile, but I'm distracted by the growing patch of darkness appearing in mid-air. It spreads rapidly until it's roughly the size and shape of a door. It must be the same thing as the hole the woman opened in the ground. The same thing that appeared on the balcony earlier when Dash took me back home.

"Is that … some kind of teleportation hole?"

"Faerie paths," Dash says, holding his hand out to me. "Although they're not really paths at all. It's this dark empty space that exists somewhere outside of our world and yours, and it can be accessed by opening magical doorways. All you have to do is think of your destination or say the name of the place you want to go to. So much easier than cars and planes."

Easier, perhaps, but far more foreboding. Reluctantly, I take Dash's hand and walk forward. On his other side, the woman happily loops her arm through his. I look over my shoulder as the edges of the doorway spread toward each other, closing the gap, and then we're in complete and utter darkness. "Can people get stuck inside here?" I whisper as we walk forward, which is an odd thing to do when I can't feel anything beneath my feet.

"No. I've never heard of anyone getting stuck. Although I think, if you know the right magic, you can stay here for longer than usual. I've heard of people hiding inside the faerie paths if they're trying to get away from someone."

"Stop thinking," the woman mutters. "I'm trying to direct the paths, and they're not going anywhere with all our thoughts tugging in different directions."

I clamp my mouth shut and try to *not think*, but light appears up ahead before I've figured out if I'm doing it correctly. We walk forward into a small room, sparsely furnished with a mirror, a sideboard displaying painted plates, and a rug covering the wooden floorboards. I pull my hand free of Dash's and step away from him. "This is your Guild?" I was expecting something bigger and more ... magical.

"Nope. This an old house in a deserted area beside a tropical beach."

I turn my withering gaze back to him. "Why is it always so hard to get a straight answer out of you?"

"He's telling the truth," the woman says, rushing to Dash's defense. I notice she hasn't bothered to introduce herself, so I decide not to bother either.

"The Guild can be a little intimidating," Dash explains, wandering over to the sideboard. "It's enormous and busy, with loads of people around at this time of day. Faeries, mainly, but other fae as well. Sometimes criminals are brought in, or stray magic escapes from the training section of the Guild. And the fact that you can't see *any* of it from the outside, and then you walk through a grand entrance that transforms itself from a tree, and you're greeted by all this sudden activity ... well, it can be overwhelming at first." He flips the plate over and examines the back before returning it to its stand. "So we take fae who are new to our world to this halfway house first."

"Oh. Okay." My brain catches hold of what is probably the least important piece of information I've heard all day. "So ... if we really are near a beach, then the ocean must be close by?"

Dash gives me a quizzical look. "Not too far from here."

The fact that I might get to see the ocean for the first time is far easier to focus on than anything else right now. I walk to the nearest window and look out, but all I see is a forest of palm trees.

"I need to get back," the woman says as I try to peer between the trees. "No message on the plate?"

"Nothing yet," Dash says.

"Well, she'll be here soon, I'm sure. She sounded in a hurry when she sent me to fetch you. Anyway, I hope it doesn't take too long to hand the girl over. I know your team has far more exciting stuff going on at the moment."

I look around in time to see her brush her hand from Dash's shoulder down to his elbow. With a half-smile, she turns away, and I resume my examination of the landscape outside, muttering, "Seriously?" under my breath. She doesn't look that much older than us, but surely there are plenty of guys in this world who are both more age-appropriate and more mature than Dash.

"Thanks," he says. Then: "Em, what are you looking for? Actually, never mind. That isn't important."

I give up on my search for the ocean and fold my arms as I walk back toward him. "Of course not. Nothing could possibly be as important as whatever it is you're about to tell me, right?"

"Right," he says, but the front door opens at that moment, and in walks a short blonde girl with orange stripes in her hair and fiery orange eyes to match.

"Oh, Dash, you're here." She gives him a bright smile.

"Uh, yes. I am. Why are you here?"

"Just checking you made it." Her eyes slide to me. "Is this Emerson?"

Dash lets out a sigh. "Yes. Em, this is Jewel. She's a member of my team at the Guild."

Jewel? They have weird hair and eyes *and* weird names? "Hi," I say uncertainly.

"Hey." Jewel gives me a smile that's way too friendly considering we just met. "Oh, hang on." She slips her hand into one of her pockets and removes what I first assume to be a phone because of the shape, but turns out to be semi-transparent and orange-gold in color. She looks at the surface, and I do a double take as tiny gold words melt into view.

"Is that a Guild-wide memo?" Dash asks. "I think my amber just pinged as well."

"Yes." As Jewel peers more closely at the honey-colored rectangle, I notice dark swirling patterns tattooed on the inside of her wrists. "A Griffin attack on a small village near Twiggled Horn. Five dead."

"Five dead from a Griffin attack? They don't normally kill people."

"Yeah, well, they're dangerous outlaws, so what do you expect." Jewel swipes her hand across the amber thing, and the words disappear.

"Griffin?" I ask. "Like the mythical creature?" Nothing would surprise me at this point.

"No," Dash says. "Although yes, griffins do exist. But in this case we're talking about people with extra magic. Abilities most normal fae don't posses. Griffin Abilities. You'll learn about them soon enough." His expression darkens. "They're pretty much a law unto themselves."

Jewel rolls her eyes before giving me a sweet smile. "Dash doesn't always explain things particularly well. These dangerous fae used to live out in the open, doing whatever they pleased, without anyone knowing they were different. But it's hard to hide a Griffin Ability these days. Testing is mandatory. The Guild just wants to keep an eye on them—understandably—but they're always going on about how they're discriminated against. So in recent years, those who managed to get away from the Guild without being tagged have banded together. Formed some kind of secret organization. And now they take out their Guild-directed anger on innocent people just to get attention."

"Unacceptable," Dash mutters.

"Exactly. So you can understand why the Guild wants to keep a record of all Griffin Gifted, right? They need to be held accountable for their actions."

She seems to be waiting for me to respond. I consider telling her I don't give a crap about faerie outlaws and politics, but decide to change the subject instead. "What's the orange rectangle thing?"

"Oh. This?" Jewel holds up the honey-colored device.

"Amber," Dash says. "Faerie cell phone."

Behind him, one of the plates on the sideboard emits an abrupt shriek. I let out an involuntary gasp and take a hurried step backward. "What the fu—"

"Seriously?" Dash says, interrupting me mid-curse. He picks up the plate and turns it over. "The situation really doesn't warrant that kind of language, Em."

I gape at him as my pattering heart rate returns slowly to normal. "You're kidding, right? What's the big deal with the no-swearing thing? I don't see any little kids around, unless you'd like to count yourself in that category."

"Very funny," he deadpans, looking up from the plate. "And if you'd had your mouth cleaned out with soap spells as many times as I have, you'd understand my automatic response to bad language. Super unpleasant spell, that one. The taste hangs around for hours afterwards."

I stare at him. "I'm trying to figure out if you're joking."

"Nope. My mother's always been deadly serious about the no-swearing policy in our household. Anyway, the Councilor's on her way. Message on the plate said she just left the Guild."

"That was the sound of a *message*?"

"It isn't supposed to shriek like that," Jewel says. "I think the notification spell is faulty."

The front door swings open, revealing a smartly dressed woman. "Oh, wonderful, you're here. I didn't have time to check with surveillance. Shall we go through to the sitting room?" Without waiting for an answer, she strides past us and opens the door beside the sideboard.

"Councilor Waterfield," Dash whispers as he takes my arm and steers me around toward the door.

I expected her to be older, being a member of this special faerie Council or whatever it is, but she probably hasn't hit thirty yet. I'm also starting to wonder if this world consists of any men, or if it's just Dash and all the females that fawn over him. I pull my arm free of his grip, muttering that I'm perfectly capable of walking into the next room without assistance.

The sitting room is pretty, with antique furniture and a large bay window on one side. I think I might be able to see something beige in color through the trees that could be a strip of sand, but Councilor Waterfield invites me to sit before I can take a closer look out the window. I choose one of the single armchairs so I don't have to sit right next to Dash or the Councilor. She sits with her back to the window, and Dash takes the armchair beside mine. I clasp my hands tightly together in my lap, feeling suddenly nervous.

"Emerson," the woman says. "I'm Councilor Waterfield. First of all, welcome to the magical realm. I trust Dash has explained the basics to you?"

"I have," Dash says before I can answer. "Only the very basics, though. She has a lot more to learn." He flashes a grin in my direction, which I wish I could scratch right off. He's enjoying this way too much.

"So, Emerson." The Councilor opens a bag at her feet and pulls out a larger version of the amber thing Jewel was using. Before she tilts it upward to face her, I see gold lettering appear across its surface. "We've been tracking you for the last ... five years? Is that correct?" She looks up from her magical device.

"Yes," Dash answers once more. "Em was twelve when we began tracking her."

"So that makes you seventeen now."

"If math is the same in this world as it is in mine," I say, "then yes."

Her smile tightens somewhat. "Numbers are numbers, Emerson, no matter which side of the veil you happen to be on. And *this side* is your side. You'll need to start referring to it as such."

"Of course," I say, when all I want to do is scream that I only just found out about the existence of this side, so give me a damn break!

Councilor Waterfield leans back, making herself more comfortable. "In case Dash didn't tell you, I'm the Guild representative for Chevalier House, which is where you'll be staying for a while. It's a school for people like you. People who've been brought up with humans and might have had access to their magic but haven't had anyone to teach them how to use it, or perhaps their magic has only just appeared, and because of some mishap or other, we've now become aware of their existence."

"What makes it suddenly appear?" I ask. "Why was my magic inaccessible before? Or—why did it come and go? Dash said it was kind of … faulty."

She purses her lips before answering. "To be honest, I don't know. If you were a halfling, it would make more sense. Their magic is highly unpredictable and can sometimes present itself later in life. But faeries … Well, I don't know. I suppose it happens every now and then."

"Wonderful. So I'm a freak even by this world's standards."

"You're not a freak, Emerson. After you've spent some time at Chevalier House, you'll be able to fit in with the rest of our world just fine."

"So basically you're sending me to magical etiquette school?"

She breathes out through her nose. I think her patience is beginning to wear thin. "It's far more than that. They'll teach you about your magic, about our world. They'll assist with the logistics of merging your old life with your new one. Whether you should return home or stay here, what story your family will believe while you're away, what you should tell your family if you decide to return home. Things like that."

I cross my arms tightly against my chest. "You should probably know that you needn't bother coming up with a story for my aunt. She'll assume I've run away, she'll be glad, and that'll be the end of it."

Councilor Waterfield looks down at her device, pausing for a moment as she reads something. "It appears that's the story she was given, actually. A guardian glamoured as a policeman has informed your aunt that you ran away. He told her that a security camera caught you getting onto a bus. Police attempted to find you on the other side, but you somehow slipped away without being noticed. They're still on the lookout for you. Your friends have been told the same story."

"But that's a lie." I sit forward. "I don't want my friends thinking I ran away."

"Well, Emerson, I'm afraid you don't really have a choice. Once you've spent some time at Chevalier House and can safely return to the human world, you can come up with a good excuse for why you ran away. We can have one of our guardians glamoured as a policeman say he or she tracked you down, if that story works for you. I'm sure you can make your friends understand."

I slump back in my chair. This woman doesn't understand, and neither will Val. She'll see right through me if I try to lie.

"Now, as I was saying," Councilor Waterfield continues, examining her device again. "All footage of last night's earthquake incident has been located and destroyed so that no one knows you were connected, and memories have been altered. An expensive cover-up—not all magic is free or cheap, you know—but we can't have humans running around spreading stories about what you did. And if you do decide to return to your old life, you can do so safely without anyone knowing what happened."

"So … so that's it? I have to go to this school for a little bit, and then I can return to my world?"

"Yes." She slides her amber device back into her bag. "Dash will take you there now."

"Um, who pays for this school?" I ask, angling my body away from Dash as I ask. Pointless, since he can still hear me, but I'd rather not see his expression if I have to admit to

Councilor Waterfield that I have absolutely no money.

"It's funded by the Guild," she says. "The program is considered part of security. It's dangerous having fae running around with magic they can't control. Far better to have you educated so you can safely re-enter society, on this side of the veil or the other side. Now." She stands and picks up her bag. "Someone will arrive here shortly to run a few tests on you before you leave for Chevalier House."

"Tests?" I shrink back against the cushions. "What tests?"

"Oh, nothing scary. Just standard procedure. To test for Griffin Abilities, magic levels, that sort of thing."

"I don't want any tests. Don't I have the right to refuse things like—"

"Perhaps," Dash says as he stands, "we could do the tests in a few days after Em has settled into Chevalier House. She's been through a lot already. And with her ... history. Her mother ..." He lowers his voice, as if whispering that one word—*mother*—instead of speaking it out loud means it won't bring up all the shock, confusion and hurt I felt earlier. I stamp down the pain as Dash continues. "I assume you remember everything from my previous reports, Councilor, so you'll understand that the concept of 'running tests' has negative connotations to her." He places his hands respectfully behind his back. As his sleeves pull up slightly, I notice the same tattoo on his wrists that I saw on Jewel's arms.

Councilor Waterfield clicks her tongue. "Fine. I'll send someone to Chevalier House at the end of the week to do the tests there."

That doesn't sound much better, but hopefully I'll be out of

Chevalier House by then. We leave the sitting room and find Jewel still hanging around near the front door. She looks up from her amber, her eyes wide. "Big news," she says. "Like, *huge*. Someone's made a breakthrough with a spell for the veil. The Guild thinks they'll finally be able to seal the tear over Velazar Island. There's a meeting in twenty minutes so they can tell us more about it."

"Correct," Councilor Waterfield says, hurrying past Jewel. "That's why I was late getting here. We received the news just this morning. Now, if you'll excuse me, I need to get back before the meeting begins." She holds a pen up to the front door, and after a few scribbled words, a dark opening appears. Even though I expected it this time, it's still horribly unnatural so see a hole of nothingness taking shape and then disappearing after swallowing a person.

"This is so exciting," Jewel says once the Councilor is gone. "Are you coming?"

Dash shakes his head. "I'm escorting Em to Chevalier House now."

"Oh, but this is important. Bring her with, and you can take her to Chevalier afterwards."

"No need," Dash says with an easy smile. "I'm sure you'll tell me all about it later. And I doubt Em wants to sit through a Guild meeting after everything she's been through in the last few hours."

Jewel's smile slips for just a second, before stretching wide once again. "You're always so thoughtful, Dash. Going the extra mile with your assignments." She leans in and gives him a hug and a quick kiss on the cheek. "See you later."

I wait until she's gone before saying, "I see you don't mind pissing off your girlfriend."

"Girlfriend? Jewel?" He laughs. "We're just friends. Wait, why did you say she's angry? She wasn't angry."

I slowly shake my head. "You're such an idiot."

He grins. "For once, dear Emerson, you are almost right. I was *almost* an idiot earlier." His gaze moves past me and up, scanning the ceiling briefly. "Fortunately, I was saved just in time."

I can't help glancing up as well, but I see nothing except a few cobwebs and a spider. Apparently those aren't unique to the human world.

At the sound of the front door opening, I look past Dash. On the doorstep stands a man with pointed ears and spiked black hair. *This is normal now*, I remind myself as my eyes refuse to move from those abnormally tapered ears. *Totally normal.*

"Emerson?" he enquires. I nod. "The professor is expecting you."

CHAPTER SIX

WE ARRIVE AT AN EMBELLISHED METAL GATE SEPARATING us from a garden of manicured maroon grass and bushes adorned in the colors of autumn. A chilly breeze raises goosebumps along the exposed part of my arms. "Is this anywhere near the house we were just in?" I ask. It doesn't feel like it, but with the faerie trails—faerie paths?—making travel so quick, it's impossible to tell.

"No," Dash says. "We're in a completely different part of the world in the foothills of a mountain range."

I peer between the metal-shaped leaves of the gate, and on the other side of the enormous house, I see snow-capped mountain peaks. The elf—I assume the pointed ears means he's an elf—opens the gate and lets us into the garden. We walk along the paved path, up the few steps to the front door, and inside. A crackling fire and a cozy atmosphere greets us in the large open entrance hall of Chevalier House.

"I'll get the professor," the elf says, heading toward the stairs.

I cross the room, my feet sinking into the thick rug as I look around. A table stands in the middle of the room, with a beautifully painted vase at its center filled with flowers I don't recognize. Richly embroidered curtains frame the windows, and painted portraits in gilded frames decorate the walls. I think about staying here, even for just a few days, and I can't quite believe it. It's a million times fancier than any other house I've ever lived in. "Of course it is," I mutter, shaking my head.

"What?" Dash asks.

"The Guild, your parents' home, this place … I guess when you live in a world of magic, everyone can have whatever fancy, schmancy house they like."

"Well, not really." Dash pushes his hands into his pockets. "Most faeries live in regular tree houses. That's how we lived until Mom got lucky with her fashion design and clothes casting. She won an award, and then this celebrity hired her to make a dress for some important event. Word started spreading about her work, and she ended up with more high-society clients. Even some of the Seelies—the fae royalty—have worn her dresses. So, yeah." He shrugs. "Now we have a fancy, schmancy house."

"Interesting. Must have been hard for you whenever you were in my world, having to pretend you lived in some crappy part of Stanmeade."

"So hard," he jokes, though his voice lacks humor.

"No wonder you still live at home with your parents. Why rush to move out and be independent when you can lounge around in a mansion for years?"

He doesn't respond, and I continue to examine the portraits on the wall. In the corner of my vision, I see someone walk into the room and out another door, but I ignore whoever it is. "So, you and Jewel aren't together, but you have matching tattoos," I say to cover the growing silence. Silence leaves space for thoughts of Mom to sneak in, and I'm not ready to deal with that. "Seems pretty serious to me. I mean, there's no going back from that, right?"

"Matching tattoos? Oh." Dash starts laughing. "You mean these?" He holds his hands up, displaying his tattooed wrists, then doubles over as laughter consumes him. I fold my arms and pointedly ignore him until he's recovered enough to say, "These are guardian markings. We get them once we've graduated."

"Wow, you actually managed to graduate? How surprising."

"Yep." He smiles proudly. "Less than a year ago."

I can't help rolling my eyes before turning back to the portrait of a young woman. I read the ridiculous name on the polished bronze plaque beneath the painting: Azure Plumehof. Seriously? Azure, Dash, Jewel … Don't these magical people know anything about normal names? My gaze slides to the date below the name, which tells me this painting is over three hundred years old. Flip. I wonder if the house is also that old.

I hear laughter behind me and look over my shoulder to see a young boy grinning while Dash writes on the boy's arm with the same pen he uses to open magic doorways. I make out a spark of light before the boy says, "Thanks, Dash!" and runs off.

I look away, pretending to examine the crystal-embellished tassels hanging from one of the curtain tie-backs. "Will they give me one of those magic pens here?"

"What magic pens?" Dash asks.

"You know." I glance back at him, nodding toward the pen in his hand. "The pens you guys use to open doorways."

"Oh." Dash snickers. "That isn't a pen. It's a stylus."

"It looks like a pen. And from what I've seen, it acts like a pen."

"Well, it isn't. It has no ink. It's essentially just a stick that channels magic."

"So … it's a magic wand?"

"Pretty much. And you'll have to prove you can safely use your magic before you'll get one."

"Fine," I mutter, crossing my arms and wandering over to the table. I lean closer to the vase and examine the oddly shaped flowers.

"Dash, Emerson!" exclaims a female voice from the direction of the stairs. "How lovely to see the two of you."

I straighten and step back as a woman with pink in her blonde hair and miniature banana earrings dangling from her ears descends the stairs. A woman I'd guess to be in her twenties, maybe early thirties. The same woman, I realize with a lurch, from the portrait. "Emerson," she says as reaches the bottom of the stairs. "So lovely to meet you. I'm Professor Azure Plumehof, but please call me Azzy." She holds her hand toward me. I stare at it, then back up at her face.

"Azure Plumehof?" I look over my shoulder at the portrait, then back. "You can't be. The woman in that painting would be over three hundred years old. She'd be a shriveled-up old prune."

Azzy laughs as she lowers her hand, apparently unperturbed that I didn't bother to shake it. "Dash didn't explain that part?"

"I guess it didn't come up," Dash says. "She was too fixated on the fact that her hair is blue."

I glance down at the pastel blue strands hanging over my shoulder that I'd somehow managed to forget about. With a blink, I return my attention to the most recent earth-shattering revelation. "Wait. You're telling me you people are immortal or something?"

"Is that so hard to believe," Dash asks, "given every other so-called 'impossible' thing you've discovered so far this morning?"

"It's—just—"

"We're not immortal, dear," Azzy says with a brief frown in Dash's direction. She clasps her hands together over her layers of loose, floaty clothing. "We live several centuries, which is a far cry from immortality."

"Several … centuries …" I murmur.

"Don't worry," Azzy says, smiling kindly. "We'll give you plenty of time to absorb all this new information. That's why Chevalier House exists—to give you a safe place to learn more about yourself and the world you're now part of. There will be history lessons, magic lessons—all the basics that young faeries learn in junior school—and interviews so you can give us information that will assist in finding your real family."

"My—what?" *Real* family? I hadn't given the idea a moment's thought.

"But we can begin all that tomorrow. For now, let me show you to your room. I'm sure you've had a trying day so far, and you probably need to rest. You'll find everything you could possibly need in your room: clothes, toiletries, makeup—if that's your thing. If you need something else that I've forgotten, or if the clothes are the wrong size, just let me know." She pauses, as if she might be expecting me to say something, but I'm a bit too overwhelmed to form words. "And if your brain is too fired up for you to rest right now," she continues, "you can explore the house and the gardens. Meet the other fae who are staying with us at the moment."

"And if you need me," Dash adds, "just tell Azzy. She knows how to get hold of me."

I blink. "Need *you*?" Now there's a ridiculous notion. "You don't have to babysit me anymore, Dash. I can get through the rest of this without you."

"I'm sure you can. Just tell Azzy everything that happened last night, okay?" He exchanges a glance with Azzy, then returns his gaze to me. "Everything. So she can help you."

I frown at him. "Obviously. What did you think I was gonna do? Pretend the whole thing didn't happen? I've tried that already, and it didn't make any of this craziness go away."

"We'll have a good chat, don't worry," Azzy says, patting Dash's arm before taking my hand and steering me toward the stairs. "Let's get you settled in, Em. Can I call you Em, or do you prefer Emerson?"

"She likes Emmy," Dash tells her. I twist my head over my shoulder and imagine sparks flying out of my eyes straight at him. Unfortunately, magic doesn't seem to work that way, and I'm left simply glaring at his smiling face. "Have fun," he says with a small wave before turning and heading for the door. And despite the fact that I want to slap him—despite telling him I don't need him—I have the sudden panicked urge to call out, "Wait, don't leave me here!" Because even though I've always hated him, he's the last tie to my normal life, and he's about to disappear through that door.

But I swallow my panic and don't say a word. I face forward and let Azzy lead me up the stairs. Because I've survived everything life has ever thrown at me *on my own*, and this will be no different.

CHAPTER SEVEN

SHE ISN'T YOUR MOTHER.

She isn't your mother.

This piece of information keeps knocking on the inside of my brain, and now that I'm alone, nothing I do can distract me from it. I examine every part of my bedroom—almost as nice as the guest room in Dash's parents' house—but fluffed-up pillows, a luxuriously soft carpet, and a four-poster bed can't keep the image of a mother who isn't my mother from branding itself onto the inside of my mind.

I open the wardrobe and discover, upon finding a mirror there, that I look terrible. My skin is pale, and my eyelids are smudged with dark makeup. I pick up some clean clothes from one of the shelves and, after peering both ways down the hall to make sure I'm not about to bump into anyone, I cross to the bathroom Azzy pointed out. What I find there is enough to startle me out of my upsetting thoughts for a time. I expected a bath or shower, but instead I find a small pool surrounded by pebbles and filled with steaming, scented water. It's the most inviting thing I've seen in ages, and I'm more than happy to push aside every thought racing through my head, strip out of my dirty clothes, and sink into the hot water.

But even this distraction doesn't last long. So after dressing myself in clean clothes that somehow fit perfectly, I leave my room. I wander around the house, through a library lined with books from floor to ceiling, into a dining room with a long rectangular table at its center, and across a kitchen larger than Chelsea's house. I explore the garden, ignoring every person— every fae … being … *thing*—I come across.

But my thoughts keep going back to Mom. I try to hold onto the picture of her I've always had, to the place she's always held in my life. The place and title of *mother*. But the idea is beginning to crumble as questions start sneaking in through the cracks of my defenses: How did she end up with me? Who do I really belong to? Why didn't she ever tell me? Who the hell am I if I'm not her daughter? And despite the fact that it fills me with guilt, I try to imagine what my 'real' mother might be like. But my imagination comes up blank. I can't picture anyone except the woman I grew up with.

When I realize I've been standing motionless in front of the same weird polka-dot plant for several minutes, staring unseeingly past it, I decide I'm done with real life for today. I can deal with all my questions, doubts, confusions, and *magic* tomorrow. I return to my room, drag the curtains closed, climb into bed, and do my best to fall asleep. When Azzy knocks on my door and says something about dinner, I pull the duvet over my head and ignore her.

* * *

"Everyone, this is Emerson," Azzy says the following morning after introducing the other seven people in the library: a faerie, an elf, and five half somethings. "Remember how uncertain you felt about everything when you first arrived here? That's how Em feels right now. So remember to do your best to welcome her."

Everyone looks at me. I slide a little lower in my chair. If I knew how to open that gap I opened in the earth the other night, I'd be tempted to do it again right now and crawl into it.

"Well then," Azzy continues. "You can get better acquainted over lunch. For now, you all need to get back to whatever you're working on at the moment. Em, you'll be with me."

I stand along with everyone else. Two of my fellow weirdos move to a table together and chat quietly as they open several enormous textbooks. The rest leave the library through the door that leads into the garden.

"So, Em," Azzy says, ushering me over to another table. "As I'm sure you've realized, this isn't like an ordinary school. We never know when someone will arrive, and everyone has a different story. Some fae have no previous knowledge of the magic world at all, like you, while others had some exposure to magic, but haven't formally been taught anything.

So as you can see, we need to tailor our lessons and training to each individual."

"Um, yes," I say after a pause, since it seems she's waiting for a sign that I'm listening to her.

"So we're going to begin with a little bit of history about this world. Momentous occasions from the past, as well as more recent events that have played an important role in shaping our world."

"Fun." I try not to sound bored, but I can tell I'm not doing a very good job. What happened to learning about actual magic?

"It is fun. Especially since I'm going to get some of the other students to explain things to you."

"What?"

Azzy gives me a knowing smile. "I thought that might get you to pay attention."

"So ... that part was a joke?"

"Oh, no, I was being entirely serious. This way you don't have to listen to me droning on for hours. I've found it to be a wonderful way of learning. It helps the students who've been here longer to remember what they've learned, it teaches *you* the most important facts, and you'll get to know each other in the process. I'll supervise, of course, to make sure they don't tell you a bunch of nonsense, but essentially it will all be a discussion."

Wonderful. So this is what I have to look forward to every day that I'm here. "So, um, when will I learn how to do some actual magic? I thought that was all I needed to know. Control the magic, then I can leave."

She smiles. "We'll start this afternoon with something easy. After you've told me exactly what happened the other night when you accidentally used magic."

I sigh as I get up and follow her to the table with the other two fae. "Why does everyone want me to tell them exactly what happened? Isn't every detail of the whole event written up in some boring Guild report somewhere?"

"I'm sure it is, but it can't hurt to explain it again. Now, you sit here with George and Aldo—" she pulls a chair out for me as the two boys look up "—and I'm going to get my tea."

I ease myself into the chair, my gaze moving warily between the two boys. "Hi," says the younger one, who looks about ten years old. "I'm George. This is Aldo."

"Okay, let me see if I remember this correctly. You're a faerie," I say, pointing to Aldo, "and you're a halfling?" My gaze moves to George.

"Yep." George nods and smiles.

I remember Dash mentioned the word halfling and saying I couldn't be one, but he didn't explain any more than that. "So what exactly is a halfling? Someone only half magical?"

"Not exactly," Aldo says. He looks a little older, fourteen or fifteen perhaps. Although age doesn't seem to make sense in this world, so I could be totally wrong. "It means two different parents. So a faerie and an elf, for example. Or a human and a faerie, even though fae laws say interaction with humans is wrong."

"That's what I am," George says, sticking his hand into the air as if volunteering to answer a question. "Faerie dad plus human mom. Dad says he got bored with this world, so he

72

went adventuring in the other one. He met my mom and he hasn't come back here since. He thought I barely had any magic when I was little, but it started increasing after I turned ten last year. Things got a little out of hand last month when I accidentally set our shed on fire with enchanted flames that couldn't be put out with water. I was sent here after that."

"Wow. Almost as dramatic as my story," I say. "So how do you tell the difference between faeries and halflings? Someone told me I'm definitely a faerie, but what if he was wrong?"

"No, you're definitely a faerie," Aldo says. "It's easy to tell because faeries have a color."

"A color?"

"You haven't noticed?" He leans forward and rests his elbows on the table. "You have blue in your hair and eyes. I have red. That guardian who brought you here has green. Azzy has pink, although she prefers to call it cerise."

"It is cerise," Azzy says as she walks back into the library and comes toward our table with a teacup and saucer floating through the air beside her. She takes a seat. "Now, Em, have you thought of your first question?"

I clear my throat and force myself to look away from the levitating teacup. "Oh, I thought they were just going to tell me stuff."

"But how will they know what to tell you if you don't ask a question?"

I raise an eyebrow. This style of teaching seems question-able, but I'm no expert, so I probably shouldn't point that out. "Um ... let's see ..." What do I want to know? I want to know if it's absolutely certain that Mom isn't my mom. I want to know how I ended up living with her. I want to know how I'm supposed to look at life and myself when I'm suddenly not the person I've always thought I was. I want to know if it's possible to have an identity crisis at the age of seventeen.

But I'm not going to ask any of those questions, of course. They're far too personal, and these kids won't know the answers anyway. "Um, well, Dash explained the faerie paths, but is that the only way to get to the other world? What if someone doesn't have one of those stylus things?" What worries me is that *I* don't have one of those stylus things, and I need a way to get out of here if things end up going badly.

"Ooh, okay, I've got this," George says, his hand shooting into the air again. "So there are gaps here and there in the veil between the two worlds, and fae can get through those gaps. I don't remember exactly where they are, though, or where they came from. I think they've always existed. Oh, and there's the tear in the veil over Velazar Island," he adds. "That's not natural, though. It shouldn't exist. Some witches created it years ago."

I glance at Azzy. "That sounds like it might have been an important event."

"It was," she says, looking pleased. I can tell what she's thinking: this group learning thing is working out just as she planned. "Can you tell us more about that event, Aldo?"

"Uh, sure, okay." He taps his stylus on the desk. "Well, there was this guy called Draven. Okay, wait, let's backtrack a bit." He frowns, then continues. "It was about, um, twenty-eight years ago when one of the Unseelie princes was trying to take over his mother's court. Instead, he and the Unseelie Queen were both killed by Draven, who was this insanely powerful halfling, and Draven ended up taking over the Unseelie Court. There was lots of fighting and brainwashing and stuff, and eventually Draven was killed. At least, that's what everyone thought."

"Dun, dun, duuuuun," George says in dramatic tones, making Azzy chuckle.

"Ten years later, the Seelie princess who'd been in prison all that time for helping Draven—because he was actually her son—"

"*Super* complicated," George adds.

"Yeah, so the Seelie princess found out that Draven was actually still alive and in hiding," Aldo continues, "and she betrayed him and handed him over to the Guild in exchange for her freedom."

"She wasn't the best mother," Azzy says with a shake of her head.

"Then the princess killed her mother and sister so she could claim the Seelie crown. So that kinda backfired on the Guild— because, you know, the Guild and the Seelie Court work together, so they lost their queen and got a horrible new one. And then it turned out that the Seelie princess was working with some witches, and they wanted to rule over the human world too. They decided it shouldn't be separate from this world anymore. So they used an ancient spell and horrible dark magic to tear through the veil, but what ended up happening was that as the hole tore wider and wider, it started consuming both worlds."

"I don't think they knew that would happen," George says.

"No, obviously not. Anyway, Draven ended up at the scene—probably to get revenge on his mother—and he was killed. For real this time. There was more fighting, and somehow the hole in the veil stopped getting bigger."

"The monument," Azzy prompts.

"Right. There was an ancient monument from the mer kingdom, and when the tear in the veil tried to pass it, the monument's magic was strong enough to hold the tear in place and keep it from getting any bigger. So now it's just there, this giant hole in the veil over Velazar Island—"

"Which is a *floating* island," George adds with a grin. "Well, two islands now, because there was a prison on the other side so the Guild chopped the island in half after the veil thing happened."

"And guardians are stationed by the hole at all times," Aldo continues, "hiding it with a glamour and making sure no one gets close enough to touch the monument."

"So there's no way to close it?" I ask.

"Scholars have been working on it ever since," Azzy says. "And I hear there's finally been a breakthrough, actually."

I vaguely remember Jewel saying something yesterday about a spell for a veil. "I think I heard about that. The Guild had a meeting about it yesterday."

"Yes, so that's quite exciting." Azzy smiles at us before picking up her teacup. "Anyway, are you keeping up so far, Em?"

"I think so. Not sure I totally understand the Seelie and Unseelie thing, though."

"Oh, the different courts." Azzy nods toward Aldo before taking another sip of her tea.

"Um, the courts rule over different parts of our world," Aldo says. "The Guild and the Seelie Court work together to kind of maintain order and peace and keep the world running. They decide on laws, and they prohibit magic that involves hurting other people. Unseelies tend to keep to themselves. They also like to ignore laws and use whatever dark magic they feel like, and the Seelie Court can't always do anything about it. I think." He looks to Azzy for confirmation.

"Essentially, yes. It's a complicated balance."

"So what happened to the Seelie princess?" I ask. "The one who killed her mother and sister and was working with the witches? The Guild didn't allow her to continue ruling, did they?"

Azzy shakes her head and places her teacup on its saucer. "No. After the veil-tearing spell, the death penalty was reinstated, and Princess Angelica—who I suppose was actually Queen Angelica at that point—was sentenced to death."

My eyes widen. "Wow. So who was left to take over the court?"

"Her sister's son. So currently we have a king in both courts. King Idrind in the Seelie Court, who is quite a young king, and King Savyon in the Unseelie Court, who's been ruling ever since Draven's first 'death.'"

More weird names, I think to myself. Out loud, I say, "This is all very interesting, but it doesn't help me get my own magic under control. That's all I really need to know, right?"

"If you decide to stay in this world," Azzy says, "then you

need to know how it works."

"But I won't be staying here."

She smiles. "No need to make that decision now."

"I'm pretty sure I've already made the decision."

Azzy laughs. "Okay, okay. That's absolutely fine, but I'm still required by the Guild to teach you some history. But I promise we'll get to the actual magic straight after lunch, okay? Now." She leans forward and watches me intently with her dark pink eyes. "Have you been told anything about Griffin Abilities?"

I remember Dash mentioning them yesterday. "Um … faerie superpowers?"

"Kinda, yes," Aldo says. He looks at Azzy.

"Well, go ahead," she says to him. "Tell Em all about them."

I sit back in my chair, and the rest of the morning passes by with explanations of what Griffin Abilities are (additional, unnatural magical abilities), where they originally came from (metal discs containing the magic of a super powerful halfling from centuries ago), and how they're passed on these days since the discs are all gone (when two Griffin Gifted have a child, although sometimes the child will come out normal).

After a few more rounds of questions and answers, Azzy finally lets us break for lunch. I stand and stretch, and am about to follow Aldo and George when I notice Aldo's stylus on the table amongst the books. After a brief glance around the room to make sure no one's watching me, I casually reach forward and pick it up. I lift my T-shirt and stick it into the waistband of my jeans, then hurry out.

The stylus digs into my chest the whole time I'm sitting at lunch, and I'm afraid it's going to suddenly open a doorway on my body or set me on fire or cast some other spell of its own accord. But I manage to make it through lunch in one piece.

Straight afterwards, Azzy tells me to put a sweater on over my T-shirt and meet her outside. "Ready to learn some magic?" she asks when I find her near a statue of a centaur pointing a bow and arrow at the sky.

It's probably the strangest question I've ever been asked. I can still barely believe magic itself exists, let alone that I have the ability to play around with it. I swallow and roll my shoulders in an attempt to relax. "Probably not, but let's go for it."

CHAPTER EIGHT

"SO HOW DOES THIS WORK?" I ASK AS WE STAND IN THE garden some distance away from the other students. "I say some magic words and something happens?"

"Is that what happened the other night when you accidentally used magic?" Azzy asks.

"Um, no, those were just normal words. My friend Val was embarrassed about something she'd said to a guy, and she made a comment about wishing the earth would open up and swallow her whole. So I said …" I swallow and wrap a few strands of hair around my forefinger, ashamed of the state I was in that night. "I was kind of out of it, because I'd had a little bit of alcohol, and apparently that isn't good for faeries, so I … I don't know, exactly, but I said something like, 'So what?

Then just let the earth swallow you whole.' And then … it happened."

"I see." Azzy nods slowly.

"Was it to do with my thoughts? Was I perhaps picturing it, and my magic appeared at the same time, so that made it actually happen?"

"You know, Em, I'm not sure. Strange things can happen when a person's magic first reveals itself after being dormant for years. But I'm going to try and find out for you, okay?" She gives me a smile that seems less enthusiastic than previously. "And it's probably best that you don't mention exactly what you did to anyone else. Not until I can find out more."

"Oh. Why—"

"In the meantime," she says before I can ask my question, "let's start with the basics. Magic exists around you and inside you. In order to get it to *do* something, you need to draw it out from within you and either release it in some form, or channel it through a stylus. A lot of our magic works that way, by writing the words to a specific spell onto something, while channeling magic through the stylus."

Part of my brain is still stuck wondering why I'm supposed to keep what happened the other night a secret, so I take a few moments to process Azzy's words. "Um, okay, so once I can channel it, can I do anything I want with it?"

"No, we have limitations, of course. Drawing upon that power tires us out, just like exercising would tire you out. If you reach the point where you have almost nothing left, then you need to rest, to regain your magical strength." She walks slowly back and forth as she speaks, her loose clothing fluttering around her. "And there are limitations to exactly what you can do. You can't just snap your fingers and have a pile of gold sitting in front of you, or a rainbow arcing across the entire sky."

"Okay. But superpowered faeries can do things like that?"

"Yes. Griffin Abilities allow people to do magic that no one should be able to do. But we'll get to the specifics of what's possible and what isn't later," she adds with a wave of her hand. "The first thing I want you to practice is the part where you actually draw upon your own magic. It will initially seem like something you have to focus intently on every time, but it will soon become instinctual. Then you'll find that you can do it automatically without even thinking about it."

"Like driving a car?"

"Well, I don't have any personal experience in that area, but yes, I suppose it's like driving a car." She stops pacing and holds her hands out palm-up in front of her. "Once you've drawn power out of yourself, if you're not channeling it through something, you can simply hold it in your hands. It will appear as a sort of glowing, swirling mass that can then be transformed into other things." As she speaks, a roughly spherical shape of light takes form above her hands, sparking this way and that like energy struggling to break free. "For now," she says, "I just want you to focus on getting to the point where you're holding it."

I swallow, then blink as Azzy's magic vanishes and she lowers her hands to her sides. "Um, okay. Should I close my eyes?"

"If that will help you focus, then yes."

My eyelids slide closed, and I concentrate on picturing a deep, hidden place inside me. I have to rid my mind of unhelpful images of intestines and other organs, but eventually I get there.

"Can you feel it yet?" Azzy asks quietly. "Humming, thrumming, vibrating. Find it, and imagine gathering some of it up in your hands and pulling it free."

I picture myself doing as she says, hoping that in reality it isn't as slippery and difficult to hold onto as I'm imagining it to be.

"There it is," she whispers.

I open my eyes, and I'm so startled to see the glowing mass hovering about my hands that I gasp and step backwards, whipping my hands away from the magic. It fizzles into nothing.

Azzy laughs. "Well done, that was good."

A breathy laugh escapes me. "I actually did it."

"You did. Now for the next challenge: can you do it again?"

I hold my hands out once more and close my eyes. I expect it to be easier the second time, but when I open my eyes, I find nothing above my palms. So I try again, taking my time, feeling for that faint humming that never used to be part of me. I tug and coax, but once again, I find my hands empty.

"Patience," Azzy murmurs. "Don't get frustrated with yourself."

I repeat the process, but I can't seem to clear my mind as easily anymore. The cold air distracts me. The chirping of insects fills my ears. I shake my arms out, breathe deeply several times, and try yet again.

Nothing.

"Ugh, this sucks! Why is it so hard?"

Azzy, standing patiently to one side, folds her arms. "Because today is the first time you've tried doing it. It will take lots of practice before it becomes easy."

"But I need to know how to do this *now*."

"Em, you need to go easy on yourself," she says with a laugh. "You have to learn everything a faerie child would spend the whole of junior school learning, and that isn't going to happen in an afternoon. Even if you're smart and dedicated, it will still take several months to—"

"*Months?*" I repeat, icy shock racing through me. "What are you talking about? I can't be here for *months*."

"Why not? Is there something important you need to get back to? I was under the impression the Guild had sorted out your story with your human relatives and friends. No one is expecting you back on that side of the veil any time soon."

"That doesn't make a—what about—there's my *mother*!" I stammer. "And I have a plan. I need to finish school and move closer to her and get a job that pays better. Then I can actually help her. How am I supposed to finish school if I'm *here* for months? I'm only supposed to be here for—I don't know—a week or two."

"I'm sorry, Em." Azzy's brow furrows in confusion. "I don't know who told you that, but this is definitely going to take longer than a week or two."

"I … just … I can't do this." I back away from her.

"Em, wait—"

"I'm going to my room."

"Emerson, please be mature about this," Azzy calls after me. "Let's just have a chat instead of you rushing off to hide from it all."

I don't look back. I run past the statues and into the house—and straight past the stairs that lead up to the bedrooms. I tug the front door open and keep running. Along the path and out the gate. I have no idea where I'm going, of course, but I need to get away from this place. I dart between trees, around bushes, and over rocks. I may not be good at magic, but I'm good at running. So I run and run and run, and eventually I trip over something and slide halfway down a steep part of the forest. I scramble up and brush my scratched and dirty hands against my jeans, allowing myself to catch my breath.

I'm far from the house now, so I pull Aldo's stylus free from my jeans. I hold it like a pen and rest my hand against the nearest tree. I've seen this spell several times now, so I should be able to remember the words. I try to focus and reach for whatever magic exists inside me while writing out the words I witnessed both Dash and Jewel writing. They spoke some foreign words as well, so I take a stab at repeating what I remember hearing.

It's hopeless. I've either got the writing wrong, or the spoken words wrong, or I'm not channeling enough magic through the stylus. Probably a combination of all three. I spin around and throw the stylus onto the ground. After a moment's pause, I drop down beside it. I cross my legs and arms and breath out a huff of air. This is so stupid. What am I supposed to do now? Keep walking until I find one of those natural openings between the two worlds? And how would I know it if I saw it? No, that's a stupid plan. Especially if there aren't many of those openings. I could be hundreds or even thousands of miles away from one. What I'll have to do instead is keep walking until I come across a person who can take me to the human world. Chevalier House can't be too far from civilization, right?

I force myself to keep moving, trying not to think of the fact that I could be completely wrong. As I walk and walk and walk, the light overhead slowly grows dim. By the time night starts to close in and I haven't yet come across any sign of either a person or civilization, genuine fear gathers at the edge of my mind. I run my hands roughly up and down my arms, trying to keep warm, but it does little good.

Then I hear something. The repetitive rustle of footsteps on leaves. Relief and uncertainty crash into me at the same time, freezing me to the spot for several moments. Then I regain my senses and slip behind the nearest tree, peeking out in the direction of the sound. In this world, it's definitely safer to check things out before waving hello.

The being that eventually comes into view looks like a man. His face is in shadow, and he wears a long black coat that reaches below his knees. When I see it isn't some form of monster, I almost step out from behind the tree and call for him. But something holds me back. A shift in the air. A feeling of unease. I notice movement across the forest floor, as if insects and tiny creatures are scuttling away from him. The sense that something here is *wrong* engulfs me.

I crouch down amongst the tree roots, covering my head

with my hands and trying to curl myself into as small a ball as possible. *Please, please, please don't see me*, I chant silently. Eventually, his footsteps fade to nothing. I allow myself to breathe out long and slow before standing and peering tentatively around the tree. I take a few steps.

And a dark shape leaps out at me.

CHAPTER NINE

I GO DOWN WITH A SCREAM, THE CREATURE ON TOP OF ME. Leathery wings flap around me, and a snarling mouth snaps at my face. I fight back with fists and elbows and knees. With a great heave, I manage to kick it off me. It leaps again—but something bright and glittering flashes through the darkness. The monster screeches as a golden blade slashes back and forth, forcing it further away from me. It swipes one wing at the man holding the blade, then darts to the side and flaps away.

The man turns around—and I see that it's Dash.

I scramble up and back away until I feel the rough surface of a tree trunk behind me. I lean against it, not trusting my own legs to keep me upright. Breathless, I ask, "How ... how did you find me?"

"Does it matter?" Dash takes a step toward me.

"Yes. Here I am trying to get back to my normal life, and my stalkerish babysitter shows up out of the blue."

He lets go of his knife, and it simply ... disappears. "I think you're probably supposed to be thanking your stalkerish baby-sitter right now."

I push away from the tree and increase the distance between us. "I'm not thanking you for anything. All you want to do is drag me back to that stupid school."

Instead of reminding me that he's just saved my life, he says, "Bad first day?"

"Of course it was bad. This place—this world—isn't for me. I don't belong here. Why doesn't anyone understand that?"

"We do understand. That's what Chevalier House is for."

"You're not listening to me. I don't. Want. To be here. Okay? I don't want to have weird lessons with strangers, I don't care about the history of this world, and I don't want any of this magic. I just want OUT."

Confusion crosses Dash's features. "But ... isn't this better than what you had before?"

"No! I don't want this!" I yell. I begin pacing, flinging my arms wildly about as I go, not caring that random sparks are escaping my fingers and burning the leaves on the ground. "Two days ago, my life was the same old crap it's always been. Now I'm magical, I'm in a foreign world, my mom isn't my mom, and basically I don't have a f—" I cut myself off before finishing. "I don't have an *effing* clue who I am or what's going on. I just want to go back to my plan where I finish school, move far away from Chelsea, and figure out how to get Mom out of that hospital. And yes, I'm well aware that it was a crappy life, but it was *my* life and I knew what to do with it."

Dash's forehead remains creased. "But you can still do all that. I mean, not exactly like that, but once you've got the magic side of things under control, you can go back to normal life. In fact, magic will *help* you with normal life, if you're discreet about it. So you shouldn't be trying to turn your back on it."

I pause, staring into the darkness and seeing nothing as my brain ticks quickly through something I hadn't considered until now. I turn slowly and face Dash. "Can magic heal my mom?"

He hesitates, his mouth open, then closes it and slowly shakes his head. "She isn't magical. It would be too risky to use magic on her body, especially on her mind. We don't know if it would damage her and make things worse."

I throw my hands up. "Then what the hell is the point in having these stupid powers? How are they supposed to help me?"

"Um, because of everything else you can do with magic?"

I fold my arms over my chest. "Can I walk through the faerie paths straight into her hospital room and take her back through them to somewhere else?"

"Well, no, you can't take her anywhere through the paths because humans can't travel that way. But *you* can go anywhere. You could visit her right now. I mean," he adds quickly, "if you thought that was a good idea."

I hesitate. Clearly Dash doesn't think it's a good idea to visit her right now, and he's probably right. I want to, of course. I want nothing more. But I don't want to go with him. I don't want him to see my mother in her current state, and I don't want him to see *me* and my reaction when I see her like that. I need to learn this faerie paths thing so I can travel there on my own. "Okay, so I can't rescue her from the hospital that way," I say. "But I could conceal myself with magic, right? And I could use magic to distract everyone while I get Mom out of the building, and magic could adjust the paperwork so everyone thinks she was properly discharged. And magic could put my name into the school system to say that I graduated, and it could help me get some money to set up a simple life somewhere and keep Mom safe. Right?"

"Yes, exactly. See? Magic is good for something. Although," he adds with a frown, "I'm not saying I advocate you doing any of those things. We're not supposed to mess around with human lives and, like, use magic to illegally get hold of money."

"You're also not saying that you would stop me."

"I'm saying …" Dash scratches his head. "I'm saying you should go back to Chevalier House and continue learning how to safely use your magic. We can consider all options after that."

I nod slowly. "Right."

He hesitates, watching me with narrowed eyes. "You're thinking about doing all those illegal things, aren't you?"

"I'm thinking about going back to Chevalier House." Which is the truth, actually, seeing as magic has suddenly become the best way to dig myself out of my crappy life and give Mom a better future than the one she's currently facing.

Dash sighs. "Well, your motives may be questionable, but if they'll get you back into Chevalier House tonight, then I've done my job."

"Great. Well done. Should we get going then?" I turn around, and something that looks like a winged lizard leaps off a branch and flies right at me. "Holy sh—"

"Sherbet," Dash says, catching the tiny creature. "Holy sherbet. That's what she was gonna say, little guy. No need to get upset."

"Holy *sherbe*t," I snap. "What the hell is that thing?"

Before my eyes, the creature begins to change form. One moment it's some kind of reptile, and the next it's a kitten. "Ah, looks like a shapeshifter," Dash says. "Formattra is the official name, I think. These little guys are quite rare. I wonder how he ended up here."

"Shapeshifters? Terrific. Are werewolves real too?"

"Well, you do get higher fae who are shapeshifters, but I think they transform into other people, not animals. You know, like another faerie transforming to look like me."

"Because who wouldn't want to look like you, right?"

"Exactly." The creature stretches out and sniffs me. I scuttle backwards out of its reach. "Hey, come on, he likes you," Dash says. "Don't you want a pet?"

"No. I don't like pets."

Dash laughs. "Impossible. Why don't you like pets?"

"They die, and it's sad." *Or they run away and never come back.*

"That is definitely not a good enough reason."

"Fine. I'll soon be leaving, and who will take care of him

then? Is that a good enough reason?"

The creature flickers between several forms so quickly I can't tell what it is until it becomes a kitten again. "He's just a baby, Em," Dash says, scratching the kitten's head. "He needs someone to take care of him."

I tilt my head to the side. "You said they're very rare, didn't you? So can I sell him for lots of money?"

Dash's face falls. He hugs the creature to his chest and covers its ears. "That's a terrible thing to say, Em. Don't listen to her, little guy," he whispers. "She didn't mean that."

"Ugh, seriously?" My hands clench into fists. "Can we go now? You said I need to get back to the house, and now you're wasting time out here with this weird shapeshifting thing."

He watches me, his mouth open as if he wants to say something. Then he shakes his head. "Yeah, okay. Let's go." As he raises his stylus to write a doorway, the shapeshifting creature leaps away and disappears into the darkness. Dash extends his hand to me, and I reluctantly take it. Whoever came up with the physical contact rule for faerie path traveling obviously didn't take into account the possibility that some people might never want to hold hands.

When the darkness disappears to reveal dim light, we're standing outside the Chevalier House gate. "You could have just taken us straight into the house, you know."

"I couldn't, actually," Dash says as he pushes the gate open. "The faerie paths don't open inside the house or anywhere in the garden."

I swing the gate shut behind us. "That's weird. Why?"

"Security measure. It's like that for most private properties.

Only the owners can open doorways inside the house itself."

"Kind of a stupid security measure if anyone can just open the gate."

"The gate won't open for just anyone, though," Dash says as we follow the path up to the house. "If you've walked through it in the company of someone who lives here—like the elf who brought us here yesterday—then you've been granted magical access to pass through the gate."

I allow a long sigh to pass my lips. "That all seems unnecessarily complicated. People should just use padlocks and keys."

Dash chuckles. "Such a human thing to say."

"Bite me," I mutter.

We walk into Chevalier House's entrance hall and find Dash's BFF teammate Jewel waiting for us. "Oh, you found her," Jewel says, a smile lighting up her face. "Well done."

"Are you also part of the babysitting team?" I ask.

She frowns. "What do you mean? I was with Dash when Azzy sent the message to say you'd run. I offered to help look for you."

"How nice of you," I say flatly.

Dash nudges me with his elbow, and I take a step away from him so he can't do it again. Azzy hurries into the room then. "Emerson." She places her hands on her hips and gives me a stern look. "Running away wasn't necessary. I hope you know that we aren't going to force you to stay here against your will. If you're completely certain you're not interested in this world, we can send you back to the Guild and they can give you one of those devices that block all magic."

"Device?" I ask.

"It's a ring or bangle or something. I'm not sure what form they're using these days. It's something that can't be removed, and it will block your magic entirely."

"Oh. I didn't know that was an option." But as Dash pointed out, magic can help me to help Mom. Especially since the kind of job I could get as a high school graduate wouldn't pay nearly as much as the kind of job I could get if I whipped up an enchanted version of some higher qualification. If I want to be better equipped to help Mom, then I need to stick around a bit longer. "I'm sorry, Azzy," I force myself to say. "I'm here to learn now. I won't run again."

"Wonderful. Now, why don't you two stay for dinner?" Azzy asks Jewel and Dash. "Or do you have important cases to deal with?"

"Our team's done for the day," Jewel says. She links arms with Dash. "We'd love to stay for dinner."

"Wonderful," Azzy says, wrapping an arm around Dash's shoulders and squeezing them briefly.

"Yeah, really wonderful," I mutter. "I'm just gonna ... clean up, I guess."

"Of course," Azzy says, nodding toward one of the doors leading off the entrance hall. "Try not to confuse it with the front door, Em. We wouldn't want you getting lost outside again."

I consider rolling my eyes, but it's too much effort. "I think I can manage."

When I'm done splashing water on my face and combing my fingers through my hair—which surprises me, yet again, with its bright blue strands—I leave the bathroom and find Jewel waiting alone in the entrance hall. She pushes away from the table. I glance around, but it's definitely me she's walking toward. "Um, hi?"

She smiles, and it seems almost genuine. "Look, I really don't want to do the whole teenage, mean-girl thing, since I know we're all practically adults around here, but I do just want to point out that Dash isn't exactly available."

I decide to play dumb. "Available for what?"

She rolls her eyes. "You know, a relationship."

"Oh." I fold my arms. "Why is that?"

"Well, look, it's not official yet, but we kind of have a thing going."

"A thing? Really? I never would have guessed that, given the way he tries to charm every female he comes across."

Jewel's smile slips a little. "Yeah, I know he's dated a bunch of girls, but none of those relationships have lasted long, and I know exactly why."

I feign intense interest. "You do?"

"Yes, it's obvious: he's searching for the right person. And he's so close to discovering that it's me, so I just don't want anything to ruin that for us now."

"Oh, wow, it's you? How do you know that?"

"Because so much of our lives have been spent together. We trained together. We grew up together. We even played together as babies. We're meant to be."

I blink. "That's the dumbest thing I've ever heard."

"Hey!"

"Who cares if you played together as babies? I doubt either

of you can remember it."

"That doesn't matter! It means we have a *history*," she snaps, all trace of her sweet smile gone. "And if we have a history, we'll have a stronger future."

"Really? 'Cause Dash and I have a history too, and it's only ever made me dislike him."

"Yes, because you have the *wrong* history. We have the *right* history, so—"

"Jewel?" I pause to make sure she's listening. "You can have him. I'm not interested."

"Oh. Really?"

"Really. I have other priorities right now." I walk past her and head for the dining room, where loud chatter and mouthwatering aromas fill the air. At the long rectangular table sit the seven other students currently attending Chevalier House, as well as a few fae I've seen walking around. Teachers, perhaps, and the man with his hand on Azzy's wrist, chuckling as he leans closer to say something only she can hear, must be her husband or partner or something of that nature.

"Emerson! You missed something exciting while you were gone," George tells me as I take a seat.

"Oh, what did I miss?"

"Another new person arrived."

"And that counts as exciting?" I pull the nearest platter of food closer and begin dishing roasted vegetables onto my plate. They smell a thousand times more delicious than anything Chelsea's ever cooked.

"That's two new people in two days," Azzy says from the head of the table. "That doesn't happen often here."

"And she's old like you," George adds.

I lower the serving spoon. "Excuse me?"

"Oh, gosh, as old as Emerson?" Dash's eyes widen. "That's seriously old."

George, sitting beside Dash across the table from me, chews his lip as his brow furrows. "Oh, I thought ... But isn't Azzy the one who's super old? And Emerson is, like, your age?" he says to Dash.

"Okay, and *this*," I say, pointing my fork for emphasis, "is why it's so flipping confusing having people who are a bazillion years old looking like they're in their twenties."

Dash shrugs. "We can't help it if we have magic running through our systems, keeping us young and beautiful."

"I know, it's so great, right?" Jewel says as she hurries into the dining room and selects the only available seat on Dash's side of the table.

"Bazillion? I'm only three hundred and four," says the man sitting beside Azzy. "I'm Paul, by the way," he adds with a smile in my direction. "Azzy's husband."

"Hi." I return his smile, pleased to discover that at least some fae have normal names. After tasting some of my food and trying not to moan out loud at how amazing it is, I ask, "So where's the other new girl?"

"She wasn't feeling so well," Azzy says. "Had a traumatizing few days. I gave her something to eat when she arrived just before dinner, and she's sleeping now. The two of you can begin lessons together tomorrow."

"Great." I'm less than thrilled about sharing lessons with someone else—what if she slows me down?—but since I've decided to commit myself fully to the Chevalier House program, I should probably be polite to everyone living here.

I turn my attention back to my food, piling a few more delicacies onto my plate when I think no one's looking. Dash catches my eye, though. I return his smirk with a glare. Spoiled brat probably has a live-in chef at home. No doubt he eats like this all the time.

At the end of the meal, the dishes rise up of their own accord and fly out of the dining room toward the kitchen. I try not to act too surprised, but I can't help pressing myself back against my chair in fright when my plate first rises into the air. I excuse myself soon afterwards and leave the dining room; all this chatter and activity over dinner isn't something I'm used to. I'd rather get to bed early so I can focus properly on all this magic stuff tomorrow.

"Em?"

I turn on the bottom step leading up to the bedrooms and look back.

"It's good that you came back," Dash says, wandering into the entrance hall. "When you're kicking butt at all your lessons in a few weeks' time, let me know so I can gloat about being the one who talked you into staying."

The only response I give him is another glare.

"Hey, come on, I'm just joking."

"You know, I've been trying to figure out why so many people like you when you're actually such a jackass."

He shrugs. "Probably because no one else is under the impression that I ruined their lives, so they're able to see me for who I really am."

"Which is what, exactly?"

"Friendly guy, charming smile, not half-bad to look at."

"I'm surprised they can see anything past that gigantic head of yours."

He frowns and raises a hand to his head. "What's wrong with my—"

"I meant your ego, dumb-ass."

"Hey, I said not half-bad. That should only give me a half-sized ego, right?"

"On you, that's more than big enough," I say as I turn and head up the stairs.

"Good night, Emmy," he calls after me.

"Shut up," I grumble beneath my breath.

I reach my door, push it open—and jump backward at the sight of a tiger sitting on my bed. The tiger flickers and morphs into an owl, then a crow, and then a kitten. Relief courses through me, followed quickly by irritation. "No," I say. "No, no, no. This isn't happening. You were supposed to stay out there in the forest." The kitten blinks. "I'm giving you to Dash. He can take care of you." I scoop the kitten up and hurry back along the hall.

At the top of the stairs, I stop. Azzy and Dash are standing close together in the entrance hall below, Dash looking uncharacteristically serious. "We have until the end of the week," he says quietly, "so there's no immediate rush. But we'll get a plan in place, probably for the day after tomorrow."

"Good. And make sure it looks like an accident."

"Of course."

I bite my lip, shrinking back into the shadows, knowing

instinctively that I wasn't supposed to hear whatever they were talking about. Before I can decide what to do about the shapeshifting animal, Dash pulls the front door open and leaves. Azzy walks back to the dining room, her lightweight, oversized top floating behind her.

"What on earth?" I whisper to the kitten. An instant later, it becomes a bunny. "Fine. Dash is gone, so you're on your own." I place the bunny on the stairs, then hurry back to my room, my mind already racing through explanations for what Dash and Azzy could have been talking about. Perhaps it wasn't anything sinister at all. *Make sure it looks like an accident.* That doesn't sound good, though. But whatever it is, I won't be getting involved. I've survived this long by keeping my nose out of other people's business, and that isn't about to change.

After visiting the steaming hot pool in the bathroom—the best thing about this house aside from the food—I climb into bed and tap the lamp to turn it off. It's powered by magic, of course—electricity doesn't seem to exist in this world—and Azzy told me to lightly tap it with my finger to turn it on and off. So far, it seems to be working.

I settle down against the pillows, finding it easier to drift off tonight than last night. I'm almost asleep when a sound—a gentle tap at the door—rouses me. So quiet I wonder if I might have imagined it. I sit up, watching the door through the dim grey light from the window and waiting. When the knock comes a second time, I know I'm not imagining it. "Yes?" I call through the darkness. My door opens slowly, revealing the silhouette of a female figure. "Who's there?" I ask, nerves fluttering suddenly in my stomach.

"Are you Emerson?" she asks. "The other new girl?"

"Um, yes." I lean over and turn on my lamp as she slips inside and shuts the door. She hurries across the room and drops onto the edge of my bed. I scoot backwards, putting a little more distance between us as I take in her appearance: a creased robe the same color as the one I found hanging in my wardrobe, pale skin, and eyes a deep blueish purple. It's the same color that runs through her dark hair, which, if I remember my lessons correctly, mean she's a faerie, not some other kind of fae.

"Please help me," she whispers, her eyes wide. "It isn't safe here. We need to leave."

PART II

CHAPTER
TEN

"UM ... WHAT?" I ASK, UTTERLY CONFUSED. "WHAT ARE you talking about? And who are you?"

"I'm Aurora. I just got here this evening. The professor told me there was another new girl, and I thought that since you haven't got too deep into their program yet, and they haven't brainwashed you, or whatever it is that happens here, we can get away together."

"Brainwash? Where'd you get that from?"

"Because I—I may not know how to use my magic at all, but I did grow up in this world, and I know things. I've heard things. About this place." She inches a little closer. "People disappear from here sometimes. Like, they just vanish without a trace soon after their training begins. And it's made to look like Chevalier House has nothing to do with it, but how can it not? People come in here, and they never leave. They just disappear. And I don't want that to happen to me. I just got my freedom, and I don't want to lose it."

If I could move any further away from this girl, I would, but I'm already backed up against the wall. "So, you're saying … they *kill* some of the people who come in here?"

"I don't know. Maybe." She tugs at the silky belt of her robe, pulling it tighter. "Or maybe it's something worse. Maybe they're prisoners somewhere. Maybe they're being experimented on."

"Do you have any proof of that?"

"Of course not, but that doesn't make it untrue."

Given what I overheard between Dash and Azzy just now, I'm almost inclined to believe this girl, but her wide, terror-filled eyes remind me all too much of Mom. Mom looking desperate and afraid, speaking about equally irrational things. "Look, Aurora. I don't mean to be unfriendly, but I don't want to get involved in whatever you're talking about. You have your issues, and I have mine. Let's just get through this Magic 101 thing, and we can both go our separate ways."

She draws back, hurt filling her eyes. "You don't believe me? You seriously want to take your chances with these people you've just met, instead of considering that I might be telling you the truth? That you and I might never get the chance to go our separate ways if something happens to us before then?"

I think again of Dash and Azzy's quiet conversation. "Okay," I say slowly. "It's true that I don't know the people here at all, but I don't know you either. You could be making this up."

She takes a deep breath. "What do you want to know? I'll … I'll tell you everything. When you understand how horrendous my life's been up until now, you'll understand why I don't ever want to be a prisoner again. I'll do anything to get out of here."

I raise my eyebrows at the word 'prisoner,' but I'm still not ready to believe this girl. If there are insane people in my world, there must be insane people in this one too. "Why don't we leave this until the morning?"

"No! Just let me explain myself. How will you know if you can trust me until you've heard what I have to say? How do you know you can trust *them*?"

I consider shouting out for Azzy, but Aurora's right. I *don't* know if I can trust anyone here. What if Chevalier House and this program is all an elaborate ruse to gather untrained magical beings? I don't know why anyone would do that, but I don't know much about this world, so there could be a reason. "Fine. Tell me what you want to tell me."

"Okay. So, I was brought up by witches—"

"Witches?" I give her a doubtful look. "Like on broomsticks? Nobody's said anything to me about witches. Are they even real?"

Her eyes narrow. "You've been in this world for all of five minutes, and you've already decided you know more than I do?"

"I just—"

"No, they don't have anything to do with broomsticks. I don't even know what that means."

"Oh. You've never been in my world?"

"The non-magic realm? No, never. Why would they have taken me there? I've spent most of my life locked up in their home. The only things I know are the things I've heard them talk about, and the things I've read in their books. I don't know how I ended up living in a house with witches, because they never bothered to tell me. They ... they treated me like their servant." She pulls her knees up and wraps her arms around them. "They never taught me how to use my magic, because that would have made me stronger. I could have used it against them. They caught me reading about Chevalier House once, when I was trying to figure out an escape plan and where I would go if I ever got away. They laughed and said that even if I managed to run away from them, Chevalier House wouldn't do me any good. Fae disappear from here all the time."

"If that were true, surely the Guild would know about it. They would have shut down the program by now." It can't be true. I need it to not be true. I need Azzy to teach me everything about magic so I can get back to my own world and help Mom.

"Unless the Guild's in on it too," Aurora says in conspiratorial tones.

"So if Chevalier House is dangerous, why did you come here?"

"I didn't *choose* to come here." She returns her feet to the floor and leans closer to me. "I finally managed to get away from the witches after months of careful planning. I was all on my own until a guardian caught me stealing food. That's how I ended up at the Guild, and they're the ones who sent me here."

I sigh. "You know this all sounds ridiculous, right? And the only thing you've got to go on is what a bunch of witches have told you. Obviously they'd want you to believe that Chevalier House can't help you. They didn't want you running away."

"Okay, so *maybe* they were lying. But are you willing to take that risk? Do you even *want* to be here?"

"Actually, yes. I do. I realized today that magic can help me far more than anything I've ever learned in my own world, and I need to know how to use it before returning home."

"If they ever allow you to return home," Aurora points out.

"Fine. What exactly are you suggesting then? That we run away together?"

"Yes. Everything's locked up now—I already checked downstairs—but we can wait for a chance tomorrow and run together. Then we can figure out what to do once we're free."

"No," I say flatly. "I'm sorry, but no. I tried that today and it didn't work. I have a different plan now, and it doesn't include running away with someone I just met."

"You're being so naive," she whispers with a fearful shake of her head.

"Am I? I don't trust you, and I don't trust them, so who am I going to go with? Obviously the side that's most likely to help me. And right now, that looks like Chevalier House. If something weird's going on, I'll figure it out soon enough and then I'll run. But for now, I'm staying put." I shove aside the tiny voice that says Aurora might be right. That the strange conversation I overheard is evidence enough. Because I *need* this program to work. Now that I've realized how much magic can do for me in my own world, I'm clinging to it as if it's my only hope for a better life.

Aurora swallows, then breathes out slowly. She tucks a few strands of hair behind her ear, leaning away from me. "Okay. I'm—I'm sorry I bothered you with this." She slides off my bed and stands. "I'll … um … I guess you're right. We should each be looking out for ourselves."

I nod, since I'm not sure what else to do or say.

"Okay, well … good night." She turns and hurries out of my room.

"So weird," I murmur as I tap the lamp, plunging the room into darkness once more. I keep telling myself I've made the right decision, but I can't help turning her words over and over in my mind, and it's a long time before I fall asleep.

CHAPTER ELEVEN

"IT'S LOVELY THAT THE TWO OF YOU ARRIVED AT THE SAME time and can learn together," Azzy says to Aurora and me as the two of us sit side by side at a library table the following morning. "It doesn't often happen that way."

Aurora says nothing, so I decide to say nothing too. I doubt either of us thinks there's anything 'lovely' about this situation. In fact, I'm surprised she's still here. She seemed so desperate last night; I thought she'd have found a way to escape the house while the rest of us were sleeping. But she was sitting at the dining room table when I got there this morning, frowning at her plate. She didn't look up once during breakfast.

"Right, then," Azzy says. "I'm going to explain glamours this morning, and after that we'll move outside to try some basic magic before lunch. No need to run away this time, Em," she adds with a chuckle. I sense Aurora's eyes on me, and I make a determined effort not to meet her gaze. "Then perhaps later, Em," Azzy says, "you can give me any information you think might be helpful in finding your real family. And you too, Aurora."

Icy apprehension shoots through my veins. I've been trying to ignore the idea that I have another family out there somewhere. It makes me sick every time I remember Mom isn't actually my mother. "Um …"

"Unless you don't want to, of course," Azzy adds quickly.

"I'm interested," Aurora says, which is surprising enough to make me look her way. I wonder what game she's playing, or if she might possibly be serious. Perhaps she hopes to discover something useful about her family before fleeing Chevalier House.

"Azzy?" I look around as Paul walks into the library. "I've just received the guardians' report." He waves a rolled-up piece of paper. "They didn't find anything suspicious."

"Suspicious about what?" Aldo asks. He's reading alone at another table in the library while George works on some practical skills outside. "Did something happen?"

"The security enchantments picked up something outside our gate in the early evening yesterday," Paul explains. "The Guild was alerted, and a couple of guardians came to check things out. They told us they didn't find anything, but they left someone stationed out there for the night anyway."

"Do you think … maybe … it was the Griffin rebels?" Aldo says. "They hate the Guild, so they would hate us too, right?"

"I'm sure it was nothing," Azzy says with a smile. "And Paul," she adds in a low voice, though we can all still hear her, "I don't think it's necessary to scare the students."

"But we have a right to know what's going on, don't we?" Aldo protests. "If there's a threat, we should know about it."

"Nothing is going on," Azzy assures him. "The Griffin rebels have absolutely no reason to attack us. We have nothing to do with them."

I look over at Aurora. Her violet eyes meet mine, and her eyebrows rise the tiniest bit, as if to say, *See? I told you something's going on here.*

"Enough about that," Azzy says, clapping her hands together. "Aurora, do you know what a glamour is?"

Startled, Aurora swings back to face Azzy. "Not really. The witches didn't tell me anything about them."

The next hour passes with Azzy explaining glamours of all types, from the simple kind I'm supposed to be able to cast over myself without even thinking about it, to the immensely complex kind that conceal buildings inside trees so they're hidden from view. I realize that this is probably what Dash was referring to when he spoke about tree houses, and it's impossible to wrap my mind around the concept. A whole house full of space hidden inside one tree trunk? *How the freaking heck?*

"Magic makes the impossible possible," Azzy says, which doesn't seem like much of an explanation to me.

Something tickles my ankle. I look down, twitching involuntarily when I see a grasshopper clinging to the bottom of my jeans. I'm about to swat it away when it flickers, drops to the floor, seems to kind of bulge out, and becomes a frog. "Seriously?" I whisper. "Leave me alone."

"Em?" Azzy asks, pausing in the middle of a description of exactly what happened to one of the Guilds years ago when its glamour magic was destroyed. "Everything okay?"

"Uh, yes. Just a frog."

"Oh, it must have hopped in from outside. I'm sure it'll find its way back out. Now, shall we try some magic?"

Excitement pulses through me as we follow Azzy into the garden. *Be patient*, I instruct myself. *Don't get frustrated. You can do this.* We stop near a three-tiered fountain. I rub my hands up and down my arms. "It's a little cold to practice outside, isn't it?"

"Yeah," Aurora murmurs. No doubt she's feeling it worse than I am. I've at least got jeans on; she's wearing a long skirt and open sandals.

"Nonsense." Azzy turns to face us. "As long as the fountain hasn't iced over, it isn't too cold. Besides, the low temperature will help motivate you to learn how to keep yourself warm with magic."

"If we don't freeze to death first," I mutter.

"Young people," Azzy mutters as she flicks her hand toward a bench on the other side of the fountain. "Always so dramatic." A retort rises to my tongue, but it freezes there as I watch the bench slide around the fountain and come to a halt behind Azzy. She sits, folds her hands together on her knees, and looks at us. "I'd like you to start by drawing magic from your core. Aurora, you said you're already familiar with how to do this?"

"Um, yes. I practiced on my own whenever I wasn't being watched."

"Wonderful. Em, you've got some catching up to do."

"Yay," I mutter. "I always love it when teachers pit students against each other to try get them to perform better."

Azzy sits a little straighter and brushes something non-existent off her sleeve. "I'm sure I have no idea what you're talking about."

"Can we just get on with this?" Aurora asks quietly. I look over and see that she's already holding a glowing sphere of magic above her palms.

Gritting my teeth, I close my eyes and repeat Azzy's instructions from yesterday. I have to stop and refocus three times before I produce a visible mass of magic, but after I've done it once, I can repeat it several times without a problem. "Okay," I say, almost giddy with elation as I hold my own power in my hands. "What's next?"

"Fire," Azzy says with a gleam in her eyes. She pulls a scrap of paper from the folds of her loose clothing and draws something on it with her stylus, using the bench to press against. Almost immediately, three long, slender candles push their way up out of the paper.

"How did you—"

"That's a lesson for another day." She stands. "Here's a candle for each of you. Now that you can call on your magic at will, I want you to shape it into a flame." She holds the third candle up in front of her face. "Some spells require written words, and some require spoken words. Some require both, or a specific movement of the hands. What we're going to do now requires a spoken word only—and of course, the subconscious nudging of your magic toward the candle."

She makes it sound easy, this 'subconscious nudging,' but I'm guessing it's one of those things that takes loads of practice and effort before it becomes instinctive.

"Repeat after me," Azzy says. She utters a strange word I've never heard before, then blows gently at the candle. A flame flickers to life.

Aurora starts practicing, and of course she gets it right on her third try. I, however, blow again and again and nothing happens. I try different ways of speaking the magical word, changing the emphasis from the first syllable to the last, but it makes no difference.

"Stop," Azzy says eventually. "I don't think you're sending any magic toward the candle at all. Don't forget that part. Pull on your magic, speak the word, and then imagine blowing that power out of your mouth and straight at the candle.

I do as she says. And nothing happens.

My patience snaps. I throw the candle onto the grass. "I don't understand. I managed to rip the ground apart without even trying, and now I can't even light a candle."

"That was different—"

"I *know* it was different. It was easy and it was English. This is … just … stupid words that don't make sense."

"Em," Azzy says, and her voice carries a warning tone.

"No, seriously. The other night I just said something and it happened."

"Emerson."

"Why can't I just keep doing that?" I bend and scoop the

candle up. Holding it high, I say, "Candle, start burning." Nothing happens. "Start burning!" I shout. Still nothing. I swing around and point at the tree. "Fall over!" Nothing. I face the fountain. "Break into a hundred pieces and put yourself back together!" A shiver ripples up my spine, and I realize those last words sounded oddly distant and yet weirdly resonant at the same time.

The fountain vibrates. Cracks form across the tiers and splinter rapidly outwards.

A pause.

Silence.

Then the entire fountain explodes.

Aurora screams as water and pieces of stone fly outward. Suddenly, we're both flat on the ground. I force my head up to see what's happening. The stone pieces freeze, reverse, and fly straight back to their starting point, all joining together perfectly. I suck in a breath as the last crack vanishes, returning the fountain to its exact original form.

More silence.

Then Aurora scoots backward across the ground. "That's not normal," she gasps. "That is *so* not normal."

"I did it," I murmur. "I used magic."

"That wasn't magic," Azzy whispers.

I twist around to look at her. "What do you mean?"

Slowly she shakes her head. "Not normal magic. Not the kind of magic the rest of us have."

I look past her and find Paul and the remainder of the students standing a few feet away, their expressions all frozen in shock. "I'll get hold of the Guild," Paul says quietly.

"Why?" I push myself onto my feet. "What did I do? What's wrong?"

Aurora stands, and Azzy looks between the two of us. "You're lucky I got you both onto the ground so quickly. You might have been badly hurt otherwise."

"Answer me," I say to her, and again, that strange ripple rushes up my spine.

Azzy jolts. Abruptly, and almost robotically, she says, "I've never seen magic like that before. No faerie should be able to do what you just did. I suspect you have a Griffin Ability. Paul's contacting the Guild now, and they'll probably send someone here immediately to test you. What happens next is up to them." Her voice cuts off abruptly, and she slaps a hand over her mouth as if to stop anymore words tumbling out. Then she breathes out slowly and lowers her hand. "Don't do that again. Don't speak again."

"But I—"

"Emerson," she interrupts. "Your voice is dangerous. Please don't speak again until a Guild member is here."

A chill races across my skin, followed by a flush of heat. Anxiety tightens my stomach. This is all going wrong. I'm supposed to learn magic and then go home. I'm not supposed to be in trouble with the Guild. I'm not supposed to be one of those dangerous superpowered faeries everyone seems to hate.

"Come, let's go inside." Azzy takes my arm and leads me toward the house. I think about fighting her, about pushing her away and running, but I'm overcome by exhaustion all of a sudden. My arms hang weakly at my sides, and a wave of dizziness passes through me. It's gone by the time we reach the entrance hall, but I still feel too drained to think about running anywhere.

Azzy ushers everyone out of the room, then hurries off to another part of the house, leaving me alone in the entrance hall with Paul. He stands with his arms crossed firmly over his chest, not once removing his eyes from me. Azzy reappears a minute or two later with a mug in her hand. "You're tired, I know," she says quietly. "This will help you regain your strength." Paul frowns, but he doesn't stop Azzy from handing the mug to me.

I take a hesitant sip, then keep drinking until the thick, chocolatey liquid is finished. It's sweet and warm and comforting, and I begin feeling stronger almost immediately. I place the mug on the table and look at Azzy. "There must be a mistake, right? I can't possibly have one of those Griffin Ability things. What happened out there ... that was just uncontrolled magic or something. Right?"

"You shouldn't be speaking," Paul says.

"Because I have a *dangerous voice*? That's absurd. I'm sure there's another explanation for—"

"Em, stop," Azzy says. "Please. I think it's safer if you say nothing."

At that moment, the front door of Chevalier House swings open and two figures stride in. A woman I don't recognize, and—

"Dash," I say the moment I see him. It's weird, but I'm actually relieved he's here.

"Emerson," the woman says, staring me down with eyes that appear to be almost bronze in color. She's dressed in a well-tailored pants suit, and her hair is pulled back tightly in a bun. I can't figure out her expression. It definitely isn't a smile, but it isn't fear or wariness or anger. "I'm Head Councilor Ashlow. Why didn't you tell us you could perform unnatural magic?"

I throw my hands up, because this is becoming too much now. "You're kidding, right? *All* magic is unnatural to me! I only just discovered it exists! How was I supposed to know that saying something and then having it happen is considered unusual in this world?"

"Not just unusual. Impossible."

"Well ... exactly. How was I supposed to know that?"

She breathes out sharply and extends her closed hand toward me. Her fingers uncurl to reveal a bright green pill sitting on her palm. "Councilor Waterfield should have tested you the first day you arrived in this world. She shouldn't have let *you*—" she pins her gaze on Dash for a moment "—talk her out of it."

Dash frowns. "I hope you're not suggesting I intentionally kept this information from you, Councilor Ashlow. I had no idea Griffin magic was involved."

"I'm not sure what to think right now." She looks at me again. "Take the pill, Emerson."

Something tells me that disobeying isn't an option, so I take the pill and place it on my tongue. It dissolves quickly. Dash's eyes rove over me, his expression darkening. I look down at myself, and my heart misses a beat or two when I see my body glowing faintly green. "So it's true," Dash says. "She's one of them."

"And you didn't know?"

"Of course not. I would have reported it immediately if I suspected she had a Griffin Ability. It's my job to protect our world from people like her." He almost spits out that last word, and for a moment I consider spitting right back at him. But then he wraps his iron-like grip around my upper arm and begins steering me toward the door, and my hatred of him is quickly replaced by ice-cold fear.

"What are you—but I haven't done anything wrong. I'm not one of those Griffin rebels. I don't want to attack people. Surely you can't hold me responsible for crimes I've never committed, or crimes that you think I *might* possibly commit in the future."

"We can, actually," Councilor Ashlow says as we reach the door. "Our laws state that the world needs to be protected from people like you. In some cases, that means tagging and tracking you. Knowing your whereabouts and activities at all times. In extreme cases, it means limiting your freedom. The Council will need to meet to discuss your case, but I'm in no doubt, Emerson, that they will find it extreme indeed. I'm sorry." She doesn't look sorry, though. If anything, she seems excited by the fact that she's just apprehended another Griffin Gifted faerie.

"But ... this ... how did it even happen?" I ask, trying to stall, trying to come up with a way out of this. "Those magical discs ... no, that can't be right. They haven't been around for years. So—"

"Both your parents must have been Griffin Gifted," Councilor Ashlow says. "That's the only explanation."

"Wait," I say as she opens the door. "Wait, please. What does limiting my freedom mean?"

"It means you'll be kept somewhere," Dash answers, forcing me out onto the top step.

"Kept?"

"Yes, like a safe house kind of thing."

I stop walking and manage to tug my arm free of his grip. "So a prison."

Dash looks back at me. "It isn't like that, Em. No one wants you to be a prisoner. It's just that you're dangerous, so you can't be set loose, either in this world or the human one. Surely you understand that."

I force back the ache in my throat and the tears pricking behind my eyes. I clench my teeth together and say, "You're enjoying this, aren't you. It's probably the best entertainment you've had in ages. You've never liked me, and now you get to see me locked up. You're doing to me what you did to my mother."

His eyes narrow and he opens his mouth, but Councilor Ashlow interrupts with a groan. "All this unnecessary drama. Just get on with it." She pulls the door shut and heads past us down the stairs. Dash tugs me against his side and forces me to follow her.

"Firstly," he says quietly, "you're the one who doesn't like me. And secondly, this has nothing to do with anyone liking anyone else. You're a threat, so we have to take precautions. That's it."

"But I'm not a threat!" My emotions are dangerously close to the surface all of a sudden, and I take a moment to swallow them down. "I mean, not intentionally. I didn't choose to be this way. This isn't fair."

He's quiet for so long that I assume he's now ignoring me. But as we walk out of the gate and find Councilor Ashlow opening a faerie paths doorway, he says, "Life isn't fair, Em. You already know that."

Councilor Ashlow looks back at us as the dark hole in the air grows larger. "Hurry up," she says. "We need to get to the Guild."

Dash's grip on my arm tightens, but he walks forward without hesitation. "Don't think about anything," he says as we step into the darkness. "It'll confuse the faerie paths, and that won't end well for any of us."

I struggle to quiet my racing thoughts, but I must somehow manage to do a good enough job, because soon, light materializes ahead of us. We walk into a small room where a man in a uniform behind an elaborately carved wooden desk greets us. I remember Dash saying something about a grand entrance transforming from a tree, but he must have been referring to a different part of the Guild because the only impressive thing in this room is the desk.

"This way," Councilor Ashlow says, gesturing to an open door on our right. Dash pushes me through it, and my mouth drops open at the site of an enormous foyer with a wide, sweeping staircase on the opposite side and glittering chandelier lights hanging here and there. My darting eyes take in men and women in dark clothing, hair of every color, gleaming white floors and twirling patterns etched into the walls—before an alarm begins shrieking in my ears.

"It's okay," Councilor Ashlow says, holding a hand up to halt the people who race toward her. "We're already aware of the Griffin Ability. I'm taking her to the detainment area now."

Get out, my brain says as my panicked thoughts return in full force. *Get out of here!* But I don't know how. What did I do the other day when the cops were trying to take me away? I must have used my Griffin Ability, but I have no idea how.

I sense Dash watching me. "I'm going to let go of you now," he says. "Can you behave?"

I nod as his grip loosens and his arm slides away from mine. Then I shove him as hard as I can and run.

CHAPTER TWELVE

I TRIP OVER MY OWN FEET—OR OVER SOMETHING INVISIBLE, since I swear I've never been that clumsy—and hit the floor on my side. My so-called useless parkour practice kicks in, and I continue rolling. Onto my stomach, my hands push against the floor, and I spring up onto my feet. I catch a glimpse of Dash sprawled on the floor with guardians tumbling over him before I take off in the opposite direction, repeating "Get away from me, get away from me!" in the desperate hope that my Griffin Ability will appear and give my words actual power. In my haste to get back to the room we entered through, I can't tell if my voice is any different, but I keep repeating the words anyway. And either it's working, or these guardians are even worse than the Stanmeade cops, because they're falling all over each other.

I rush into the entrance hall just as someone runs out—and I crash right into her. The force slams me backward, but she lunges forward and grabs my arm, pulling me upright. "Aurora?" I gasp as she pulls me into the room. "What are you doing here?"

"Trying to help you!"

Glittering rope lashes out at me and snaps around my arm, tugging me out of Aurora's grasp and onto the floor. I scrabble uselessly at the glossy surface before looking up at the guard who greeted us a minute ago. He's standing on the desk now, dragging me swiftly toward him. "Get away!" I yell, hoping it will work. Invisible power knocks him through the open door and into the foyer, yanking me sharply to the side as the rope grows taut.

Light flashes, severing the rope and leaving a small piece attached to my arm. I look up and find Aurora with a stylus in her hand. "Get up!" She rushes to the wall and writes on it. "Come on!"

I look toward the foyer, where guardians are racing toward us, flashes of magic escaping their hands. I jump up and lurch toward Aurora and the growing darkness behind her. "You can use a stylus?" I gasp as I take her hand.

"Don't think of anything," she instructs as she pushes me ahead of her into the faerie paths. "And don't let go."

"I thought you didn't know—" My words cut off as Aurora's hand is torn free of mine. I swing around to see what's happening and find two guardians hauling her backward.

"Emerson!" she shrieks, one hand reaching out for me.

I hesitate, conflicting parts of my brain screaming *Save her!*

and *Save yourself!* And in that moment, the darkness of the faerie paths closes around me. I try to remember what I'm supposed to do now, what I'm supposed to focus on or say, but then I'm falling backward through the darkness. I land hard on the ground as tangled trees and overgrown bushes take form around me. I groan and cough and try to suck in air as I sit up. I have no idea where the faerie paths have dumped me. For a moment, I wonder if I might have been lucky enough to end up back in the normal world, but as two minuscule people-shaped beings with wings flit past me, my hope dies. "Brilliant," I mutter as I climb to my feet, leaves rustling beneath my shoes.

I look around, but Aurora is nowhere to be seen. Guilt mingles with my relief at having escaped. I should have tried to pull her back into the paths. The only reason she was there was to help me. I press my fingers against my temples and try to convince myself that nothing bad will happen to her. It's not like she's Griffin Gifted. They'll just send her back to Chevalier House, and once she's finished training, she'll be free. Although, now that I think about it, does she even need training? Last night she said she didn't know how to use her magic, but she had no problem cutting the rope around my arm or opening a faerie paths doorway.

I lift my right arm and frown at the sparkling piece of rope still attached to it. I try to undo the knot or loosen it enough to pull my hand free, but it won't budge. So after one last glance around the forest, I pick a direction and start moving. The air is warmer here than in the garden we were training in this morning, which tells me I'm probably nowhere near Chevalier

House. Unfortunately, that might mean I'm right next to whichever tree conceals the Guild, so I'd better get away from the area as quickly as possible.

I start running, swerving between trees, launching my body easily over giant tree roots, and giving a wide berth to an exotic bush with large, blood-red thorns. I throw the occasional glance over my shoulder, but nothing seems to be following me. Eventually, I slow to a quick walk. Something tickles the side of my neck, and I swat at my skin, afraid that some dangerous magical insect is biting me. A screech rips through the air right beside my ear. I leap away, letting out my own startled yelp and spinning around to face whatever's attacking me. A fluffy bird that might be an owl flaps as it descends clumsily toward the forest floor, morphing into a kitten as it reaches the ground. Sad, high-pitched mews fill the air.

"Holy sh … sherbet." I rub my ear as the adrenaline rush subsides. "You nearly deafened me. What are you doing here, you weird little thing? You're supposed to be back at Chevalier House." The kitten flashes between several unrecognizable forms before settling as a fox cub. It walks over to me and begins nuzzling my ankle. I step away and fold my arms over my chest. It looks up with wide, pleading eyes.

And I give in.

"Fine. You can stay with me. But I'm not giving you a name. It'll all be downhill from there." I tuck the soft, furry creature beneath my arm and continue walking.

And almost fall over in fright when someone steps out of the air in front of me. "*Dash?*" I stumble backward, the shapeshifting creature transforming into something tiny as it leaps away from me. "How did you find me?"

"Doesn't matter. We—" The space ripples beside him. He steps hastily away, raising his hand. A knife appears in his grip as he places himself between me and whatever threat we're about to face.

"Oh, you found her," Jewel says, walking out of the darkness. "Well done."

"Jewel?" Dash says. The knife vanishes as he lets go of it. "How did you—Why are you here?"

Hurt flashes briefly across her face as I carefully inch away from the two of them. "Just trying to help," she says. "You still have that tracking spell on your amber from the other night in the spider tunnels."

"Right." Dash retrieves his amber, drags his finger across the surface in a series of weird patterns, then shoves it back into his pocket. "Don't need that anymore."

"What's the big deal? I thought you needed help finding her."

"No big deal. I can handle it, that's all." He grabs my wrist before I can move too far away and twists it behind my back.

"Can you really handle it?" I ask in taunting tones as he ties my hands together. "It didn't seem like it back at the Guild. Are you guardians always so useless?"

Dash comes back around to stand in front of me, his expression showing genuine amusement. "No. They're not."

Huh. Maybe my Griffin Ability worked after all. "Ropes, untie," I instruct. Nothing happens. Dash quirks an eyebrow, then starts laughing.

"What's she doing?" Jewel asks.

"My guess is she's trying to make her Griffin Ability work."

"Oh." Jewel's brow puckers. "Maybe we should tape her mouth shut."

"Nah, she doesn't have the first clue how to use her Griffin Ability."

Heat rises to my face. "I'm gonna strangle you with this rope when I finally get it off. Rather that than end up a prisoner for the rest of my life."

"As I've already explained," Dash says slowly, "you won't be a prisoner. You just won't have the same level of freedom as everyone else."

I blink, unable to believe he's this stupid. "Are you listening to yourself? Do you know what the definition of prisoner is?"

"Em, it isn't that bad, I promise. Look, I know you're worrying about your mother—"

"Don't you dare bring her up right—"

"—but I'm sure the Guild will let you visit her under supervision. And our researchers are working all the time on trying to find a way to remove Griffin Abilities. That could happen soon, and then you'll be free again. Please try to understand." He throws a quick glance at Jewel before returning his gaze to me. "We're trying to keep the rest of the world safe, and this is unfortunately one of the precautions we have to take."

"Come on, Dash, you're wasting time," Jewel complains. "We need to get her back to the Guild." She pulls her stylus out and raises it.

"Don't," I say, and when I feel that odd tingle spreading rapidly throughout my body and my voice echoing oddly in my ears, I rush to add, "Don't open a doorway! Neither of you open a doorway!"

The rush of strangeness passes, and Jewel frowns at me over her shoulder. Then she presses her stylus against a tree and opens her mouth. After appearing to struggle for several seconds, she says, "I—I can't do it. I can't say the words."

Dash swings around to face me. "Oh, *come on*. You did not just do that."

I let out a shaky laugh. "I think I did, actually."

"Now none of us can go anywhere."

I nod slowly as I take in a deep breath. "Good."

"Undo what you just did," Jewel says, pointing her stylus at me.

"No way. Even if I wanted to, I have no idea how this Griffin Ability thing works."

Dash lets out a long sigh. "Oh well. Time to walk, I guess."

"Dash!" Jewel exclaims. "How are you not seriously pissed off right now?"

He shrugs. "We've been through worse. You know that. A *lot* worse." He starts walking. After several moments, the rope pulls taut between us and I'm forced to follow him. "Try to keep up, Emmy. Wouldn't want to get yourself eaten by some kind of dark, sinister creature." Despite his nonchalance, I notice the way his fists clench periodically at his sides. He's definitely angry with me. No doubt he's already in trouble for letting me get away from the Guild. Hopefully he'll wind up suspended or, even better, fired. If he's going to continue to ruin my life, I can ruin his too.

"We're near the edge of the forest, right?" Jewel says. "On

the side with the waterfall?" Dash nods, and Jewel scribbles something onto her amber. "Okay, Councilor Ashlow and a bunch of guardians will meet us there in a few minutes.

"Good." Dash writes something on his amber too, then adds, "Do you want to run ahead and meet them?"

"Yeah, okay." Jewel takes off through the trees, and the moment she's out of sight, Dash stops.

"Okay. We don't have much time. You—"

The air ripples so close I almost feel it move. A dark hole opens up, and a child tumbles out and crashes into me. "Oh, oops, sorry," he mumbles, pushing himself away from me and staggering backward.

"Are you flipping kidding me?" Dash demands. "What the heck are you doing here, Jack?"

The boy, who can't be more than ten, gives Dash a wide smile. "I wanted to be part of the mission. I listened to where everyone was going, but … I don't know. Where is everyone?"

"Jack, you need to go home immediately. Your parents are—" Dash looks up at the sound of crunching leaves up ahead. "Hide," he whispers, shoving the boy behind the nearest tree and dragging me forward once more.

"Dash, hurry up," Jewel calls as she comes into view. "They're waiting for us."

"Coming," Dash says before muttering something else under his breath. I keep my questions to myself as my mind races to figure out what's going on. Dash is afraid of something, and there must be a way I can use that to my advantage.

We catch up to Jewel, and after walking another minute or

so, we reach the edge of the forest. The trees thin out and come to an end. A short distance away, on a grassy patch of open space, Head Councilor Ashlow and several guardians are waiting for us. A stream runs past them and disappears over the edge of what must be a very high cliff, since I can't hear the water hitting the bottom.

"Well done for finding her, Dash," Councilor Ashlow says. "Although the fact that you haven't gagged her makes me question your intelligence."

"It was a fluke that she managed to use her Griffin Ability on us," Dash says. "I'm confident it won't happen again soon. But I'll gag her now to be safe." He brings me to a halt in front of the Councilor, but a collective murmur racing abruptly through the group distracts him before he can tie anything over my mouth. We both turn, and I see another group of people walking out of the trees. I assume at first that these are more guardians, but the sudden flash of glittering weapons all around me proves my assumption wrong.

"Well, well," Councilor Ashlow says. "The Unseelies have decided to show their faces."

"And why wouldn't we?" A man says, walking forward. I sense a change in the atmosphere—something I can't quite explain—and I wonder if that's how the Councilor knows these faeries are with the Unseelie Court. "A particularly interesting Griffin Ability has come to light," he continues. "We thought we should take a closer look."

"No need. We have everything under control."

"Of course you do. You probably plan to hand this girl over to the Seelie Court to be used as their own personal weapon."

Councilor Ashlow smiles. "What we plan to do with her is none of your business."

"It is our business when she could turn out to be one of the most powerful weapons in existence. What's to stop you from using her against us?"

"I suppose you'll have to trust that we like to keep the laws we make, unlike the members of your court."

"Trust?" He laughs. "I don't think so."

"Well, at the risk of sounding petty," Councilor Ashlow says, "we found her first. So we certainly won't be handing her over to you."

"Of course not. And I suppose you wouldn't like it if we took her from you by force."

"You could try, but I doubt you'd be successful."

The man's expression becomes thoughtful. "Since we can't come to a mutually beneficial arrangement, perhaps neither of us should possess this weapon. Perhaps she should be killed."

Perhaps WHAT? My heart rate kicks up notch.

"The only way we'll be killing her," Councilor Ashlow says, "is if *you* get your dirty talons on her." She looks around at her guardians, lowering her voice as she adds, "Don't let that happen. If it does—if it looks like they might get away with her—you have my permission to kill the girl."

"What?" I gasp, finally finding my voice. "That can't be legal."

"Yes, Councilor," Dash says, along with his fellow guardians.

I tug and twist and try to face him. "Are you kidding me? Are you really such a monster?"

Dash doesn't move, but his eyes dart around the clearing, between the trees and up to the canopy tops. "Sometimes," he mutters as the Unseelies advance on us, "we have to be monsters to protect the rest of the world." He tugs me backward as his companions spring forward.

Shouts and grunts and the clash of blades soon fill the air, along with a confusing mix of sparks, wind, glass shards and cackling birds. I wriggle and kick and yell, "Get away from me!" But it doesn't work this time. I try to focus on the core of magic deep inside me, just as Azzy instructed, but it makes not difference. Dash's hands remain firmly attached to me.

Two of the Unseelie faeries break through the line of guardians and come racing for us. "Stop them!" Dash yells, backing further away toward the edge of the cliff. One is tackled to the ground. The other launches forward. Dash spins me out of the way. "I'm sorry about this," he says. And then he shoves me clear off the edge of the cliff.

CHAPTER THIRTEEN

I BARELY HEAR MY SCREAM AS I PLUMMET TOWARD MY DEATH. Foamy water and jagged rocks rise rapidly to meet me. Faster, faster, faster—

Then my body decelerates abruptly and a dark shadow swoops below me as I come almost, almost, *almost* to a halt. Then I'm tumbling out of the air and into a pair of strong arms, and someone's saying, "Don't worry, I've got you." I land clumsily on the back of a creature with wings and find myself sandwiched between it and whoever it was that caught me. An arm wraps around my stomach. I squeeze my eyes shut and cling more tightly to that arm than anything I've ever held onto. I don't care who or what it is. I don't care if it's an Unseelie faerie or a guardian who wants to lock me up or some kind of new being I've never met. My brain cares about only one fact right now: I'm not falling anymore.

We begin moving upward. It's a jerky, flapping motion, but at least it's up and not down. I don't open my eyes. I don't want to see anything. Up and up, sideways, and up some more, and all the while I silently repeat, *Don't let go, don't let go, don't let go.* Then we plummet downward, and an involuntary gasp escapes me. But it's over, and we're landing amongst the trees, and that strong pair of arms is pulling me off the winged creature. "She's fine," he says to someone as he deposits me on the ground. "We were almost too late, but she's fine."

My legs are shaking so badly they can't hold me up. I land on my butt, blinking and gasping and taking in the people around me in disjointed snapshot moments. Three faeries. *Blink.* A man, dark blue, bending closer to me with concern on his face. *Blink.* A woman, purple, saying something I can't hear. *Blink.* Another woman, watching something through the trees, hair of actual gold sliding over her shoulder. Dark tattoos weave across her arms and reach up the side of her neck.

"Emerson? Emerson!" I refocus on the woman who's now crouching beside me. The one with wide eyes of vibrant purple who somehow knows my name. "Can you hear me?"

I try to speak, but words won't seem to come out of my mouth. Every time I blink, I see water, rocks and death rushing full-speed toward me.

"You're safe now," she says, her hand reaching toward me. I jerk away, my body still shaking uncontrollably. 'Safe' doesn't mean a thing to me anymore. Her companion may have saved my life, but didn't Dash save my life too? And a day later he tried to kill me.

"Vi, they're coming this way," the golden haired one says. "No time to get the gargoyle back into the paths. Can you keep Emerson quiet while they pass?"

The woman in front of me nods. "Emerson," she says, leaning a tiny bit closer, but not attempting to touch me again. "We're all going to turn invisible now. It's nothing to freak out about. Just an illusion to hide us while the guardians pass. But we need to keep quiet, okay? Completely quiet."

I nod jerkily, despite the fact that her warning isn't necessary. Even if my brain was capable of manufacturing words right now, I wouldn't make a sound while anyone from the Guild runs by. Not after they so readily tried to dispose of me. A moment later, all three faeries vanish. I look down—and manage to hold back my squeak of terror when I find that my body is gone. I know she said 'invisible,' but I didn't realize I wouldn't be able to see myself either. I thought ... I don't know what I thought.

At the sound of hurried footsteps, I look up. I almost scramble backward when I see the guardians running straight for us, but they swerve and continue running past. "... might not have been this way," Councilor Ashlow is saying to the rest of her guardians, "but we have to check. Especially if the rest of the team can't find her body. And find out who that cloaked person was. It didn't look like he or she was with the Unseelies."

We wait in silence for at least a minute after the guardians pass. Then: "I think that's fine, Calla," the guy who caught me says. The three of them reappear. When I look down, I'm relieved to see my own body once more. I'm not shaking as much as when we first landed, so I push myself up onto my feet. I still feel weak in the wake of more adrenaline than my body's ever produced in one go, but at least I can stand now.

"Sorry about the dramatic rescue," the man says, reaching over and patting the leathery winged creature I haven't looked at properly until now. Ridged horns curve out of its head, and fangs protrude from its wide mouth. "We ran out of time to get a better plan in place. Vi, can you open a doorway? We should get going."

"I—I'm not—um—" I cut myself off when it becomes clear I can't utter more than a few stammering words. I hate sounding so weak and confused. It isn't me. I'm *stronger* than this, dammit, but everyone has a limit to what they can endure without completely breaking down, and I think I'm fast approaching mine. I swallow and breathe in deeply before trying again. "I'm not ... I'm not going anywhere with you. Thank you for saving me, but I don't know who you are."

"Right, sorry," the man says. "I'm Ryn, and this is Violet." He gestures to the woman with the dark purple hair. With a nod toward the tattooed, golden haired woman, he adds, "And that's Calla."

"You can trust us," Violet says. "We know everyone's been after you since you arrived in this world, and we can keep you safe."

I press my hands over my eyes and suck in a shaky breath. "I don't trust you," I whisper, finding myself dangerously close to tears. "I don't trust anyone. Everybody wants to lock me up or kill me."

"Emerson." I lower my hands and find Violet right in front of me, staring intently into my eyes. "You *can* trust us. You know why? Because we're exactly like you."

I shake my head. "What do you mean?"

"We're all Griffin Gifted."

CHAPTER FOURTEEN

"CRAP." I STUMBLE BACKWARD IN MY HASTE TO PUT SOME distance between me and these faeries. "You guys are part of that Griffin rebel movement, aren't you."

"Yes." Confusion crosses Violet's face. "Which is a good thing. It means we're on your side."

"But … you're the bad guys."

"Uh, no we're not," Calla says.

"That's what the Guild—what everyone in this world— says."

"Of course that's what the Guild says. They don't trust us. They want to track our every move or lock us up so we can't use our 'dangerous' magic without supervision. They just tried to do the same thing to you."

I hesitate, because she's right, of course. "They … they said you attack people."

Ryn's expression darkens. "Is that what they're telling people now?"

"They'll twist any story to their advantage," Violet says. "They want people to be afraid of us."

Calla's head whips around. "Guys, I think they're coming back this way."

"On it," Ryn says, already raising a stylus and scribbling invisible words in the air.

"Are you coming?" Violet asks. "Please, you can trust us."

I swallow. Perhaps this is all a lie and I'm being tricked yet again, but I don't exactly have anyone else to turn to. "Can you help me?" I ask. "With ... everything?"

She takes my hand and squeezes it. "That's what we do."

* * *

Hot air dances across my skin as the darkness of the faerie paths evaporates around us. My feet sink into soft sand. I turn slowly on the spot, squinting against the harsh light as my eyes take in the same scenery on all sides: rolling sand dunes that go on and on, seemingly forever. "You guys live in a desert?"

Calla smiles. "Yep. You wouldn't think to look for us out here, would you?"

"I guess not," I say, keeping the rest of my thoughts to myself. My thoughts of how unpleasant it must be to live amidst all this sand and heat.

"This way," Ryn says, nodding to his right and leading the gargoyle by its reins. I have no idea how he knows which direction to go in since every sand dune looks the same to me. We've barely taken a few steps, though, when the faint outline of something dome-shaped comes into view. I blink a few times, but the outline only grows stronger. I'm afraid to ask if I'm imagining things, so I keep my mouth shut. But a minute or so later when the dome is right in front of us and I can make out the hazy shapes of trees and buildings within, I figure it must be real.

"This," Violet says, "is our oasis. An enchanted piece of land beneath a dome of magic. And once you've passed through the dome layer—" she takes my hand and pulls me through after her "—you now have a spell placed upon you that means you can never speak about this place. Even if you're questioned under the influence of truth potion, you won't be able to say a thing. Which means everyone here will always be safe."

The air is immediately cooler, and the fresh scent of plants fills my nostrils. I'm aware of a small smile on my lips as I slowly look around. Grass and bushes and streams, fountains and flowers and a few small buildings, plus a number of enormous trees with houses built into the upper branches. "Actual tree houses," I murmur. "Not the glamoured type I learned about this morning."

"Yes," Violet says. "I lived on Kaleidos for a little while, and they have tree houses like these. I really liked them, so I suggested we do the same thing here."

"And we spent years before this living in glamoured trees or Underground or inside mountains," Calla adds, "so when the Guild forced us to run and we had to make a new home somewhere, we decided we didn't want to live in concealed houses anymore. The outer dome keeps us hidden, so our actual houses don't have to be hidden."

"It's really cool." I push away the thought that if I could just get Mom safely into the magic world, she and I could happily live here for the rest of our lives. She'd love the gardens, the fountains, the flowers. But I don't know if that's possible, so I'll leave my dreams for another day. Another time, when I've figured out if I can really trust these people. "What do you guys do here?" I ask, watching Ryn hand the gargoyle reins to a bald man with eyes that don't look normal.

"We rescue Griffin Gifted and hide them from the Guild," he says, turning back to me. "We also help people in other ways. Basically, we do what the Guild does, but on a smaller scale."

"It's also non-official and illegal," Calla says. "So, you know, that's another reason the Guild doesn't like us."

"Oops," says a small voice behind us. We all turn, and there stands the boy who appeared in the forest before Dash dragged me out to the edge of the cliff. "I was hoping I'd get home before you."

After a pause filled with shocked silence, Violet walks forward, takes hold of the boy's shoulders, and makes sure her face is right in front of his before asking, "Where have you been?"

"Um …"

"Did you leave the oasis?"

He blinks. "Maybe. I just … wanted to help with the rescue mission."

"Jack Linden Larkenwood," she says, "you're grounded." She straightens and lets go of him. "For the next decade."

"What?"

"For the next *century*."

"Mom!" Jack lets out a dramatic groan and turns to Ryn. "Da-ad," he whines.

Ryn folds his arms. "Do you want me to add another decade?"

"Ugh, you guys ruin everything!"

"No, ruining things is what you did when you decided to disobey the rules and leave the oasis," Violet says. "Now please give me whoever's stylus you decided to steal."

Jack mumbles something too quiet for anyone to hear before handing over a stylus, crossing his arms, and sticking his lower lip out. Calla covers her mouth to hide a smile before turning away. Looking past her, I see the bald man walking back toward us. When he reaches Calla's side, I realize why his eyes look strange: his pupils are vertical instead of round.

"Lord Sedon wants to arrange a meeting with the two of you," he says to Ryn and Violet. "He's on hold on one of the mirrors."

"Great, we'll come speak to him now," Ryn says.

"Is Chase back yet?" Calla asks.

"No," the bald man says. "You missed a mirror call from him earlier, though."

"Oh, I'll see if I can get hold of him now." She hurries away.

"Jack," Violet says, "please take Emerson to one of the empty rooms and then show her around a bit while Dad and I do some work."

"Will you un-ground me if I do that?"

"No. You'll do it because you want to be friendly and welcoming to Emerson."

"Fine," he groans.

"Great. Emerson, we'll see you a little later," Violet says. "We can meet for ..." She hesitates, then laughs. "Sorry, it always takes a moment to readjust when traveling between time zones. It's afternoon here, isn't it, so we can meet for sundowners by the hammocks."

"That sounds ..." Like the kind of vacation I've only ever dreamed about. "That sounds nice."

I watch the two of them walk away. When they're out of earshot, Jack turns to me and grins. "I actually am friendly and welcoming."

"Okay. Good to know."

"Come, you can choose a room."

I walk with him, slowing my pace to match is short stride. "Who set up this whole place?"

"Dad and Uncle Chase. They said it took them like a year to get all the right enchantments in place. But that was before I was born, so obviously I don't remember any of it."

"Who's Chase?"

"Aunt Calla's husband."

I nod. "So ... are your dad and Chase the ones in charge?"

"I guess. But so are Mom and Aunt Calla. And Uncle Gaius. Although he's not really my uncle, he's just Uncle Chase's friend since forever, and he doesn't come out of his house much anymore, since he's sick. I think they're all in charge. Well, they set the rules, and I get in trouble with all of them if I break them, so they must all be in charge."

We reach the base of one of the giant trees. Steps have been carved into it, starting from the bottom and curving around the side of the trunk as they climb higher. Jack leads me up, moving as quickly as his short legs will take him. "How old are you, Jack?"

He drags his hand along the trunk as we climb. "I'm eight and a half. How old are you?"

"Seventeen. Eighteen in a few months."

"Did you go to school where you're from? 'Cause you can do that here. I have lessons with the other kids who live here, and mostly it's fun. You can join us if you want, although you'll probably be with Junie because you're older."

I sigh and say, "No, I'd probably be with you." *In fact,* I add silently, *if there's a class lower than yours, that's probably where I belong.*

"So this is our house," Jack says as we reach the first large structure built into the branches. "It's got more rooms, like a kitchen and lounge and stuff, and then higher up are just bedrooms and bathing rooms for new people. Then if they stay and they want other rooms, Merrick just adds them on."

I stop for a moment and look up at the smaller wooden structures built above us. "I probably shouldn't ask about how bathrooms work all the way up there. I mean, I guess magic takes care of all the ... plumbing?"

Jack shrugs. "I don't know. I guess." He continues moving up, and I follow him, grateful for all the physical activity Val and I have done over the past couple of years in our quest to teach ourselves parkour.

"Looks like you have to be quite fit to live here," I comment. "It's a long way up if you forget something when you leave your house in the morning."

"I know!" Jack exclaims. "And I haven't learned how to boost myself with magic yet, so it takes like forever. Mom and Dad can get up here in seconds if they have to. It's so unfair."

"Well, you'll probably be able to do that soon, right? I mean, you know how to do the faerie paths thing." I'm still particularly interested in that spell. The sooner I learn it, the sooner I'll feel more in control of my situation.

"Oh, yeah, the faerie paths. I'm not supposed to know that one yet. But I've always paid attention when Mom and Dad do it. I'm a fast learner." He looks back at me with a proud smile, then increases his pace a little, as if spurred on by his own words. "Okay," he says a little breathlessly after we've passed four smaller tree houses. "This one's empty. Or you can go higher if you want. There are another three that are empty. Merrick always adds more on when he has time."

"This one's fine." I place my hands on my hips and look around as I give myself a few moments to catch my breath. The branches up here are wide enough to walk along without having any balance issues. Good thing I'm not afraid of heights, though. The distance from here to the ground is enough to cause some serious damage to anyone who might freak out and slip.

"Okay, come see," Jack says. He skips along the branch and pushes the door open. I follow him into a bedroom, plainly furnished with nothing more than a bed, a wardrobe and a chair in the corner. It's still nicer than the room I've always slept in at Chelsea's house, though. At least I don't have to climb over boxes of hair products and share my shelves with tiny bottles of strange concoctions.

"Is that a bathroom?" I ask, pointing to a closed door on the other side of the room.

"Yeah. So this is just the basic stuff they put in all the rooms. It's kinda boring, so you can change whatever you want. You can even change the shape of the room, if you'd like something different. Merrick will do it. He's an architect faerie. And Junie—she's an elf—is a designer. So if you tell her what you want your bed to look like, she can easily change it. Or, like, if you want that chair to be a swing hanging from the ceiling, she can do that too. She did that in my room, but then I fell off one night when I was supposed to be sleeping, not playing, so Mom and Dad made her change it to an armchair, which isn't nearly as fun. But Junie made it dragon-shaped, so I guess it's not that bad."

I smile at this outburst of information. "Sounds cool." I walk to the window, and my smile stretches a little wider at the sight of the orchard, the river, and the sun going down in the distance. I've never imagined having a view like this from my own bedroom. *And you still don't*, a small voice reminds me. This isn't really my bedroom, and I probably won't be here for long. Nothing this amazing could ever last.

"The wardrobe's empty now," Jack says, "but Mom will put some clothes in it later. Dash's mom is a clothes caster, and she sends *tons* of clothes here. Some of them are weird, and Mom hides those ones, but most are normal. Oh, where did that come from?" I swing around and look to where he's pointing. In the corner, sitting on the chair, is a kitten.

I cross the room with a sigh. "This little guy is a shapeshifting creature that keeps following me everywhere. I thought he ran away when Dash found me in the forest, but he must have just shifted into something really small and climbed into one of my pockets or something." The creature shifts rapidly back and forth between two forms I can't identify, like an old TV flickering between channels. Then it settles as a kitten again.

"Cool, he's just like Filigree!" Jack says.

"Filigree?"

"Yeah, Mom's pet. He doesn't shift much anymore 'cause he's super old and Mom says he doesn't have the energy now, but he used to change into all kinds of things. He was even a dragon once, but then he slept for like three days solid after that 'cause it used so much of his magic." Jack crouches in front of the chair. "What's this one's name?"

"He doesn't have one."

"Ah, can I name him please?" Jack begs, his eyes widening in delight as he looks over his shoulder at me.

"Sure. He'll probably end up staying here anyway. It's not like he's *mine*. He just seems to like following me." A strange twist, given that my first pet had the opposite reaction and ran away after only a few days.

"Yay." Jack scoops the kitten up and cradles it against his chest. "I shall name him ..." Jack squeezes his eyes shut as he thinks. "Bandit. His name will be Bandit."

I nod slowly. "Sounds cool."

We walk back down all the stairs—my legs getting a good workout in the process—and Jack shows me around the rest of the dome, pointing out a greenhouse, a school, a vegetable garden and orchard, an outdoor gym area, and a building that apparently contains a laboratory and some other 'out-of-bounds' places Jack doesn't know much about. "It's stuff to do with their work and how they help people. That's all I know."

"There's a lot here," I say as we stop beside a narrow river with a swan-shaped boat floating near the bank. "It's bigger than I first thought."

"It was smaller when I was little," Jack says, "but Merrick keeps adding onto it. He gets bored when he isn't helping Mom and Dad with cases. Anyway, come see the playground." He grabs my hand and tugs me away from the river. "I kept it till last 'cause it's my favorite place here. The swing is amazing. You have to try it."

The playground turns out to be filled with the same kind of equipment I'd expect to find in my world. The swing, too, looks pretty much normal. "It doesn't just go backwards and forward," Jack says when I ask what's so special about it. "See, you strap yourself in, and the swing goes all the way around. As many times as you want."

"Wow, okay. That is cool. It's enchanted, I assume?"

"Yeah, obviously. Do you want to have a go?"

"Uh, maybe another time. It's just … this is a lot. I'm still getting used to all the magical stuff."

"Oh, right, sorry. You're from the other world. I remember now. So what do you do for fun there?"

"Oh. Um …" I push my hands into my back pockets. "Well, I hang out with my friend Val. We taught ourselves this thing called parkour. It's kind of like a sport. You use whatever environment you're in—like buildings, walls, stairs, whatever—as an obstacle course. There's lots of jumping and running and climbing. And falling, but falling the right way. Like landing on your shoulder and rolling and standing up."

"Okay. Is it fun?"

"Yeah. You have to be creative about getting from point A to point B. It's like an art, actually. The art of rapid movement despite obstacles. An ordinary person might take the stairs out of a building and then walk along the road to wherever they're going. Instead, we'd figure out how to jump or climb down, and then vault over walls and through gardens to get to the destination the quickest way possible."

"Cool. Can you teach me?"

"Uh, sure. If you can teach me how to open the faerie paths."

"Okay." He wraps an arm around one of the swing's chains. "But we'd have to use someone's stylus. Without them knowing. And … I don't really wanna get grounded again."

"Right. Yeah. You should stay out of trouble." Those last few words come out sounding unexpectedly deep and resonant, and that same strange shiver from earlier ripples up my spine and across my arms.

"What was that?" Jack asks, pulling his head back as he eyes me with suspicion. "You sounded weird."

"Um …" I'm not sure if he knows about my Griffin Ability. "Probably just some escaping magic. I don't really know how to use it yet." He nods slowly while I look around for something else to talk about. "So where are the hammocks? I think I'm probably supposed to meet your parents there soon."

"This way," he says, taking off in another direction. I hurry after him, grateful for the lasting effects of the chocolate energy drink Azzy gave me before letting the Guild take me away. I probably would have passed out from exhaustion long ago without it.

Jack leads me to a collection of hammocks strung between trees near a round, open-sided pavilion. Large couches sit beneath the pavilion's decorative roof. "I think I'll wait over there," I tell him.

"Cool. I'm going to find some food for Bandit."

I watch him wandering away until a familiar voice behind me says, "Hey, you got here safely."

I spin around, my heart thundering in my chest. "Dash." I jerk away from his outstretched hand. "He's found us!" I yell. "The Guild's found us!"

CHAPTER FIFTEEN

"WHOA, HEY, CALM DOWN." DASH BLINKS, CONFUSED. "I'M on your side. How have you not figured that out yet?"

"It's okay, Emerson," Violet says, running up to me. "He's telling the truth. He's on our side."

"How can he possibly be on our side?" Anger rushes hotly through my veins, escaping in violent sparks that shoot away from me and aim straight for Dash's face.

"Ow!" He ducks and bats the magic away with both hands. "What the heck, Em?"

"You tried to imprison me! And then you pushed me off the edge of a cliff!"

"Jeez, Em, I'm the only reason you got away from the Guild. You never would have escaped without my help." He straightens as my magic stops attacking him. "You don't think guardians are normally that clumsy, do you? And the cliff ..." He shrugs, looking a little sheepish. "Well, we ran out of time, so I had to improvise. But I knew Ryn and Vi were out there. I knew someone would catch you."

"*You knew someone would catch me?*" I repeat in disbelief. "I almost died!"

"But you didn't. You're fine. And now you're safe, which was the plan from the very beginning."

"What plan?"

"You know, to get you here to the Griffin rebels."

"Wait." I blink and hold my hands up. "You knew all along that I had a Griffin Ability, and you didn't say anything to me?"

Dash's eyes flick toward Violet before returning to me. "Well, we weren't certain. That's why I kept trying to get you to tell me exactly what happened that night at the party, but you weren't interested in talking about it."

"Are you kidding? If it was so important—if having a Griffin Ability is so dangerous—you could have forced the information out of me. Told me, 'Em, this isn't normal magic. You could be in danger because of it. You have to tell me what happened, for your own safety.'" I throw my hands up in complete exasperation. "Did you consider that option, Dash?"

He folds his arms over his chest, his expression growing stormier by the second. "Perhaps you don't clearly remember the occasion on which you completely freaked out and ran away from Chevalier House, but you weren't exactly in the mood to be forced into anything. And forgive me, but I kinda thought you had enough to deal with at that moment, having just found out about, you know, *everything* else. I thought I was being *kind* not dumping another horrible revelation on your shoulders. And I figured Azzy would get the truth out of you soon enough—which she had already done, actually. I didn't know it, but she'd already contacted Ryn by the time I got you back to Chevalier House. We just didn't manage to get you safely away before you revealed to everyone what you can do."

"Hang on. Azzy's in on this whole thing? That's what the two of you were whispering about last night?"

"You heard that?"

"Yes, Prof Azzy's on our side too," Violet says.

"Then why the hell did Paul call the Guild to come get me?"

"Because Azzy is the only one who's in on this," she explains. "Paul isn't. He's firmly on the Guild's side, just like everyone else working at Chevalier House, so his automatic response was to contact them."

"Okay fine. Fine!" I face Dash again. "But you still didn't explain a damn thing to me after I accidentally revealed my ability. If your Griffin friends were planning to come and rescue me, why didn't you just tell me?"

"I tried, Em, but we weren't alone for long enough after that. I couldn't say anything with other guardians around. If the Guild gets even the tiniest hint that I'm not entirely on their side, things would turn out very badly."

"Looking after your own skin, I see," I mutter.

"Emerson—"

"Not just my skin," Dash snaps, interrupting Violet before

she can get any further. "I'm looking out for everyone else who lives here. Protective magic might keep me from being able to tell the Guild about this place if I were ever questioned, but I know far more than that. I know what Azzy's doing and about all the people who come in and out of here. Can you imagine what would happen if the Guild got that information out of me?"

"Then why bother working at the Guild if it's such a gigantic risk?"

"Hello! Because Vi and Ryn and everyone else here need people on the inside. They wouldn't know what's going on otherwise. They wouldn't have known about you, or about what the Guild was planning to do with you."

"It's true," Violet says. "The information Dash gives us about the Guild is extremely valuable. And aside from that, he *wants* to be a guardian. He wants to help people. He shouldn't have to walk away from that just because he's connected to us."

I cross my arms tightly over my chest, wanting to say that other people have to give up their dreams all the time, so what makes Dash so special that he gets to keep his? But my childish, petty thoughts aren't helpful, so I manage to remain quiet.

Violet's gaze shifts between the two of us. "Should we ... perhaps ... sit down?" she suggests after several more moments of silence have passed.

With a terse nod, I follow her up the pavilion steps. I wait for Dash to sit so I can choose a spot far away from him, but he nods at me to sit first. Idiot. Is he pretending to have good manners or something? I take a seat on a blue-and-white-striped couch and hug one of the fluffy white cushions against my stomach. Dash has the decency not to sit right next to me. "So, are we okay now?" he asks. "You and me?"

I shrug. "As okay as we ever were, I guess."

"Cool. So you still don't like me, but at least you don't believe I wanted to kill you."

I nod. "Pretty much."

"Great," Violet says, waving to Ryn as he walks toward the pavilion with a tray of glasses floating in the air beside him. "As long as the two of you don't want to kill each other, everything should be fine."

"Dash," Ryn says as reaches us. "Thanks for helping out with the rescue." He shakes Dash's hand, as if pushing me off a cliff was some great accomplishment. "I know Emerson wasn't too pleased about the way it happened, but you had to keep your cover somehow."

"Thanks. It's good to know that *some* people appreciate my sacrifice." He gives me a pointed look.

"Yeah, whatever. *Such* a sacrifice, I'm sure. And you guys can stop calling me Emerson," I add. "Em is fine."

"Or Emmy," Dash says.

I clench my teeth together. "I will hurt you."

"I will hurt you," he mimics in a high-pitched voice.

Violet sighs and lowers herself onto one of the couches. "Were we ever this immature?"

"Of course not," Ryn says, taking a seat opposite her. "Well, you might have been, but I'm sure I wasn't."

She laughs. "That is definitely not true."

"Dash, I heard you had a small problem getting here," Ryn

says, neatly changing the subject. "Calla said she got a message from you asking her to go meet you somewhere and bring you back here."

"Uh, yeah." Dash turns his gaze to me. "So, I have a small problem."

"And why is that my problem?"

"Because it's your fault. I can't use the faerie paths anymore. It's impossible for me to travel anywhere if I'm alone."

"Aaaaand I still don't see how that's my problem."

"Em, come on. It's your Griffin Ability that did this to me. You need to fix it."

"I don't know how. And even if I did, wouldn't that look suspicious to the Guild? I'm supposed to be dead, right, so how could I fix your faerie paths problem?"

"I don't know. I guess I could say the effects of your magic wore off."

"And when Jewel still can't use the faerie paths? That's going to look seriously suspicious, Dash."

"She has a point," Ryn says.

"Just try it, Em. Try right now. Say, 'You can open doorways to the faerie paths.' And if it works, then we can get you to sneak up on Jewel while she's sleeping and do the same to her."

"That's really creepy, Dash."

"Just try!"

I lean back, cross my arms, and say, "You can open doorways to the faerie paths."

He sighs. "Perhaps you could put a little effort into it?"

"Who says it works that way?"

"I don't know, but it certainly didn't work the way you just said it. Your voice didn't go all … weird."

I uncross my arms and fiddle absently with the sleeve of my sweater. "Weird how? What does my voice sound like when it happens?"

"Sort of … deeper. A little distorted. And kind of … not like an echo, but it was as if I could hear it in the air all around me."

I nod slowly. "It kinda sounded like that to me too."

"Do you want to try again?" Violet asks. "Focusing this time, instead of just saying the words."

Since it isn't Dash asking, I agree to try again. I try several more times, even closing my eyes and focusing intently on pulling out that power from deep inside me as I tell Dash he's allowed to open doorways to faerie paths. But just like at the edge of the cliff, nothing happens. My voice remains normal.

Eventually I slump back against the couch and hug the fluffy cushion closer to my chest. "See? Can't do it."

"Well, no need to stress about it," Violet says. "We can definitely help you."

"Really?"

"Yes. And in the meantime, Dash will just have to figure out another way to get around."

"Ugh, seriously? I'm going to have to be *taken* everywhere like a child," Dash complains.

"Good thing you work in teams at the Guild," Ryn says. "One of your teammates should be happy to help you and Jewel, right?"

"It's still extremely limiting."

"Poor you," I say without a shred of sympathy.

His eyes narrow as he looks at me. "You're enjoying this."

I shrug. "You pushed me off a cliff."

"Is that going to be your comeback for everything?"

"Probably. I feel like it's never gonna get old."

"So," Violet says loudly. "Would anyone like a drink?" She gestures to the tray of glasses Ryn brought with him, which is sitting on a small round table beside his chair.

"Okay," I say, pointing to one containing alternating layers of green and pink. "As long as it has no alcohol manufactured by humans."

"No alcohol at all," Ryn assures me as he hands over the glass. "Dash? Would you like something?"

"Nah, I'm actually gonna go say hi to Gaius if he's awake. Haven't seen him in a while. And I'm sure your conversation with Emmy—" he winks at me as he stands "—will be more pleasant if I'm not around."

"Finally," I mutter as Dash walks away. "He doesn't hang out here often, does he?"

Violet shakes her head and pushes her hair back away from her face. "Not too often."

"Thank goodness for—Oh. Those marks on your wrist." My eyes follow her arm as she lowers it. "They're the same as the ones Dash has. Isn't that supposed to mean you're a guardian?"

"Yes."

"But ... you have a Griffin Ability, so ... oh, was this before they came up with a way to test for Griffin Abilities? Sorry, the age thing is confusing. You look so young but you could be a hundred years old for all I know."

"Not quite," she says with a laugh.

"Not even close, actually," Ryn adds.

"But yes, I was a guardian. Ryn, Calla and I were all guardians before we were outlaws. Well, Calla never actually had the chance to graduate, but Ryn and I did. We worked for the Guild for a number of years without anyone knowing we were Griffin Gifted. Then the Guild developed a way to test for Griffin Abilities, and we were revealed as 'traitors' along with all the other Griffin Gifted. We ran before the Guild could deactivate our marks, though, so we still have access to our guardian weapons. You may have seen them? Gold and sparkly. They appear when we need them and disappear when we let go."

I nod, picturing the fight at the edge of the cliff. "Are those guardian-specific?"

"Yes. Only guardians have access to weapons like that."

"So now you basically do what you did before, but without the Guild's approval? So ... you're like vigilantes?"

Her smile is wry. "Pretty much. Not something we ever planned to be, but the Guild kinda forced us into it. Especially since their system doesn't function as well as it's supposed to."

"What do you mean?"

"They work with Seers. Fae who have an ability to glimpse the future. They See things that will go wrong, and the Guild sends guardians to prevent those things from happening. The problem is, there are too many of those visions. There are never enough guardians to deal with them all, so the visions that are deemed less important are thrown out. We have a Guild contact, however, who gathers those up and gets them to us as quickly as possible. We deal with anything that hasn't already happened."

"Cool." I lapse into silence, thinking through everything she's explained. Then I remember that I'm holding a drink, so I take a sip. It tastes like a mixture of pine needles and something fruity, which isn't a bad combination. I wait for Ryn or Violet to ask me a question, but it seems they might be waiting for me to steer the conversation. Either that or they're having their own silent conversation with their eyes.

"Anyway," I say eventually, "what do you guys want to chat about? My Griffin Ability? The fact that I can't perform even the most basic magic? The fact that my mom isn't my mom?" Violet raises both eyebrows, and I inwardly curse myself for letting that last one slip out. "Griffin Ability," I say hurriedly. "Let's go with that one."

"Uh, yes," she says. "I'm very interested to hear more about your Griffin Ability. I've never come across anyone who can speak things into being. That's incredible."

"You mean dangerous, right? That's what everyone else seems to think."

"Dangerous, yes, if you can't control it. But we're all dangerous if we can't control our magic. And you've only just discovered yours, so of course you don't know what to do with it yet. But we'll do whatever we can to help you, I promise."

I chew on my lip and slowly shake my head. "Perhaps I should stop speaking altogether, because I never know when something I say is going to come out as a magical command. Also …" I place my glass on the floor before pressing my hands together. "There's a possibility Jack is never going to be in trouble again."

Ryn tilts his head. "What did you say to him?"

"I think my exact words were, 'You should stay out of trouble.' And my Griffin Ability randomly switched on at that moment. So … I'm not really sure what kind of effect that's going to have on him."

Violet bursts out laughing. "Well, I'm looking forward to seeing the results of that one."

"Yeah, but what if I'd said something different? Something bad?"

Ryn pushes a hand through his hair. "Yes, there are definitely risks as long as you don't know when the ability will kick in. But completely muting yourself isn't practical. Perhaps just think about everything you want to say before you say it, and make sure it isn't a command or instruction."

My shoulders slump. "That sounds even less practical. I'm sure it would be easier to tape my mouth closed than to tell myself I have to think about every word before it leaves my mouth."

"It won't be a problem for long," Violet says. "We can start working on it tomorrow. Well, the next day, I suppose. You'll need to go to the lab tomorrow so Ana can take a sample of your magic. The elixir to stimulate your Griffin Ability should then be ready the day afterwards."

"Lab?" Cold, hard fear takes shape in the pit of my stomach. "I—that's—I'm not very—"

"Of course, I'm sorry. Dash mentioned you have a fear of all things medical. But don't worry. There are no needles or anything. It's just a simple spell, and you won't feel a thing."

I pluck at the hairs of the fluffy cushion, unable to get rid of my frown. I hate that Dash has been talking about me to these people. What else has he told them?

"Seriously, Em, it isn't a big deal," Ryn says. "We need to take a sample of your magic so we can create an elixir that will stimulate your Griffin Ability. Once you get used to what it feels like having that particular part of your magic switched on, you can hopefully figure out how to do it without the aid of the elixir. It needs to be specific to your magic, though, which is why we need the sample."

I lick my lips, reach forward for the drink at my feet, and take a long gulp. "Okay," I say after I've set it down again. "I guess that makes sense." That doesn't mean Ryn and Violet aren't lying to me, though. They might intend to use my magic for something else.

Violet leans forward, her amber now clasped between her hands. "Do you want to tell us anything about your mom?"

Suddenly, this feels like an interrogation. "Um …"

"What's her name? What hospital is she at?"

I scratch at a dirty mark on my jeans. "Daniela Clarke. And she's at Tranquil Hills Psychiatric Hospital. It's … well, the setting is tranquil. The inside isn't."

Vi nods and scribbles something onto her amber with a stylus.

"What are you writing down? Are you telling someone? Dash said those amber things are like cell phones, so are you messaging someone?"

"Em, calm down," Ryn says. "She's taking notes, that's all."

Violet sits back. "I know Dash told you that it isn't possible for your mom to be your biological mother. That must have been a huge shock for you to find out."

I nod but say nothing.

"I'm really sorry, Em. It's a lot to take in all at once, I know. Finding out that you're not who you thought you were and that you might have a whole new family somewhere out there. Do you want us to try find out more about them?"

I shake my head. "My mom's my only family. I don't need to know about anyone else."

"Okay. Just let us know if you change your mind."

"Yeah." I won't be changing my mind.

"Em, you don't have to freak out." It's Ryn who leans forward this time, watching me intently. "I'm serious. We only want to help you. If you really don't want us to take a sample of your magic, we're not going to force you. And if you don't want to talk about your mother, that's fine. We won't mention her again. We want you to feel safe here, that's all. We're hiding from the Guild just like you are. We understand what it's like to be hunted. We understand what it's like to want nothing more than a safe place to call home."

I realize I've been holding my breath while he's been speaking, and I slowly let it out. I think I believe him. I *think* I do. The only problem is … "This isn't ever going to be my home," I say carefully, hoping they understand I don't mean to offend them. "I have a life somewhere else. And a mother who needs me. I need to get back to that world when my magic is no longer a danger to everyone around me."

Ryn nods. "Then that's what we'll help you do."

CHAPTER
SIXTEEN

I SPEND AN HOUR OR TWO THAT EVENING IN MY ROOM WITH
Junie, the elf Jack mentioned earlier, trying not to stare at her
ears while she creates linen for the bed and curtains for the
windows, and changes the chair from a hard wooden thing into
a soft armchair with flower-patterned fabric. Bandit takes an
immediate liking to the new armchair and promptly curls up
on it and falls asleep. Junie asks if I want anything else, and
when I ask about getting a clock so I won't be late for breakfast
in the morning—no more cell phone alarm to wake me up—
Junie paints the time onto my wall. A minute later, when the
number magically increases by one digit, I suck in a breath.
Even after several days in this world, magic continues to
surprise me.

While the room is more rustic than the one I had at

Chevalier House, I prefer this one. When I'm finally left alone, I spend a while at the window, staring at the tiny lights in the trees and the millions of stars visible through the dome layer. But eventually my eyelids become too heavy, and I climb into bed.

I sleep better than expected, waking to the sound of singing coming from the direction of the painted numbers on my wall. After using the pool in my little garden-themed en-suite bathroom, I head down the many stairs on the outside of the tree to Violet and Ryn's house. I tap on the half-open door before pushing it open and walking into what appears to be their kitchen. The scent of something baking fills the air.

"Oh, morning, Em," Violet says, smiling at me over her shoulder. She's standing at a counter where the contents of a jug seems to be stirring itself, and a knife is neatly slicing through an apple. Her hand hovers above three mugs, and though I can't see inside them, I assume something magical is going on. "You can take a seat at the table," she says. "Coffee?"

"Oh, thank goodness. I was worried coffee might not exist in this world."

She laughs, picks up the three mugs, and carries them to the table. The jug carries on stirring itself behind her. "It isn't quite the same as the coffee you're probably used to, but hopefully you'll like it."

Jack runs into the kitchen, shouting, "Morning, Em! Did you bring Bandit with you?"

"Jack, please," Violet says. "You don't have to be so loud indoors."

"Sorry," Jack whispers with a mischievous grin as Ryn walks

into the room behind him.

"Hey, Em," he says to me. Then to Violet: "Sorry, I got distracted. I was going to finish the coffee."

"All under control," Violet tells him. She gives him a quick kiss as he slips his arm around her waist. "Can you get the muffins out?"

"So did you bring Bandit?" Jack asks again, climbing onto a chair.

"Actually, he went back to sleep after I got up. He's probably still upstairs in my room."

"Oh." Jack deflates, then perks up when his mother places a small glass of something brown in front of him. "Ooh, chocolate, chocolate, chocolate."

"Hey, can I join you guys for breakfast?" The question comes from the direction of the door, and it's Calla who's peering around it. "Chase isn't back yet."

"Of course." Violet motions to one of the empty chairs. "Are you worried about him?"

"No, I'm sure he's fine. Things sometimes take longer than he expects, that's all. Hey, Em," she adds with a wave in my direction. "Ooh, are those muffins?" She slips quickly into a chair, rubbing her hands together as Ryn places a plate of steaming muffins in the center of the table. Violet adds a plate of sliced fruit beside it—at least half of which I don't recognize—while I try to remember if Chelsea, Georgia and I have ever eaten anything that doesn't come out of a cereal box at breakfast time. I don't know how to bake, and I doubt they do either.

"Something to drink?" Violet says to Calla.

"No, don't worry. I'll help myself to something in a minute."

Violet joins the table, and Jack proceeds to tell Calla all about Bandit, the 'new Filigree,' while everyone helps themselves to food. He then turns his attention to me and gives me a detailed outline of what Bandit's diet should include and how many times a day I should feed him. "I can help you, if you want," he adds.

"Thanks. You can actually keep him if you—" Violet cuts me off with a quick and vigorous shake of her head. I backpedal quickly. "I mean, um, you can keep visiting him. As much as you like. And I'm sure he'd love it if you bring him food." I risk a glance in Violet's direction, hoping I've successfully fixed my blunder. She smiles and gives me a brief nod.

Beside her, Calla mutters something and lowers her amber onto the table beside her plate. "Everything okay?" Violet asks.

"That was a message from Perry. He says there was an attack at a faerie boarding school last night, and another one at that village near Twiggled Horn. That's the second one at that particular village this week. Something bad is going on out there."

"I think I heard about that," I say, at which Calla looks across at me in surprise. "Well, the first one," I add. "Not the one that just happened. I only remember because the name of the place is so strange."

"It's the name of an oddly shaped mountain," Ryn says. "What did you hear about the first attack?"

I try to recall the details Jewel passed on to Dash when she received the message. "They said five people were killed, I think. Oh, and they said it was a Griffin attack. I remember now. That was the first time I heard about Griffin Abilities."

Calla's mouth drops open. "What? That's one of the stories the Guild is spreading around? But we were nowhere near Twiggled Horn. And we don't kill people. Ugh, the Guild makes me so mad sometimes. I can't believe they pinned that on us."

Her amber buzzes briefly across the table again. She picks it up and reads it. "Oh, brilliant." Her hands fall to her lap in exasperation. "The Guild's official message is that no one has claimed responsibility for these recent attacks, but they have reason to believe they were carried out by Griffin rebels."

I watch Violet's hands clench tightly around her knife and fork. Ryn's expression darkens. "Such lies," he grinds out between his teeth. "They know it isn't us, so they'd damn well better be doing whatever they can behind the scenes to figure out who's really responsible."

"Sounds just as messed up as our law enforcement system," I mutter.

"Dad," Jack says uncertainly. "I thought we weren't supposed to say 'damn.'"

A small smile breaks past Ryn's frown. He reaches across and ruffles Jack's hair. "You're right. Thanks for reminding me."

"Yeah, I guess we shouldn't let this get to us," Calla says, pushing her amber away and selecting another muffin. "The Guild's been spreading lies about us for ages. This is hardly any different."

"True," Violet says. "Although they definitely need to find out who's behind this."

"Hopefully they can manage without our help," Ryn says with a superior smile that reminds me, just for a moment, of Dash.

Calla's amber shivers yet again. She frowns at the latest message. "Perry says there's something extra weird about the way these fae were killed. Says I should meet him so he can explain properly." She stands. "I guess I'd better get going. Oh, but I want some of that chocolate cinnamon stuff Jack loves so much first." She hurries to the counter.

"Morning, everyone."

We all look toward the door. At the sight of Dash, I suppress a groan. "Dash?" Violet says. "Can you use the faerie paths again?"

"No, but I have other friends here who are happy to help me out."

"Don't you have a job you should be at right now?" Calla asks.

"Yeah, I'm heading to work in a few minutes. Just stopped by to say hi."

Calla places a hand on her hip. Behind her, the jug that was stirring itself with a spoon earlier pours some of its contents into a glass. "You stopped by to 'say hi?' Why don't I believe you?"

"I don't know. I'm a friendly guy. I'm not sure why you'd doubt my desire to wish everyone a good morning."

She shakes her head as she picks up the glass and moves toward him. "Well, good morning, then. And goodbye. I'm heading out now."

"Stay alive," Dash calls cheerfully after her as she leaves.

"Stay alive?" I repeat. "Is that a common greeting around here?"

Violet throws a quick glance at Jack before quietly saying, "It's a common sentiment, even if we don't always say it out loud."

Dash walks into the kitchen. "How nice of you to welcome Em to the oasis with baked goods." He leans past Violet and grabs a blueberry muffin. "I approve."

"Dash," I say, deciding to be civil. "Do you know what happened to Aurora after I got away from the Guild yesterday?"

He leans his hip against the table. "Aurora?"

"The other new girl from Chevalier House. The one who showed up at the Guild and helped me escape. Guardians got hold of her before she could get into the faerie paths with me."

"Oh yeah." Dash chews and swallows. "They put her in a detainment cell for a few hours. Then they sent her back to Chevalier House after questioning her."

Guilt twists in my gut. "Questioning her?"

"They wanted to know why she'd come to help you. As far as they knew, there was no connection between the two of you."

"There wasn't—isn't," I say. "I have no idea why she came to help me."

"Who is this girl?" Ryn asks.

"She arrived at Chevalier House the day before yesterday. She seemed super suspicious of the whole setup. She said she'd heard that people disappear from there sometimes—which I suppose makes sense now that I know Azzy helps Griffin Gifted people."

"Do you think this girl also has a Griffin Ability?" Violet asks.

I lift my shoulders. "No idea. I suppose Azzy will let you know soon enough if she does. Anyway, what's weird is that she was supposedly a slave to a bunch of witches who never taught her how to use magic. But she somehow got to the Guild on her own, used magic to cut my ropes, and opened a way to the faerie paths."

Ryn considers my words. "Maybe she picked up some basic magic skills around the witches. Although," he adds with a frown, "witches don't travel through faerie paths."

"So witches are real? That part wasn't made up?"

Ryn exchanges a look with Violet. "Witches are very real." He pushes against the table and stands. "I'll contact Azzy now. She can tell me if there's anything we need to be suspicious about."

We start clearing up then, partly with the use of magic and partly—at least for Jack and me—by hand. He and I are drying the dishes washed by one of Violet's spells when I realize Dash and Violet have gone into the next room. I think I hear my name mentioned, and my anger flares up immediately. Hasn't Dash told these people enough about me and my personal life already?

"… can help her, right?" Dash is saying. "Come on, you can find anyone."

"No I can't, and I don't want you telling her that. You

know how it works. I need to touch something that belongs to—"

"To her parents, right. I've thought about that. *She* belongs to her parents. So just touch her, and you'll be able to find them."

"Dash, she hasn't belonged to her birth parents for a very long time," Violet says. "That isn't going to work. Besides, she's not interested in finding them."

"Exactly," I say, loud enough to startle them both. They look around with guilty expressions. "So thank you, Dash, for sticking your nose where it doesn't belong, but as you can see, I don't want your help."

He opens his mouth as if to argue, but then he sighs and raises his hands in surrender. "Sorry. I thought I was helping. I'll stay out of it."

"Probably best," Violet says quietly.

"Cool, well, I guess I'll head to work then." He raises his hand and makes a fist, holding it in the air in front of Violet as he grins at her. "Have a good day saving lives."

She rolls her eyes and bumps his fist with hers. "You too." She watches him leave, then turns to me. "I'm sorry about that. I hope you know I wasn't going to do anything without your permission."

I nod hesitantly, wanting to believe her. "What were you guys talking about? Being able to find someone ... Is that your Griffin Ability?"

She nods. "Yes. I can find people. If I know the person I'm looking for, it's easy. The connection's already there. If I don't, then I need to be holding something that belongs to that person."

"That's so weird," I murmur. *No less weird than being able to speak things into being,* a tiny voice reminds me. "Hang on," I add as something occurs to me. "Is that how Dash found me yesterday after I escaped the Guild? And the other night when I ran away from Chevalier House? Did you tell him where I was?"

She nods, looking guilty once again. "Azzy sent a message to say you'd run. I searched for you, then told Dash where to find you."

"That's …" I shake my head. "I … I don't even know how to feel about that."

"Like your privacy's been violated?"

"Kind of, I guess. Like I can never truly hide anywhere, even if I want to."

She nods. "I know. I hate making people feel like that. I only do it when it's necessary. In your case, we were worried for your safety."

"Wait, how did it work if you didn't have anything that belongs to me?"

She closes her eyes for a moment and rubs the back of her neck. "Now you're really going to think we violated your privacy." She opens her eyes. "I have a hairband that belongs to you. Dash took it off your wrist the night he brought you home after you passed out at that party. He figured we might need to find you at some point."

I cross my arms and stare at the floor. "Yeah. This is all very weird."

"I should probably tell you about Ryn too. Get all the weirdness out of the way in one go."

"Oh dear. That doesn't sound good."

"And just so you know, none of these abilities are a secret. We don't want people to think we're hiding things from them, so we're very open with those who live here."

"Okay, so what can Ryn do?"

"He can sense your emotions."

I blink. "That's … not cool. At all. What if I don't want him knowing what I'm feeling?"

She shrugs. "Try to not feel what you're feeling?"

"Is that even possible?"

"Not really. Trust me, I have years of experience in this area." She looks briefly over her shoulder as Jack calls for her. Something about a book he can't find. "Anyway," she says, turning back to me. "It isn't such a big deal. Most of the time, people's emotions are evident in their expressions and actions. Ryn's ability just makes him a little more intuitive than most, that's all."

I bite my lip and frown some more at the rug on the floor. Perhaps she's right, but that doesn't make me feel any more comfortable about being around him.

"I'm sorry, Em. I know this is all quite overwhelming. There's plenty more I want to explain, but I need to help Jack get ready for school, and then I've got some work things to deal with. I thought you could take today easy—just look around, hang out in the hammocks, practice whatever Azzy taught you before you left Chevalier—and tonight we can talk about the best way to teach you everything you need to know, including your Griffin Ability."

Fabulous. Sounds like you've got everything perfectly worked out. I push my sarcastic, bitter thoughts aside. "Okay. I guess that's a plan. And … can I ask one more thing?" Now's probably the best time, while she's still feeling guilty about using her Griffin Ability on me. I swallow and peel my gaze from the floor. "Can you take me to visit my mother?"

CHAPTER SEVENTEEN

"IT'S BEEN ALMOST A YEAR SINCE I SAW HER," I RUSH ON, suddenly feeling like I need to convince Violet this is a good idea. "I saved up—I was going to take a bus—and then my aunt found my stash and took it. And then everything went to sh—I mean, um, everything got messed up."

"Almost a year?" Violet repeats with raised eyebrows. "Em, that's horrible. I'm so sorry. I can't imagine how hard it is to be separated from her for so long."

"But now I don't have to be, right? Traveling through the faerie paths is quick and easy. But I can't do it myself yet, so I need someone's help."

Her expression becomes conflicted, and I can sense that tiny voice inside me getting ready to yell, *See? I knew it! They don't really want to help you.* "I understand how desperate you must be to see her," Violet says carefully, "but you have to understand that it will be risky. The Guild knows all about her. They probably already have someone watching to see if you'll go there."

"Wait, seriously?" I hadn't considered that. "You really think someone's hanging out at Tranquil Hills just in case I show up?"

"Yes. Your power is valuable to the Guild. They'll want to get it back if they can."

"But they think I'm dead."

"Do they? You might not know this yet, but it's hard to kill a faerie, Em. Our magic can help us survive a great many things that would kill a human. If the Guild doesn't find your body, they'll assume you survived somehow."

"Mom! I still can't find the book," Jack shouts from somewhere in the house.

"Just keep looking," she calls over her shoulder.

"Okay, this is bad." I can't keep still so I start pacing. "So the Guild is probably watching my mom. Do you think they'd hurt her? You know, try to use her against me?"

"I highly doubt it. I know they seem like it, but they're not the bad guys."

"Really?" My voice is laced with sarcasm. "They certainly seemed like the bad guys when they were trying to kill me yesterday. And if my magic is so valuable to them, why would they think twice about threatening a sick human woman who means nothing to them?"

"Em, one of the major purposes of the Guild is to *protect*

humans. They don't mean—"

"And what about the Unseelies? They somehow knew about me and my Griffin Ability, so they probably know about Mom too. Won't they try to take her? That's villain move number one, right? Use a person's loved ones against them. They've probably taken her al—"

"Em, calm down." Violet grips my upper arms and gives them a reassuring squeeze. "We're one step ahead of you. I already sent someone last night to check that your mother's okay. That's why I asked you the name of the hospital yesterday. He reported back that she's fine. He couldn't go into her room in case someone was watching, but he saw her from a distance."

"Oh. Okay." My rising doubts shrink back down. "Thank you." I tuck my hair behind one ear as she lets go of me and steps back. "So, can I visit her? I mean, I know someone from the Guild might be watching, but I can disguise myself. I'll be really careful."

I expect her to argue about it not being safe—that's what grown-ups do, right?—but instead she nods. "Yes, we can help you do that, but like I said, it will be dangerous. If your mother has no other family or friends that regularly visit her, then the Guild will expect that anyone going to see her now is associated with you. So even if Calla creates an illusion that makes you appear entirely different, the Guild will likely be suspicious. That's her Griffin Ability, by the way. Casting illusions."

"Wow. Oh yes, she made us invisible yesterday."

"That's right."

"Can she make me appear invisible to everyone except my mother?"

"She can, although it tires her out much faster to project an illusion onto some while keeping it from others. So as long as you understand that you may have to get out of there on short notice, we can make this work."

I nod fervently. "I can do that. A short visit is better than nothing."

"Okay. Later, then? Calla's schedule's full for the day, but she'll be able to take you late this afternoon."

"Thank you." Excited anticipation rushes suddenly through me. I'm going to see her. I'm actually going to see Mom.

Jack appears in the doorway, hefting a heavy book. "Look, Mom, I found it."

Violet claps her hands together. "See? I knew you could do it. Come on, let's get you to school."

* * *

Late in the afternoon, when I'm tired of practicing pulling magic out of myself, and my brain is almost bursting with all the things I want to talk to Mom about, I wait for Calla in the pavilion. As people I don't know wander past, I slide a little lower on one of the couches and avoid making eye contact. I watch Jack running by in the company of several children. They slow near the hammocks and jostle as they try to decide who gets which one. Jack tries to jump onto one, but it ends up flipping over and depositing him on his stomach on the ground. I stand quickly, unsure if I should run over to check he's okay, but he pushes himself up a moment later, laughing along with his friends.

"Hey, it's Emerson!" he shouts suddenly, grinning and pointing my way. They all start running toward me, which I find a little alarming. "Emerson," Jack says when he reaches the pavilion. "Remember you were saying you know how to fall the right way?"

I stare down awkwardly at five young faces. "Fall?"

"Yeah, when you and your friend do that park stuff."

"Oh, parkour. Yes."

"So can you teach me how to fall out of a hammock the right way? So that I look cool?"

I can't help laughing at that. "I'm sorry, Jack. I don't know if there's *any* way to fall out of a hammock that looks cool."

"See?" says a girl whose eyes have vertical pupils like the guy I saw yesterday when I arrived here. "Such a dumb idea."

"Hey, don't be such a witch," another boy says.

She gasps. "That is *so mean*."

"You can't talk about witches in front of Jack, remember?" a second girl says.

"It's fine," Jack tells them with a dramatic sigh. "It's just my mom and dad and Aunt Calla who don't like talking about witches."

"Why not?" I ask, wondering what terrible blunder I made when I spoke about Aurora and witches earlier today.

"They killed my sister," Jack says, so matter-of-factly that at first I wonder if he's making a terrible joke. But the other four children nod, their expressions serious.

"That's—oh my goodness. That's horrible. I'm so sorry, Jack."

"Yeah." He looks down. "I didn't know her. It happened a long time ago, way before I was born."

"Hey there, guys." Calla jogs up to the pavilion steps. "What happened way before you were born, Jack?"

"Nothing." He gives her a wide smile. "We're gonna go back to the hammocks." He runs away, followed closely by his friends.

"Okay then," Calla says, watching them for a moment. "So." She turns to me. "Ready to go?"

I suck in a deep breath, trying to figure out how to answer her. She probably doesn't realize what a loaded question that is. "Yes," I say eventually, despite the fact that I doubt I'll ever feel ready.

"We need to leave from outside the oasis," she says. "And I want to talk to Ryn quickly before we go."

"Okay." I fall into step beside her as we leave the pavilion behind. "Are there a lot of people living here?" I ask, glancing up at a faerie couple walking hand in hand in the other direction.

"Yes, quite a few. Most end up leaving if we can help them live safely somewhere else, but there are individuals and families who decide to stay. We now have over a hundred fae who call this place home."

"All Griffin Gifted?"

"Not all, but mostly, yes."

"Okay here's something I don't understand: How are there so many fae who ended up with Griffin Abilities? I was told it started with magical discs someone created long ago, but weren't there only six of them? I know they were passed around to various people, but seriously? How did those discs get into the hands of so many?"

Calla pushes her gleaming gold hair over her shoulder. "It may seem like a lot, but the number is small in comparison to the population of our world."

"Okay, sure, but still. All these people from six discs of magic?"

"Think about the fact that those discs were around for centuries. They granted power, which means others coveted them, which means they were frequently stolen. Add to that the fact that two Griffin Gifted can possibly pass on Griffin magic to their offspring, and you wind up with even more of us."

"I suppose when you take into account the fact that you guys live so long, it makes more sense. I'm still having trouble accepting that part. Or at least, applying it to myself. I can't imagine still being alive in a few hundred years time." And I can't imagine how I'm supposed to deal with all my human friends and family growing old and dying while I still look like a twenty-year-old. "Is Jack Griffin Gifted?" I ask, forcing my mind in a less depressing direction.

"No, thank goodness. If he wants to leave here one day and join the rest of the world, he can do so without having to hide a secret ability."

"Good afternoon, ladies."

I slow to a halt as Dash waves and walks toward us. "Ugh, really?" is all I can bring myself to say.

"Interesting to see you back here so soon," Calla comments. "The Guild definitely isn't working you hard enough."

He shrugs. "They tell us to take our first year easy."

"They do not." She eyes him suspiciously. "What are you really doing here?"

"I was updating Vi on something earlier and she mentioned that you're taking Em to see her mom. I thought—"

"You're not coming with," I tell him.

"Hey, I just thought you guys could do with some extra protection. You'll be focused on your mom, and Calla will be focused on whatever illusion she's using to cover you. Don't you think you need a third person to keep an eye on things? In case a doctor or another guardian shows up?"

"No."

"Actually," Calla says, "that's a perfectly sensible plan. But I was going to ask Ryn to come with us."

"Ryn's out with Vi at the moment. I was just up there looking for them." He nods toward one of the giant trees. "And everyone else who's mission-approved is busy." He grins. "Looks like it's a good thing I showed up."

I manage to keep myself from groaning out loud. "Fine. Whatever. Just stay away from my mother. She doesn't need you ruining her life any further."

Calla frowns, opens her mouth, then appears to think better of whatever she was going to say. "Okay then. Let's go."

Once we're out in the desert, Calla opens a doorway to the faerie paths and tells me to focus firmly on picturing the outside of the hospital. Though complete darkness surrounds me, I shut my eyes anyway, imagining the high walls, the security gate, the discreetly small sign with the hospital's name on it, and mountain peaks in the distance.

"Well done," Calla says.

I open my eyes and look across an empty street at the exact scene I just pictured. "That's amazing," I murmur.

Dash raises the hood of his jacket and pulls it over his head. "What?" he asks when I give him an odd look. "I don't want my face showing up on any Guild surveillance orbs."

"Surveillance what? And you're going to be invisible, aren't you?"

"Invisible to people, yes. Not to bugs. I don't know if they're watching, but it's good to be careful."

"Am I supposed to know what you're talking about?" At that moment, a shiver sends goosebumps racing up my back and into my hair. "Oh—um—you can—" I grab Dash's arm, in case my ability has any doubt who I'm talking to. "You can open doorways to the faerie paths," I blurt out.

Dash stares at me with wide eyes. Calla looks equally startled. "Well that came outta nowhere," she says.

Dash quickly removes a stylus from inside his jacket and crouches down. He writes on the tar, muttering those words I still can't clearly make out. Darkness appears, spreading rapidly into a large hole leading to the faerie paths. "Yes! Finally! Thanks, Em." He rises and puts his stylus away. "Now we'll have to come up with a way for you to fix Jewel as well."

"That was pretty darn cool," Calla says.

"Yeah. When I'm saying something useful."

"True. Okay, let's focus on the hospital again. Do you remember anything about what the inside looks like?"

"Yes, I remember the waiting area. But I don't remember where Mom's room is. It's been a while since I was here."

"Not a problem," she says. "The guy who checked things out for us last night said she's in room twenty-six. I'm sure we can find it. All you need to do is picture the waiting room so we can safely get inside." She opens another faerie paths doorway.

"Wait," I say before we step into the darkness. "Are you absolutely sure we'll be invisible on the other side?"

"Yes. I'm focusing on invisibility. You're focusing on the waiting room. Dash, you're emptying your mind." She gives him a half-smile. "Should be easy."

"That's why I'm here, right?" he says without missing a beat. "Empty-minded muscle."

I shake my head, link arms with both of them, and walk forward. I squeeze my eyes shut and picture the waiting room. The rows of chairs, the hard-angled reception desk, the confusing abstract paintings, and the tall monochrome flower pots. I smell it before I see it: detergent and something sour. As if someone threw up in here recently.

I look down, and instead of seeing my body, I see the polished floor. I cling more tightly to Calla and Dash. "Okay," I whisper. I look around, the memory of my last visit coming back to me. "We need to get through that door on the right. The one that looks like it requires an ID tag."

"I guess we'll need to go through the paths again," Calla says.

One of the women behind the main desk looks up, frowning in our direction. "Move quietly," Calla instructs, her whisper barely audible now. I feel a tug pulling me to my left. Calla leads us around the corner to an alcove with another few chairs and a window onto the garden. When we're out of view of the desk, we suddenly become visible again. "Quickly," she says, opening a doorway. We hurry into it. Moments later, we're on the other side of the security door.

We head along the corridor, arms still linked so we don't lose each other. Bright sunlight streams in through the windows, illuminating more canvases of colorful art. The gardens themselves, visible through the windows, are neatly manicured. From here, I can see a group of patients sitting on the lawn in a circle. Tranquil Hills is pretty and serene, but that's part of what makes my skin crawl whenever I'm here. It's like icing on a cake that has worms crawling through it. Perfume sprayed over rotting garbage. Nothing can hide the true nature of this place.

We pass silently through an open living area where people sit in twos or threes at small tables playing board games or card games. They're all watched by nurses around the room. This is where Mom was the first time I came to visit. We sat here together and played Go Fish while Chelsea waited for me in the reception area, refusing to see her 'crazy sister.' A shiver races across my skin at the memory. "Okay, Em?" Calla whispers.

"Yeah."

We enter another corridor on the other side of the room. Fewer windows and less light. Closed doors lining the right hand side. "Okay, here's a number twenty," Calla says. "I guess we just keep going and we'll find twenty-six."

My heart leaps, pounding faster with every step we take. Nervousness makes me nauseous and light-headed. I still can't believe I'm about to see her. "There it is," I whisper as a door with a number twenty-six on it comes into view.

"I haven't seen anyone suspicious yet," Dash says. "Anyone I recognize from the Guild, I mean."

"Can I go in?" I ask, stopping outside the door.

"Yes," Calla says letting go of me. On my other side, Dash moves away. "We'll keep watch out here, and I'll make sure you appear invisible to anyone who walks past."

I swallow. If I could see my hand, I'd probably find it shaking. I fumble a moment with the door handle— misjudging the distance and bumping the door with my invisible knuckles—before finding it and wrapping my hand around it. I push down, take a deep breath, and slowly open the door. Too scared to take a step forward, I peer inside.

The room is empty.

My head pounds as disappointment and relief collide. "Where is she?"

I sense movement beside me, then hear Dash's voice: "Perhaps she's eating a meal. Or having some kind of social time. Or a bathroom break. Is she usually restricted to her room, or does she only come back here to sleep?"

"I don't know." My words come out harsher than I intended. "I haven't been here in a long time."

"We'll just have to wait," Calla says. "It's okay. I'm only projecting one illusion right now, and it's a simple one, so it isn't too tiring."

"Okay. Thank you." One of them bumps into me as I move

to the side, and after a moment of shuffling, we're all leaning against the wall beside door number twenty-six. There's no way I'm waiting inside that room on my own. The corridor will do just fine. As the seconds tick by, my anxiety begins to rise again. Up and up, my insides twisting tighter and tighter.

"You aren't going to say anything to her about magic, are you?" Dash asks eventually, breaking the silence.

"Firstly," I tell him, "you don't get to tell me what I should speak to my mother about. And secondly, no. I'm not so stupid that I'm going to tell her I'm a faerie with magic. I don't even know if I'm going to tell her I know she isn't my real mother. There are dozens of things I *want* to say, and I probably won't end up saying any of them because I don't want to freak her out."

Like last time.

We're quiet for a minute or two as someone in the company of a nurse walks slowly past us and into one of the other bedrooms. The nurse leaves soon afterwards.

"Vi told me it's been a long time since you saw her," Calla says once we're alone again. "You can probably talk to her about whatever's happened in your normal life up until a few days ago. Stuff you did at school. Updates on your friends."

"All the parkour skills you and Val have learned," Dash adds.

Val. Val who's probably confused and angry that I ran away and left her behind.

"Yeah, maybe," I say. "But also … well, I like to chat to her about the good old days." I stare past the blank wall ahead of me and picture Mom as she used to be, smiling and happy. "I think she likes remembering our pretty garden, and the little house we lived in, and the ornaments she collected. I've often imagined taking her back there one day. Returning to the simple, happy life we used to have. It always seemed impossible, but now with magic …" I trail off, coming back to the present with a jolt and remembering who I'm with: Dash, who doesn't deserve to know my private thoughts and wishes, and Calla, who probably wouldn't approve of any of the things I plan to do with my magic once I know how to use it.

"With magic?" she prompts.

"Nothing. Wait, is that … Oh, heck, I think that's her." Two people are walking toward us. A nurse and a woman with dark messy hair, not quite as tall as I remember, and dressed in sweatpants and a hoodie. My heart rate rockets upward and my conflicting emotions reach a peak. I think I might throw up right here. But I manage to breathe through it as Mom walks closer. *It's her!* my mind shrieks as she passes me and goes into her room. *It's really, really her!* She's right here, after so many months. I'll finally be able to speak to her, hug her, let her know I think of her every single day and that she won't have to be here for much longer.

The nurse stops in the doorway. "Just lie down and I'm sure it'll pass soon," she says to Mom. Her voice lacks feeling, as if the words mean nothing to her. Or, I wonder briefly, as if she's spoken those same words a hundred times before. "You know you can call one of us if you start feeling any worse."

Mom gives her a distant smile and a nod.

The nurse closes the door and walks away.

I take another dizzying few breaths before moving forward and grasping the handle. As I push the door open, I suddenly become visible again. Mom looks up. She blinks and frowns. A smile spreads rapidly across my face, turning into a laugh. "Mom." I walk into the room—

—and an alarm begins blaring.

CHAPTER EIGHTEEN

MOM SCREAMS AND SCRAMBLES BACKWARD ACROSS HER bed. Calla and Dash, visible now, rush into the room. Calla goes immediately to the wall and scribbles across it. "We have to go," she calls to me.

"What? I don't under—"

"It's a Guild alarm. It was set for you."

"But I only just … Mom, it's okay, it's me." I ignore Calla and Dash and approach Mom cautiously. "Everything's fine, Mom. Don't worry about the alarm." I reach for her, but she shrinks back, slapping wildly at my hands. "It's okay, it's just me. It's Emmy. Your daughter. I came to—"

"Em, we gotta go." Dash takes my arm and pulls me toward the faerie paths.

"No!" I wrench my arm free. "I need to get her!"

"What? No, we can't take her with us."

"I won't leave without her!"

"You can't take her through the paths, Em!" Calla shouts above the alarm.

"Then we go out the front door with her!" I shout back.

"And then what? We'd have to find somewhere safe for her in this world. Someone who knows how to care for her. And what about her medication, her treatment?"

"The medication makes her worse!" I gesture to Mom, now hiding under her blankets, curled up and wailing, rocking back and forth.

Movement in the corridor draws my gaze away. Dash throws his hand out, and the door slams itself shut. He runs to it and begins drawing big glowing patterns across it. "This won't hold them for long," he says as the door shudders beneath an assault from the other side.

"Em, we will come back for her," Calla says firmly. "I promise. But we're not taking her anywhere until we have a solid plan." She reaches for my hand. "Dash, stay here and keep watch. Make sure no one does anything to—Actually, no. You go with Em. I'll stay. You can't risk your cover, and I can more easily hide myself."

"Got it." Dash grabs my arm as Calla pushes us both toward the gaping hole leading to the faerie paths.

"Mom." The word is a half-whisper, half-sob as I throw one last look over my shoulder before the darkness consumes us. I stumble through it, Dash pulling me along, until soft orange light appears ahead of us. I breathe in the rapidly cooling evening air of the desert as sand shifts beneath my feet. I pull away from Dash.

"Em ..." He reaches for me, but I smack his hand away.

"Don't touch me." His hands fall to his sides while I wrap mine tightly around my body. I need to hold myself together.

Quietly, Dash says, "She didn't recognize you, did she."

Thanks, Dash, I want to yell. *THANK YOU FOR POINTING THAT OUT!* Instead I bite my lip until the tears recede. There's no point in screaming at him. He doesn't know about the nerve he's struck. He doesn't know that the last time I visited Mom, she ended up cowering in the corner of her room and screaming about the stranger—me. He doesn't know that several nurses had to hold her down while I left the room in tears, and he doesn't know how desperately I hoped this time would be different.

"Emerson—"

"Don't."

"I'm sorry I did this to you." His tone is pleading, and his hands are clasped tightly together beneath his chin.

"What?"

"I'm sorry! She's in that hospital because of me. I've always denied it, and some logical, defensive part of my brain still argues that she would have been institutionalized at some point anyway, and that you can't really blame me, but ... you can. It was my fault. On that day, in that moment, she went completely over the edge because of me. And ... I'm sorry."

I blink, look down at the sand, then back up at him. "What do you expect me to say to that?"

"I ... I don't know. I just needed you to know how sorry I am."

"Why? It doesn't change anything."

"It might change how much you hate me."

I shake my head. "Get over yourself, Dash. This isn't about you." I turn away, looking for the faint outline of the dome. It's almost invisible, but I manage to spot it. I start trudging across the sand, picturing the hidden world within the dome. Lush vegetation, twinkling bugs, and the gentle scent of flowers. A peaceful scene contrasting starkly with the repeating memory of a bare white room and Mom screaming while scrambling away from me.

Again.

Again.

Again.

I frown and blink and look away, desperate to push the image from my mind. The tension in my chest eases the moment I pass through the magic layer and into the oasis. I hate that I'm glad to be back here. It feels like a betrayal to Mom. I shouldn't enjoy a single moment of this sanctuary while she's trapped between four blank walls. Trapped inside her own mind.

"Em, wait," Dash calls as I stride away from him. I swing around, still walking backward, wanting nothing more than to be alone right now.

"We're going to get her out," he says. "We couldn't do it today, but that doesn't mean it won't happen. We'll give her a better life somehow, I promise."

"Thanks," I say, "but you shouldn't make promises you don't know how to keep."

* * *

I don't come out of my room that evening to join anyone for dinner, but I hear Violet and Ryn outside my door, speaking quietly to one another. Calla joins them at some point. I press my ear against the door long enough to hear her say that Mom is okay and the guardians who were waiting for me didn't do anything to her after I left. Then I move back to the bed.

The Guild knows I was there. They'll probably increase the number of guardians hanging around, and if I try to visit again, it'll be even more likely that I'll be caught. Not that I have much hope of convincing Calla to take me back. She and her companions are probably regretting offering to help me. I could have got her caught. Ruined Dash's cover. Maybe the three of them are standing out there trying to come up with a kind way of telling me they can't do anything more for Mom. And it's not like I'd blame them. They don't owe me anything. They'll probably forget about me as soon as the next desperate person arrives at the oasis.

Which suits me just fine, since I'm used to taking care of things on my own.

CHAPTER NINETEEN

THAT IMAGE OF MOM SCREAMING, WILD TERROR IN HER eyes, floods my mind first thing the next morning. I make a conscious effort to focus on something else: My Griffin Ability. I need to learn how to use it. Last night could have turned out so differently if I'd been able to calm Mom down with just a few words. If I'd been able to tell that magical alarm to turn itself off. I need to get past my fear of all things medical and hand over a sample of my magic. I need that elixir.

Mom. Cowering. Her mouth open in a silent scream.

I shove the memory aside yet again and turn over—and find Bandit snuggled beside me in kitten form. I'm about to push him away from me, but he looks so darn cute curled up with his nose tucked beneath one paw. And it's oddly comforting to realize I haven't been alone all night. I reach out and stroke two fingers from his head down his back, hoping he doesn't turn out to be just like the puppy that ran away.

My stomach grumbles. I wonder if Violet's breakfast invitation was only for yesterday morning, or if it extends for as many mornings as I'm here. Hopefully the latter, since I have no food in this room. I get dressed and check the enchanted numbers on my wall—I'm later than yesterday morning—before hurrying down the stairs, one hand trailing against the tree trunk to steady me if I trip over an uneven step. I slow down before reaching Ryn and Violet's door. It's open, which is a good sign, and the heavenly aromas wafting through the door start my stomach grumbling again, but I'm still not sure if I'm welcome here a second time. Especially after freaking out at the hospital yesterday and putting Calla and Dash at risk.

I move a little closer and see Violet, Jack and Calla at the table. Jack straightens, jumps off his chair, and runs toward me. "I'm sorry, Emerson!" He wraps his arms around my middle and squeezes tight.

"Oh, um, okay." I pat his back awkwardly. "What are you sorry for?"

"I don't know. Mom and Dad were talking about you this morning and they sounded worried, and when I asked Mom what was wrong, she said you probably just need a big hug."

"Jack," Violet scolds, rising from her chair and then standing there hesitantly. Color appears in her cheeks. "You should ask before you do things like that. Some people don't like to be hugged by people they don't know well."

Confusion crosses Jack's face as he pulls back. "But Em

knows me. We walked around the whole oasis together."

"It's fine," I say hurriedly, leaning down and hugging him quickly, despite the growing awkwardness. I'd prefer to keep my personal space to myself, but I don't want to hurt Jack's feelings.

"Would you like to join us?" Violet asks, gesturing to the table and still looking somewhat embarrassed.

"Yes, thank you. I wasn't sure if, um …" I shove my hands awkwardly into my back pockets as I hover near the table. "Well, I know you invited me yesterday, but I wasn't sure if that was just a first-day thing, like for everyone who's new, or—"

"Oh, that was for every morning while you're here," she says with a smile, sitting again.

"Yeah, we don't want you to starve all the way up there in the top of the tree," Calla adds.

I pull a chair out and take a seat. "Do you cook amazing breakfasts every morning?"

"Dad actually made the pancakes," Jack tells me before helping himself to another one.

"And no, we don't do breakfasts like this every morning," Violet says. "But when things are less busy and we have time, then we do."

I help myself to two pancakes and reach for a small jug of what looks like syrup, but could very possibly be an exotic magical alternative. I prepare myself for the possibility of it tasting very different. Ryn walks into the house as I finish drizzling it over my pancakes.

"Okay, everything's sorted," he says as he joins us at the table. "Em, we're going to get your mom out of hospital today, if it's all right with you."

"I—yes. Of course that's all right with me." I pause with a fork and a piece of pancake in the air in front of me and shake my head, giving myself a moment to take in the news. "Today? Already? That's amazing."

Ryn laughs. "Yes, today."

"I mean, I know Calla said we'd go back for her, but ... I just figured that would take a while. I'm sure you have plenty of other priorities, and my mom's just ... a human stuck in a hospital."

Ryn lowers the mug he just picked up and looks directly at me. "She's your mother. That makes her a priority. And if she's been stuck in that hospital for years, then it clearly isn't doing anything to help her. We were talking about getting her out as soon as possible, and then Dash called last night to tell me it had to be today and that he plans to help. So today it is. Everything's been planned."

"You know, I'm seriously starting to wonder if the Guild is going to fire Dash soon. He's spending more time on cases for us these days than the job he's paid to do."

"Don't worry about him," Violet says, reaching for a glass of something green. "He works a lot harder than you think."

"Works hard?" Calla snorts. "You think so? That boy is far too chilled. He's probably sitting back and letting his team do all the work."

"Just like he does with the ladies," Jack says.

Violet chokes on her drink. "Excuse me?" She sets her glass

down. "What exactly are you talking about, young man?"

"That's what he said to me," Jack tells her, his tone defensive. Then he deepens his voice, probably in an attempt to impersonate Dash. "I just sit back, and the ladies come flocking."

Violet blinks at Jack while Calla bursts out laughing. Ryn tries to keep the smile off his face as he clears his throat and says, "I hope you realize, Jack, that that's not the way to find the right girl."

Jack screws up his face and reaches for another pancake. "I'm not looking for any girl."

"Good," Violet says as I chew and wait patiently for a moment to ask for more details about Mom's rescue plan. "And when you do, you'll find out it takes a lot more effort than just sitting back and waiting." She looks across the table at Ryn, her frown replaced by a small smile.

Ryn winks at her. "Like glow-bug asses in the sky."

Violet flicks her fingers, and a spark bounces off Ryn's shoulder. "Don't say ass," she whispers.

"Mom and Dad said ass!" Jack shouts gleefully.

Violet rolls her eyes and Calla starts laughing again. I smile and wait for the laughter to die down before saying, "So, uh, what's the plan for getting my mom out of Tranquil Hills?"

"Right, sorry," Ryn says. He takes a sip from his mug, then continues. "Calla and Dash will go into the hospital and retrieve her. Dash doesn't have a Griffin Ability, so he won't set off the alarm the Guild put on her room. He'll need to sedate her so she doesn't put up a fight. Obviously not with magic, so he'll use something herbal that doesn't contain any magical elements. Then they'll use an illusion of invisibility and carry her through the building and out the main door."

"And the door that requires an ID tag?" I ask.

"They'll wait for someone to go through and then follow them before the door closes. Same with the main gate. Vi and I will be waiting for them outside, mainly as backup in case anything goes wrong. Then, since we can't get your mom through the paths, we'll need to drive to one of the natural openings between this world and that one."

"You can drive?" I ask, doubt very much evident in my voice.

"No, but one of our Guild contacts has a sister—a halfling with no magic—who's always lived in that world. She's agreed to drive us. So we'll meet her down the road from the hospital, and we've calculated it'll take about five days to get to the nearest opening."

"Five *days*? Surely you can't keep her sedated the entire time?"

"No. I assumed you'd want to travel in the car with her. When she wakes up, you can explain everything to her so she doesn't panic."

I hesitate, not wanting to have to explain what happened last night. The fact that my own mother didn't recognize me.

"I know," he says gently. "Calla told me what happened. You're worried she still won't recognize you. But we were hoping it might have been the stress of the alarm going off, and two other unfamiliar people in her room. It will hopefully be easier once she's away from the hospital."

"She …" I swallow and push my hand through my hair.

"She didn't recognize me last time either. When I went almost a year ago. I hoped last night would be different, but it was just as bad."

"Perhaps something in her medication confuses her," Calla says. "You said yourself that the medication makes her worse."

"It's just that after she moved there, she always seemed a bit ... spaced out. We played a card game the first time I visited, and her responses were so slow."

"Well, we'll take it as it comes," Ryn says. "Two of us will always be with you in the car. Not necessarily Vi or Calla or I, but two people from the team. Possibly people you haven't met yet, but they're all a hundred percent trustworthy. We'll swap out every few hours over the five days. If your mom panics, someone will be there to help you calm her down."

"And when we get to this world? Then what?"

"There's a healing institute we plan to take her to. White Cedars. It's private, has nothing to do with the Guild. We've sent people there before, and the Guild's never known anything about it. Hopefully someone there can figure out if it's possible to help your mom."

I lean forward. "Do you think there's a chance? Dash said we can't use magic on her because she's human. Was he wrong?"

"He wasn't, but our healers don't always work with magic. I don't know their methods in detail, but we may as well ask them to try. Nothing in your world has worked so far."

I nod vigorously. "Yes. I agree. Thank you."

"Sure. Shall we enjoy the pancakes now before they get too cold?"

"I've had three," Jack announces.

"Little piggy," Calla tells him.

I cut into my second pancake—and out of the blue, that tingle I'm becoming familiar with rushes up my spine, into my hair and down to my fingertips. I grasp for something harmless to say, to test this thing, and blurt out, "Pass the syrup."

There's a beat of silence, and then four hands reach out simultaneously, knocking into each other and toppling the syrup jug onto its side. Together, in a fumbling, sticky mess, the four of them slide the fallen jug across the table to rest in front of my plate.

Calla is the first to snatch her hand away. "What was that? Was that your Griffin Ability?"

"Wow, that was weird," Violet says, pulling her hand back.

"Mom, what's going on? What just happened?" Jack holds his sticky hand up in front of his face. Violet reaches for a cloth and passes it to him.

"I'm sorry," I say in a small voice. "I suddenly felt it coming on, and I wanted to test it, and I tried to think of something silly and safe. I didn't think it would make a mess."

"It's fine," Violet says. "Not a big deal."

I look at Ryn, because he's the only one who hasn't said anything yet. "You think it's a big deal, don't you."

"Not the mess," he says. "The Griffin Ability. The power to make other people do things with just a simple command. That's a big deal."

"Yeah. I know." Using my fork, I push a piece of pancake around my plate, no longer interested in eating it. I half expect Ryn to give me that clichéd line about great power and great responsibility, but he doesn't, which makes me like him a little more. "So, I should probably go to that laboratory you mentioned and hand over a sample of my magic."

"I'll take you after breakfast," Violet says. Then she briefly explains my Griffin Ability to Jack—"That's so cool!" is his response—and the atmosphere around the table slowly returns to normal after that.

"I need to finish a few things before we get going," Ryn says, standing. He clears a few items from the table and gets a cleaning spell going in the sink. "I'll be in the mountain if you need me. Otherwise, we'll meet at the base of the tree at eleven?" He glances at Violet and Calla, then at me.

"Sure," I say. It's not like my schedule is full.

"Oh, hey." Ryn stops to greet someone in the doorway. "I didn't know you were back. How'd it go?"

"Uncle Chase!" Jack shouts.

Calla pushes her chair back immediately and runs to the door. The man standing there pulls her into a hug. "Oh, you know how it is," he says to Ryn over her shoulder. "Things got a little complicated, but it all worked out in the end."

"Great. Looking forward to hearing more about it. I need to get to the mountain now, but Calla can fill you in on what's happening today." As he leaves, the man in the doorway gives Calla a quick kiss and says something in a voice too low for the rest of us to hear.

She nods, then turns around and gestures to me. "This is Emerson. Em, this is Chase." I walk a little closer as she introduces me. "Remember the girl Dash was keeping an eye on for the Guild? Her magic finally kicked in properly and it turns out she's Griffin Gifted."

"Welcome to the club," Chase says, reaching forward with a tattooed arm to shake my hand. He pauses, gripping my hand for a moment too long as his eyes dart quickly across the room before returning to me.

"What?" I pull my hand back quickly. "Please don't tell me you can read minds or something, because I'm not sure I can handle that. Having someone feel all my emotions is weird enough."

His expression relaxes into a smile. "No. Nothing to do with minds. I have a knack for controlling the weather."

"Really? That's weird."

"It's come in useful at times. What's yours?"

"I say things and then they happen."

"She told the earth to split open and it did," Calla adds.

Chase's brow rises. "Impressive. You must be at the top of the Guild's most-wanted list right now."

I nod. "Pretty much."

"Okay, we need to get to the lab," Violet says. She sweeps her hand through the air past the table, then ducks as the remaining dishes fly into the sink. "Jack, please dry the dishes when the spell's finished washing them, and make sure you're ready for school by the time I get back."

"Aah, Mom, but I wanted to introduce Em to Filigree. She hasn't met him yet."

"Em needs to come with me, and Filigree's being a grumpy old sloth right now. It isn't the best time."

With a downcast expression, Jack walks to the sink and

reaches for a dish cloth. "Here, I'll help you," Calla says. "Don't be grumpy like Filigree."

As Violet and I walk out and head down the stairs, I ask, "Is there a mountain somewhere inside this dome that I've missed?"

"A mountain? No. Why would—Oh." She chuckles. "Because of what Ryn said on his way out. No, that's just what we call the building that has the rooms we meet in to plan and discuss missions and Seer visions and everything else. The lab's there too. Chase used to run things from a mountain, back when Ryn and I were still at the Guild. Then we all ended up here, and some of the people he worked with previously started calling that building the mountain. It's silly, I know, but the name stuck."

I put my hand out and run it along the tree as we descend. "Silly, but it makes an interesting story, at least." We pass a person with greenish scaled skin walking up the stairs, and Violet introduces me quickly before we continue. At the bottom of the tree, I push my hands into my back pockets. "Can I ask you something more serious?"

"Yes, of course."

It's an awkward subject, but less awkward—hopefully— than if I'd asked at the breakfast table. "Um, how do I earn my keep here?"

Her smile turns bemused. "Earn your keep? You don't have to earn your keep, Em."

"But, I mean, nothing in life is free, right? Everything costs something. So if I'm not contributing, then how does that work?"

She shakes her head. "Don't you worry about that. We have paying clients. They help us keep things running."

"Really? That's it? I don't have to pay anything?"

"Nope, not a thing," she says with a laugh. "If you decide to stay here, then we can find a way for you to contribute. If you end up leaving, then just consider this all a gift. Either way, you don't need to worry about it now."

Stay here ... with Mom. Didn't I wish for that the moment I first walked into the oasis? I shove the thought aside quickly, not wanting to somehow jinx the possibility.

"Can I ask you something now?" she says.

"Yeah, okay."

"What's up with you and Dash?"

My internal defenses go up immediately. "What do you mean?"

"Well, he's been talking about you for years—this not-so-human girl he's been keeping tabs on for the Guild—but he failed to mention that you ... dislike him? Hate him? Hold a grudge against him?"

"Can I tick all of the above?"

She laughs. "How interesting. Most girls seem to fall all over him trying to get his attention."

"I've noticed. And I've never understood why."

"So what unforgivable thing did he do to you?"

I look at her. "You said he's spoken about me. Didn't he tell you what happened with my mom?"

She nods. "He saved her life, didn't he?"

"Saved? More like ruined."

Surprise colors her expression. "Oh. What happened?"

"Well, it's because of him that my mother was taken away to a psychiatric hospital."

Still looking completely lost, she says, "Um … how?"

I raise my eyes to the treetops and let out a frustrated sound. "Okay. Dash obviously never gave you the whole story, so here it is."

CHAPTER TWENTY

"I WAS TWELVE, ALMOST THIRTEEN," I TELL HER. "ONE OF my friends had a birthday party at the park. Mom had been okay for a little while. She had episodes sometimes, but at least they all happened when she was at home. No one knew about them. Anyway, the party was going well. I was happy, Mom was interacting with people.

"Then Dash showed up out of nowhere. I'd never met him before. Didn't know who he was. And suddenly he started running toward us for no reason, launched himself right over the table, and crashed directly into Mom. I was standing near her, and he managed to knock us both down at the same time. I got up and started yelling at him. That's when Mom lost it." I wrap my arms around myself and focus on the river as we walk alongside it. "I realize now that she couldn't see him.

That she thought I was yelling at nothing. Or maybe she saw something I didn't. One of the imaginary people always out to get her. Maybe that's who she thought I was yelling at, I don't know. Anyway, she ended up completely freaking out. She was cowering on the ground, sobbing and rocking, wailing about someone coming to get her and her daughter. Everyone in the park was watching her—and me. Dash had somehow vanished by then.

"Some of the other grown-ups in the park tried to help her. Tried to figure out what was going on. But she screamed at them to get away. To stop trying to hurt her. And then she started scratching at herself, trying to get something invisible off her skin. Someone must have called an ambulance, because the next thing I knew, paramedics were strapping her to a gurney—I guess to stop her from hurting herself—and carrying her away. I was allowed in the back of the ambulance with her, and that was the last time I saw my friends. I still remember the looks on their faces just before the ambulance doors slammed shut. The fear, the confusion. The whispers to one another.

"I went to live with Chelsea after that, and unlike before with the previous episodes, Mom never got better. It was like the incident in the park was the trigger that sent her off the edge completely. I don't know. Maybe it would have happened anyway because of something else, or maybe she would have stayed the same if there had been no incident that day.

"Then I saw Dash a few months later in Stanmeade. I thought it was a cruel coincidence that we ended up living in the same crummy part of the world. I had no idea, obviously, that he was there because of some magical assignment, or that he later hung around because he was keeping an eye on me. All I knew was that I hated him for ruining my life and my mother's life. It could have been so different if not for what happened in the park."

Violet touches my shoulder, and I realize we've come to a standstill beside the river. "I'm so sorry. It must have been traumatizing to see your mother like that."

I nod slowly, breathing in a long breath and exhaling all the memories. At least, that's what I'm trying to do. It doesn't seem to be working.

"But didn't Dash tell you why he was in the park that day?" she asks. "I realize he couldn't tell you as long as you didn't know anything about magic and our world, but has he told you in the past few days?"

"Something about an assignment? A group assignment, I think. He didn't give me details."

"He and some of his fellow trainees were there because a Seer had a vision of that park. A vision of several trolls running through and injuring people. Humans wouldn't have been able to see the trolls, of course, so I suppose it would have appeared as a tremor, with people falling and getting hurt. The assignment was given to a group of first years and their mentor because the Guild didn't think it was a serious threat. The trainees were meant to divert the trolls. They almost succeeded, but one got away. Dash saw it heading for your mother. If you don't remember seeing it, then perhaps it was behind you. Anyway, Dash knocked you and your mom out of the way, and his mentor chased after the rogue troll. Then you got up and confronted Dash, who was so shocked that you could actually see him that he couldn't come up with an explanation." She chuckles. "I remember him telling us about it in great detail. He said it was the most exciting assignment he'd had so far."

I take a few moments to absorb this information before responding. "So ... you're saying ... he actually *saved* my mom?" This is a difficult concept for my brain to wrap itself around, given that I've spent years blaming Dash for putting Mom in a mental institution.

"Yes. I mean, she would have been badly injured otherwise, or worse. Humans have been killed by trolls before. So it's a good thing he got her out of the way. What happened afterwards, though, was horrible. I'm not trying to diminish that in any way."

I shake my head slowly. "No. I know." I cross my arms, then drop them to my sides, then start pacing along the bank as confusion and frustration tangle around each other. "Why didn't he tell me this?"

"I'm not sure."

"Ugh, now I have to be *grateful* to him. How am I supposed to do that?"

"Uh ... I don't know."

I stop, let out a huff, and say, "Sorry, let's keep moving. I know we're supposed to be at the lab now."

"Yeah, okay." We continue walking, and eventually Violet says, "Thanks for telling me what happened. I know it can't have been easy."

I nod. Then, since I don't seem to have left my frustration

behind just yet, I blurt out, "What is it about him that makes so many females fawn all over him? I mean sure, he's good-looking, but that doesn't make up for being a gigantic asshat most of the time. And yes, I realize that he's now an asshat who saved my mom, but he's still an asshat."

A snort-laugh escapes her. "Asshat?"

"Yes."

She sighs. "If you've only ever hated him, then you've never had a chance to see the side of him everyone else sees."

"Which is?"

"He's friendly and charming, and he has a way of paying attention to people and showing an interest in their lives that makes them feel … special, I suppose. It's just part of his personality, but some girls read too much into it. They like it when a handsome guy pays attention to them—even if he's a few years younger, which, you'll soon find out, doesn't mean much when you live for centuries—and they end up wanting more than Dash ever intended to give."

"Okay, all I'm hearing is that he uses his charm to manipulate people, and then he acts like he has no idea what's going on when they want more from him."

Violet smiles and shakes her head. "I've known him since he was born, so I'm probably biased in the other direction, but I'm pretty sure he isn't manipulative. I've seen that he's respectful toward his parents, that he's honest, that he's extremely hardworking when he thinks no one's watching." She rolls her eyes. "Granted, he can be a little too full of himself at times, but on the whole, he's a good guy. He genuinely cares about people. He likes to put them at ease, make them laugh. And that's why they end up liking him and enjoying his company."

"Well, you're right that I haven't seen that side of him."

Violet directs me toward a bridge. "Perhaps you'll get a chance to see that side of him now."

I almost say, *I certainly hope not*, but I realize that sounds a little too negative. We cross over the river and head for a large building on the other side. It looks like the kind of ordinary house one would see in a nice neighborhood in the human world. We walk up the steps and onto the porch, and Violet opens the door. The first room we pass is taken up mostly by a long rectangular table and chairs, but the wide bay window and the plants spread across the windowsill give it more of a homey feel than a boardroom feel. The rest of the doors we pass are closed—I remember Jack saying something about out-of-bounds areas—until we reach the end of the passage, where the last door is ajar.

Violet pushes it open and gestures for me to walk in. My first thought is of the labs at school, but this is a far more interesting version. The counters around the edge of the room are covered in jars with colorful liquids and oddly shaped ingredients, laboratory equipment like test tubes, beakers and burners, all interspersed with scattered cogs, levers, pipes, and gadgets I don't recognize. The three parallel workbenches across the center of the room are slightly tidier, with flames, bubbling beakers, and steaming pots indicating live experiments in progress. Except they're probably not experiments, now that I think about it. They're probably ... potions?

"Oh, hey there." A woman comes sliding toward us on a

wheeled chair. Except it isn't a wheeled chair, I realize when she stops in front of us. The chair has no legs at all, and it's floating in midair. The woman, who has pointed ears and an interesting hairstyle of thin braids twisted around each other and piled on top of her head, stands and places her hands on her hips. "You're Emerson, right?"

"Yes. Um, I'm supposed to give you a sample of my magic?"

"Yes, for the Griffin Ability elixir."

"This is Ana, by the way," Violet adds.

"Right, yes. I'm Ana." She walks to one of the shelves and removes an empty glass sphere. "It's pretty simple," she says, returning to me. "Hold the orb in your hands, I'll recite the incantation, and by the end of it, some of your magic will have been drawn out of you and into the orb."

"Does it hurt?" I ask.

"No, but you'll feel a kind of tug. The important thing is not to resist."

I nod. "All right."

"Just relax. Seriously, this isn't a big deal. Close your eyes and chill."

I do as she suggests, blocking out the beakers and gadgets and the glass ball in my hands. The words she begins chanting are foreign, so I have no idea what she's saying. As she slowly repeats them, I begin to feel the tug she spoke about. A strange, slow pull in the region of my chest. I try not to resist. I think I might even be leaning forward a little.

"Okay, all done," Ana says.

I straighten and open my eyes. The orb is filled with the same glowing, sparkling mass that appeared in my hands when

Azzy taught me how to access my magic. "Cool," I murmur.

"I should have the elixir done by tomorrow," Ana says, taking the orb from me. "So what's your Griffin Ability?"

I scoop my hair back, twist it, and pull it over my shoulder. "Sometimes, when I say something, it actually happens. Like if I told you to drop that glass ball on the floor, you'd have no choice but to do it. And if I told the river outside to dry up ... well, I think it would dry up."

Ana's eyes widen. She nods slowly. "Hectic. That's a big one."

"Yeah. I discovered as much. Now I need to know how to control it so I'm not a danger to everyone. Honestly, though, I'd be happy if you guys could just get rid of it." I frown. "That isn't an option, is it?"

Ana's gaze flicks to Violet for a moment before returning to me. "It used to be, but Gaius isn't well anymore. His Griffin Ability is that he can remove and transfer others' abilities. He did it many times, for those who didn't want to be Griffin Gifted. And slowly, he started getting sick." She moves to the other side of the room and places the glass orb in a box. "He didn't connect it to his Griffin Ability until a few years ago," she continues, walking back to us. "He started realizing then that each time he removed another one, it made him sicker. He's very weak now. Doesn't often come out of his house. This lab—all the inventions and the potions—used to be his." Her eyes slide across the counters and shelves. "He taught me everything."

"And we're very grateful you stepped up," Violet says.

"Yeah, yeah. Okay, go away now. You people keep giving

me too much to do." She plops back onto her chair and glides away.

"Thanks, Ana," Violet calls after her.

On the way back to the tree, we talk about what kind of lessons I need in order to learn all the ordinary magic I still know nothing about. I joke that I might not need to learn anything if I can just get my Griffin Ability right. And then I wonder, as Violet continues talking through a plan for my magical education, if there might be some truth to my joke. If I can make things happen with a simple verbal command, shouldn't that be enough?

When we get back to the base of the tree, Calla and Ryn are already waiting for us. "Ready for the rescue mission?"

CHAPTER TWENTY-ONE

"OKAY, THIS IS FAIRLY STRAIGHTFORWARD," RYN SAYS AS THE five of us stand hidden amongst the trees a good distance down the road from the entrance to Tranquil Hills Psychiatric Hospital. "We'll wait until Perry and his sister get here. Em, you'll stay with them. Calla and Dash will go into the hospital, and Vi and I will wait outside near the entrance. If anything goes wrong and you're followed out by guardians, we'll be ready to fight. That shouldn't happen, though, since you'll be invisible."

"Is she in her room now?" Calla asks.

Ryn produces something that looks like a small round mirror. "Yes. Still in her room."

"What's that?" I ask, leaning closer.

"I left a spider in her room yesterday," Calla says. "Not an actual spider," she adds quickly. "It's a little enchanted surveillance device. It didn't look like the guardians were going to do anything to your mom when I left yesterday, but I thought we should keep an eye on her anyway."

"The Guild probably has some of their own in there," Dash says, "in addition to that Griffin Ability detector."

"Anyway, the spider is linked to the mirror," Calla says, handing it to me so I can take a closer look. "So when the charm is on, we can see into your mom's room."

A jolt passes through me as I look down at Mom sitting on her bed, paging through a magazine. She seems so normal. So completely different from yesterday. Her head jerks up suddenly, her gaze pointing across the room at the door. It doesn't open though. She stares at it for a while, hugging the magazine to her chest. Then her lips move, saying something we can't hear, before she returns to reading the magazine.

In the awkward silence that follows, I hand the mirror back to Ryn, then turn to face Dash. "Please don't scare her."

"I won't, I promise. She won't even see me."

"How are you sedating her?"

"Calla's going to make me appear as one of the nurses, and I'll take her a drink."

"And if that doesn't work?"

He flips his hood up over his head. "Then we'll figure something else out. Don't worry, Em. Everything will be fine."

At the sound of a car slowing down on the road, I turn and peer through the trees. "Is that them?"

The car comes to a stop. Ryn holds a hand up for us to be quiet as the front passenger door opens and a tall guy with green in his hair climbs out. "Yes, that's Perry. And that must be Hannah," he adds as a woman gets out the other side of the car. We walk toward them, and Perry waves when we come into view.

The introductions are quick, then Calla says, "Right, let's get this done."

"Okay, Vi and I will be waiting near the entrance," Ryn says, raising his amber and glancing at it. He frowns.

"What is it?" Vi asks.

"Message from Azzy. The girl who tried to help Em escape, Aurora, disappeared from Chevalier House this morning. Azzy assumes she ran away."

"Not surprising," I say. "Aurora spoke about running away the night she got there. She wanted me to go with her."

"Interesting." Ryn pushes the amber into a pocket. "Anyway, we can wonder about that later. Let's get moving."

Calla and Dash disappear through one doorway, then Ryn and Vi head through another one to wait further up the road near the hospital entrance. Perry bids them a cheery farewell, then turns to me with interest. "So. You're Em."

"Yes. I am. You, uh, might have seen me when a whole bunch of guardians chased me through the Guild foyer."

"I missed that, unfortunately, but I've heard all about your magnificent Griffin Ability."

"Magnificent, huh? Well, I'd offer to give you a demonstration, but I don't really know how. This thing seems to switch on and off by itself."

"Probably best not to try it," Hannah says, placing her hands on the roof of the car and resting her chin on them.

"Things could get scary."

I lean against the car and face her. "So you grew up knowing about magic, but you don't have any magic yourself?"

"Yeah. Kinda the opposite of your experience."

"I used to go visit her and show her all the spells I'd learned," Perry says.

"And I'd show him my computer and the Internet and the best shows on TV. It was fun."

We chat for a while about their respective childhoods, but nothing can distract me from the fact that time is ticking by and Calla and Dash haven't returned yet. "Do you think everything's okay?" I blurt out eventually, interrupting Perry in the middle of a description of his first time using a TV remote. "They're taking a while. I thought they'd be out by now."

"I'm sure everything's fine," he says. "And if it isn't, Vi and Ryn would have gone in to help them."

I push my hair back, then start winding some of it around and around my finger. "I hate this. Just ... waiting and not knowing."

"Do you want to play a game?" Perry asks. "I'm sure we can come up with—"

"Wait. I hear something." Something like feet slapping against tar. I walk into the road and try to see further up the hill past the curve. So far, no one's come into view. I can definitely hear them, though. I clench my hands together and press them against my chin as I hold my breath, barely blinking.

Then I see them. All four of them running, Ryn and Dash easily carrying Mom between them. I take off up the hill to meet them. "Yes, glass," Calla pants when I reach them. "Or crystal, I don't know."

"But who the hell was it?" Violet asks.

"I don't know!"

"Is Mom okay?" I ask, running faster now to keep up with them.

"It was that hooded, cloaked person who showed up with the Unseelies by the cliff," Dash says. "I'm sure of it."

"She's bleeding!" I gasp, noticing the trail of blood running down Mom's arm. "Why is she bleeding?"

"She's fine," Dash says.

"She's cut!"

"She's *fine*, Em. Why aren't you in the car? Perry, Hannah," he shouts. "Get in the car."

"Who are you running from?" Perry shouts back.

"Get in the car!" four voices yell at the same time.

He tugs the driver's door open, pushes Hannah inside, then runs around to the other side.

"What the hell happened?" I ask as we reach the car.

"Someone got there before us," Calla pants. She pulls open one of the back doors. "But I think we—"

"Everybody, stop."

I whirl around. On the other side of the road, stepping out from the shadows, is a figure in a silver hooded cloak.

CHAPTER TWENTY-TWO

"YOU HAVE SOMETHING I WANT," THE FIGURE SAYS, AND though her face is hidden in shadow, the pitch of her voice tells me she's a woman. As her cloak billows around her, a memory flashes to the front of my mind: A person in a silver cloak just like this one, standing in a road in Stanmeade and turning a man into a solid crystalline statue.

"Shield," Violet whispers, and in unison, she and Calla raise their hands. Something almost invisible shimmers in the air in front of us. At once, the woman raises her hand. Glass shards, jagged and deadly, fly straight at us. Instinctively, my arm flies up to protect my face. But the glass stops, embedded in the invisible layer that hangs in the air in front of us.

I look behind us, hoping the guys have got Mom into the car by now, but their hands are in the air as well, and Mom is

226

draped over Ryn's shoulder. Perry rushes around the car to join them, while Ryn swears under his breath. "Why isn't it working?"

I whip my head back around to see that the woman has increased her assault on us—and some of the glass shards are twisting their way through the shield. The first piece slices free on this side and flies straight for my face.

Perry's hand strikes out, diverting the glass to the side before it reaches us. In the car, Hannah is screaming.

"Be ready when the shield goes down," Violet shouts. "You know the drill."

Glass shoots past me and sinks into the metal part of the car door. Hannah's screams intensify. Then the air is filled with the screech of tires as the car reverses rapidly. The hooded woman sweeps her hand toward it, and a blizzard of broken glass flies from her fingers.

"No!" Perry yells, throwing his hand out. Not toward the woman, but toward the car. It spins out of the way, and the glass embeds itself into several trees. Frenzied revving fills the air, and then the car is speeding away.

"Attack!" Violet yells.

The woman, striding confidently toward us with her hand already raised, is tossed into the air. She spins, flies sideways, and drops onto the ground on the other side of the road. Sick with horror, I take a few hurried steps backwards to where Mom's lying on the ground. Ryn must have put her down so he could fight. I look up and see him crossing the road with Violet. Calla falls into step with them.

The woman rolls onto her side and extends her hand. Glass

pieces skitter across the tar toward us. Ryn sweeps them aside with a wave of his hand, but I drop onto my knees in front of Mom, shielding her just in case. Dash hovers hesitantly at my side, and Perry hurries across the road to join the others.

The woman pushes herself up.

"Don't let her touch you," Calla says. "Do *not* let her touch you." A shimmering shield appears. On the other side, the woman lifts both hands above her head and, with an unearthly scream, releases a spray of glittering glass into the air. It shreds through the tops of the trees and rains down around her.

"Magic ..."

My heart almost stops at the sound of that one quiet word. I look down. Mom's eyes are half open. She's staring across the road, but not at the woman or the falling glass or the sparkling guardian weapons now visible. She's looking at her own outstretched hand—where glowing sparks are drifting lazily around her fingers.

I pull back in fright. "What the actual freak?" I whisper. I blink several times, but the magic is still there. My heart thunders and my mind races. "You have magic. We can use the paths." I clear my voice and shout, "We can use the paths!"

Dash looks down. "No, your mom can't—"

"We can. She can." I jump to my feet, taking Mom's arm and trying to pull her up. "Open a doorway quickly."

"But she—"

"Open it!" I struggle to get Mom into a sitting position, but as soon as I let go of her, she falls back down again. She must still be partly sedated. "Help me." I call to Dash as he writes a doorway spell onto the road. A dark hole grows beside him as he reaches for Mom's other arm.

"Are you sure about this?"

"Yes, I saw her—" I cry out as a sharp pain slices across the side of my neck.

"Crud." Dash throws a look over his shoulder. "The glass is getting through again. Are you—"

"I'm fine," I say with one hand pressed against my neck. "Get Mom into the paths."

Together we pull her to the edge of the opening, and just before we fall into it, I see Dash look across the road one last time. I know he's worried about the others, but as selfish as it is, I care only about Mom right now. I lean into the darkness, tugging Mom and Dash with me.

"I don't know where we're going," I say as silence presses against my ears and Mom becomes weightless beside me.

"I've got it," Dash says, and seconds later we drop onto grass. I stumble as Mom's sudden weight drags me down, and all three of us end up on the ground. A quick glance around at the night sky above us and the unfamiliar building nearby tells me I'm in a new place. "This is the healing institute," Dash says. "White Cedars. You'll be safe here. I need to go back." He pushes himself quickly to his feet. "They might need help."

I nod, propping Mom up against my side. "Yeah. Be careful."

He lifts his stylus, but the air ripples nearby, and Violet, Ryn, Calla and Perry run onto the grass a moment later. "Oh, you're all right," Dash says, his expression brightening. "Thank goodness."

And then suddenly we're all talking over each other:

"Is your mom okay?"

"Yes, she—"

"What happened to that woman?"

"She got away. Fled the moment she saw you were gone."

"*Why the faerie paths?*" Violet asks, her eyes wide with worry. "How did you know she'd survive?"

"She has magic," I say, and finally everyone stops talking. "She woke up, and I saw it in her hand, sparking around her fingers." My lips stretch into a wide smile. "She is my mother after all."

PART III

CHAPTER TWENTY-THREE

EVERY STARTLING REVELATION OVER THE PAST SEVERAL DAYS has given me emotional whiplash—and this one is both the worst and best. I had just begun to accept the fact that Mom wasn't my real mother, and suddenly that truth has been flipped on its head entirely. It sends my brain spinning once more. It leaves me wanting to sob with relief.

But I don't have a moment for that, because soon after we arrive on the grass outside White Cedars Healing Institute, several faeries come rushing out to help us. Mom is barely conscious, so they carry her quickly inside. Someone cleans the blood on my neck and tells me the cut will be totally healed within the hour, and then they disappear, along with Mom, into a room I'm not allowed to be in.

The rest of us end up in a waiting room that reminds me

more of a spa than a hospital, with its gentle lighting, herbal scents, and plants that seem to form part of the building itself. Not that I've ever been to a spa, but I've seen movies.

"That was the same woman who appeared just before you guys rescued Em," Dash says, pacing across the wooden floor. "By the cliff, when the guardians and Unseelies were fighting. I mean, I didn't see her face, but that silver cloak looked the same, and there were glass shards flying about that day. I assumed they were part of someone's offensive magic, but it must have been this woman."

"Did you see what she did in the hospital?" Calla says. "Before we got Em's mom out?"

"Yes."

"She touched one of the nurses and he transformed instantly into a frozen glass structure. One touch, and that was it. Then she pushed him over, and he shattered into a million pieces."

Violet sucks in a quiet gasp and covers her mouth with her hand.

Perry looks up. "That's what happened at that boarding school and the village by Twiggled Horn. Those attacks I told you about."

"I know," Calla says. "That's what I thought of the moment I saw it."

"Plus several more incidents from the past few months," Perry adds. "Cases of missing fae where the only thing left behind was shattered glass. We couldn't understand what those were all about until eyewitness explained what happened in that village a few days ago."

"And then you realized those people weren't missing after all," Ryn says, his voice grim. "They *were* the shattered glass."

"Yeah."

"What's the connection between all the attacks?" Violet asks.

"It may be a coincidence," Perry says, "but the only connection so far is that most of those who've been killed either worked at the Guild in the past, or were related in some way to Guild employees, either past or present. But again, it could be a coincidence, since some of the deaths were fae unrelated to the Guild in any way."

"They could have been collateral damage," Violet says.

Perry inclines his head. "Possibly."

"So either this woman in the silver cloak is the one carrying out these attacks," Calla says, "or there's a group of fae who all dress the same and attack with the same magic."

"That can't be," Violet says with a frown. "This must be a Griffin Ability, right?"

"Must be," Ryn says. "Any faerie can transform things into glass, and our magic itself can be shaped into glass if we choose, but to transform living beings? That shouldn't be possible. At least, not by any spell I've heard of. It must be a Griffin Ability."

"I think I've seen her before," I say, finally speaking up. "The same day my magic revealed itself. The day of the party, when I accidentally used my Griffin Ability. I was heading home, and I saw a cloaked person touch a man, and he turned into crystal or glass or something."

Dash brings his endless pacing to a halt. "You didn't mention that before."

"Well, to be honest, I didn't believe my eyes. I had no idea magic existed yet. I thought I was, you know, starting to lose my mind like Mom. So … I just ignored it. I ducked behind a building, and when I looked again, it was all gone. And so much has happened since then that I didn't remember it until just now when she appeared on the other side of the road. I didn't notice her the day the Guild and the Unseelies were fighting over me." I give Dash a pointed look. "Guess I was preoccupied with the fear that I was about to be killed."

He rolls his eyes and looks away. Perry gets to his feet. "Well, uh, I'm going to check on Hannah."

"Did she get away safely?" I ask.

"She did," Perry says, not meeting my eyes. "I went to find her while the healers were getting your mom into a room. I … I'm sorry she panicked and fled. She's never been in a situation like that before."

"It's okay," Ryn says quietly. "We don't blame her."

I chew on my lower lip, deciding not to comment. I was horrified when I watched what I thought was Mom's only safe escape route speed into the distance. But I get why Hannah did it. She was looking out for herself—a skill I've been honing for years.

After Perry leaves, Violet turns to Ryn. "I think we need to get home too. Check on Jack, make sure those other Seer visions were dealt with." She looks at me. "We'll come back a bit later and keep you company."

"I'll stay here with Em now," Calla says.

"Oh, I don't mind waiting on my own," I tell them. "Seriously. Calla, your husband just came back from … somewhere. Wouldn't you rather be with him?"

"Sure, but I can see him later."

"No, it's fine, really. I'm happy on my own, and I know you've all got stuff to do." Violet and Ryn exchange a glance. "Seriously," I repeat.

"Okay," Violet says, "but we'll be back a bit later." She leaves through the faerie paths with Ryn and Calla. I look at Dash, expecting him to leave through another faerie paths doorway, but he walks to a chair a few seats away from me and sits. He shifts his body to face mine.

"Seriously, Dash. I don't mind waiting on my own."

"How's your neck?" he asks. "It looks almost better from over here."

I'd forgotten about the cut, actually. I place my fingers gingerly against the area. There's no pain, and a raised line of skin tells me a scar has already formed. "Holy crap. It healed so quickly. I thought they were exaggerating when they said it would be better within the hour."

Dash smiles. "And you know the scar will heal too, right? That will also be gone within the hour."

"That's amazing."

"Also …" He leans forward on his knees. "I'm sorry the rescue plan for your mom turned into such a mess. The rest of us deal with that kind of magical confrontation all the time, but for you and Hannah, it must have been scary. Things could have gone badly wrong."

"But they didn't. Everything worked out in the end." I

smile, which seems easier now than it's been in a long time. "I'm just so happy Mom's out of that hospital. I'm happy we're in the same world again, and that all that stuff about her not being my mom was just a nightmare."

He nods. "Yeah. Hopefully."

My smile slips a little. "What do you mean *hopefully*? She's my mother. How could she not be?"

"Well, I just mean … you look like a faerie and she doesn't, so how does that work?"

"But I didn't look like a faerie either before my magic broke out, right? You said you couldn't always see my blue hair. So obviously Mom is the same."

"Yeah …" He shakes his head. "I still don't understand why it happened that way for you. Faeries don't grow up with blocked or inaccessible magic. Halflings do, sometimes, but you're not a halfling."

"Okay, so maybe Mom and I are some strange type of faerie you've never come across before. That could be possible, right?"

He lifts one shoulder in a slow, uncertain shrug. "I guess."

"What other explanation is there? Actually, never mind. In this world, there are probably a whole host of strange, complicated explanations involving different kinds of magic. And I don't care to know any of them."

Dash looks down at his hands, then quietly says, "I'm not trying to make you upset again. And whether she's biologically related to you or not doesn't change who she is to you. I just thought you would want to know the truth about the situation, whatever it happens to be."

I lean back, pull my legs up, and wrap my arms around them. "You think I might want to know the truth? That's interesting, considering you never told me what really happened in the park that day."

A frown pulls at his features, but he doesn't look up at me. "What do you mean?"

"You know what I'm talking about." My arms tighten around my legs. "You saved my mother's life. There was something else there that day. Something I didn't see because you knocked us both out of the way. Something that might have ... killed her."

Dash slowly leans back, rubbing one hand along the side of his neck. "Who told you?"

"Violet."

He nods, but says nothing.

"So? Why didn't you tell me? I realize you couldn't explain it before, but since everything happened in the past few days, you still haven't told me."

"Because ... I mean ... how would that conversation have gone? You would have said, 'You ruined my mother's life.' Then I would have said, 'Actually, I saved it.' And then you would have told me, 'Spending the rest of her days in a mental hospital is *not* the same as saving her life.' Then we'd probably argue some more, and you'd still hate me."

I'm quiet for a moment, because I have to admit there's a strong likelihood things would have gone that way. "Maybe. Or maybe I'd hate you less. Or ... I don't know. Maybe I'd be grateful she's still alive. I *am* grateful she's still alive. There's a chance, at least, for her to get better. But you've known all this time that you actually helped her that day, and instead of letting me in on that little secret, you allowed me to blame you for landing her in hospital."

"Wait." He straightens a little. "Are you *angry* with me?"

"Yes!"

"But I thought we just established that I actually saved your mom's life."

"Yes, so now I have to be grateful to you. Which sucks because I don't like you. So the whole thing just … pisses me off!"

He stares at me another moment, then doubles over with laughter.

"Oh, fantastic. This is all just hilarious, is it?"

"You have to admit," he says between breaths, "that it is."

"I don't have to admit anything." I cross my arms, but there's a smile tugging at my lips, and I'm finding it impossibly hard to fight it. So I give in and let it stretch across my face. I think a small laugh might even escape me.

Eventually when we're quiet again and I'm staring at my hands, I lace my fingers together and slowly let out a long breath. It frustrates me that I have to be grateful to him, but that doesn't change the fact that I *am* grateful to him. "Thank you for saving her," I say, and though my voice is small, I know he hears it.

"You're welcome, Em." He looks over at me and grins. "See? We can be mature. Isn't it nice?"

My smile is back again. "I guess it isn't *completely* overrated."

He stands and pushes his hands into his pockets. "Do you

want to go find something to drink? Or eat?"

"Hospital cafeteria food? No thanks."

"This isn't your world, remember? The vast selection of hot drinks available in this world is mind-blowing."

"Mind-blowing? Really?" I place my hands on the arms of the chair and push myself up. "One would think I've had enough mind-blowing experiences in the past few days, but I guess not. Let's go find a hot drink."

"Great. It's a date."

"It is most definitely not a date."

"You know what I mean," he says as we walk out of the waiting area.

"No, I know what *I* mean, and I'm making sure that you also know what I mean."

"Miss Clarke?" Just outside the waiting room, a healer stops in front of us. "Can I speak with you?"

I can't help the dread that begins to form in the pit of my stomach. "Yes. Definitely. Is my mom okay?"

"Shall we sit?" She gestures to the chairs behind us.

"Why?" Panic rises rapidly into my throat. "Do you have something bad to tell me?"

She smiles. "Not at all. It's just more comfortable."

"Oh. Right. Of course."

We return to the waiting area, and as the three of us sit, she asks, "Are you happy for us to talk in front of the gentleman, or would you prefer to speak alone with me?"

My brain stumbles over the word 'gentleman'—Dash? A gentleman? Ha!—before getting to the actual question. "Um …"

"That's okay. I'll wait outside while you guys talk," Dash says, saving me from having to answer.

"Is she awake?" I ask the healer once Dash is gone. "Can I talk to her?"

"She isn't awake, unfortunately. She became very upset and confused after we brought her in, and we ended up having to sedate her again. We ran a few tests then, which revealed that even though we can't sense any magic in her, she is in fact a faerie. She also tested positive for a Griffin Ability."

I pull my head back in surprise. But then I tell myself that this makes complete sense. If she is indeed my mother, then obviously she has a Griffin Ability.

"This is a somewhat baffling case," the healer continues. "We haven't encountered anything quite like it before, so if you tell us everything you know about her, including the mental illness you mentioned when we brought her in earlier, then we'll do everything we can to figure out what's going on."

CHAPTER TWENTY-FOUR

SWITCHING TIME ZONES SO OFTEN IS MESSING WITH MY mind. I feel like it should be the middle of the night by the time I leave the healing institute with Dash—because it *is* the middle of the night there—but it's early evening when we reach the oasis. Violet and Ryn are preparing dinner while Jack sits at the kitchen table doing homework.

"She's a faerie," I announce to them as I walk in. "She's a faerie with a Griffin Ability, but they can't sense her magic, and she doesn't *look* like a faerie, and she's currently too confused and upset to explain anything to anyone, so ... yeah. That's the situation."

"And the plot thickens," Dash says, rubbing his hands together.

"Dash!" I punch his arm. "This is my *life*, not some mystery novel."

"Jeez, sorry, I know." He walks into the kitchen and looks over Jack's shoulder at whatever he's working on. "It is a mystery, though. You and your mom both are."

"A mystery we're happy to help you solve," Ryn says, looking across the kitchen at me, "if you'd like our help."

"I'd definitely like to solve it. Where should we start?"

"With whatever you can remember from before she ended up at Tranquil Hills," Ryn says.

Violet leaves a wooden spoon stirring a pot and steps away from the stove. "Dinner will still be a while, so why don't we sit in the living room and start solving this puzzle?"

"Awesome," Dash says. "You guys sit. I'll get drinks. I know my way around this kitchen."

Jack gathers his books and follows Ryn, Vi and me into the next room. He spreads his work out on the floor and carries on. "Have you noticed Dash hanging out here a lot more than usual?" Ryn says to Violet.

"I have." She looks at me. "I can think of only one reason for that."

I raise an eyebrow. "I hope you're not suggesting it's because of me. Because that's the most absurd answer you could possibly have come up with."

"From where I'm sitting, it looks like the only answer."

I pull my legs up and cross them beneath me. "In the unlikely event that you happen to be right, I'm sure it's only because it's a brand new challenge for him to be around a girl who has zero romantic interest in him."

Violet laughs. "You could be right. That would definitely be a new experience for him."

"Actually," Dash says from the doorway, "I'm hanging around more than usual because I've been following Em's case for longer than anyone else, and I'm extremely curious to get to the bottom of all this mystery."

"Hey!" Violet flicks her hand. A cushion flies across the room and knocks Dash against the side of his head. "Eavesdropping is rude. I know your parents taught you that." With a laugh, he disappears back to the kitchen.

"Hey, look," Jack says. "Filigree and Bandit are playing." I follow the direction of his pointing pen and see two animals: a squirrel sitting beneath one of the side tables, and a kitten bouncing back and forth in front of it, swiping at the air with its paws, then leaping away. The squirrel blinks and remains motionless. "Well, Bandit's playing," Jack corrects. "Filigree's being a grumpy squirrel."

"Cute," I say. "Although I hope Bandit doesn't irritate Filigree too much."

"Don't worry about it," Violet says. "Filigree needs to learn to chill out a bit. He's getting too uptight in his old age."

"Okay, have we begun solving the mystery yet?" Dash asks, coming into the living room with a drink in each hand and another two floating beside him. They're all blue, and I'm certain I've never tasted whatever's inside them.

"I don't know how we're supposed to solve anything," I tell them. "I just had this conversation with the healer, and nothing useful came up. She asked me about my childhood and my father, but I don't know a thing about him except that he's supposedly been paying for Mom's hospital bills. And I can't remember anything strange from my childhood. Unless you count Mom's delusions, but those didn't have anything to do with—Well, now I wonder." I lean back and stare at the opposite wall with a frown. "Maybe they weren't delusions after all. Maybe she could see things I couldn't see because my magic was blocked. But she didn't ever look any different—her hair, I mean—so doesn't that mean her magic was always blocked too?"

"I would think so," Violet says, absently playing with a lock of her purple hair.

"When she had these delusions," Ryn asks, "did she seem rational? As if she was speaking normally to someone who just happened to be invisible?"

I slowly shake my head. "No. She didn't seem rational to me at all. She usually ended up in a highly panicked state."

"Hmm, okay."

"Do you remember any friends of hers that we could possibly try to track down?" Dash asks. "If any of them turn out to be magical, we can question them. I mean, in case your mom is still confused for a while and can't explain things herself."

I shake my head. "Not really. There was just ... well, I wouldn't classify her as a friend because she and Mom always fought whenever she came over, but I guess they must have been friends at some point."

"What was her name?"

"Um ... I just remember ..." I push my hand through my hair. "Line."

"Line? That's not a name."

"I know, but that's all I remember. It was a long time ago, okay. I would hear them shouting at each other through the wall, and I remember Mom saying "line" a lot."

"That's weird," Dash says.

"What did this friend look like?" Violet asks.

"I don't know. I never saw her. Mom would always say, 'My friend's coming over now. You need to go to your room.' And then she'd close me in my bedroom, and soon after that I'd hear them arguing."

"Doesn't sound like much of a friend," Dash says.

"What did they argue about?" Ryn asks.

I sigh. "I don't know. I couldn't hear much. I tried to just ignore them and play with my dolls." I twist my hair around my finger, feeling awkward beneath all these questions. "See? I told you I can't remember anything useful."

"When your mother was taken to hospital and you were sent to live with your aunt," Ryn says, "what happened to all the things in your house?"

"Uh … I don't know, actually. I think my dad must have cleared stuff out, and then a few weeks after I got to Chelsea's, some boxes arrived. Chelsea opened one or two, then closed them back up and put them away somewhere. Probably my bedroom, since that's where she likes to store stuff."

"Then that's where we start looking," Ryn says. "Do you want to go take a look tomorrow morning before you go back to White Cedars?"

"I can go with you," Dash volunteers immediately.

"Of course you can," I say, "because apparently you never

have to do any work for the Guild anymore."

He shrugs. "Work is flexible. Plenty of time in the field. They'll think I'm working on one of the many other ongoing cases we have."

"Just don't blame me when you get yourself fired, okay?"

He places a hand over his heart. "Your concern is so touching, Em."

I turn to Violet. "Can you teach me that cushion throwing thing?"

"Ooh, I'll do it!" Jack sweeps his hand wildly through the air, and four different cushions soar off their seats and pummel Dash's head.

"Hey, stop, I surrender!"

"More cushions!" I cry, urging Jack on. And soon Dash is buried beneath almost every cushion in the living room. Bandit leaps on top of the pile, and even Filigree comes over to check things out. By the time we move to the kitchen for dinner, my stomach and cheeks are aching, and I realize I've laughed more in the past few hours than I have in ages.

CHAPTER TWENTY-FIVE

"IT FEELS A LOT LONGER THAN FIVE OR SIX DAYS SINCE I WAS here," I say to Dash as we stand in the back parking lot of Stanmeade Elementary School. "And I don't know if I'm doing this glamour thing correctly." Violet gave me a lesson last night, and another one this morning, but I'm still not really sure what I'm doing.

"Unfortunately we'll only know if it isn't working if a human looks over and sees you," Dash says, "and by then it'll be too late."

"It would have helped if you'd brought us out of the faerie paths a little closer to Chelsea's house. Like in her backyard, perhaps."

"Okay, so here's something you may not know yet, Em," he says, leaning against a car and facing me. "It takes a lot of focus to land in exactly the right spot when using the faerie paths, and the further away the destination is, the more focus in requires, so—"

"So we do this step by step. Got it. We first come to the edge of Stanmeade, then we go to Chelsea's house."

"Right."

"Oh, careful. Don't let Mrs. Pringleton see you." I pull him down between two cars as Mrs. Pringleton steps out of the back door. She raises a cigarette to her lips and lights it.

"I have a functioning glamour, remember," Dash says. "You don't need to worry about anyone seeing me." He peers around the edge of the car. "Ah, the splotchy faced teacher. I've always been afraid of her, and I never even went to school here."

"Don't be rude. It's a birthmark or something."

"Right, sorry. Can't be rude about things like that."

"Exactly." I rub my left shoulder through my T-shirt. At the sound of a faint ping, Dash reaches for his amber. "What's up?" I ask as his eyes scan the surface.

"Just another Guild-wide memo updating us on the spell that's supposed to fix the veil. Finished testing … everything looks good … still setting a date and organizing a ceremony for the actual closing of the tear." He sighs. "I don't know why they want to waste time with a ceremony. They should just send a few people out there and fix the darn thing. That hole's been in the sky almost as long as I've been alive."

"Then I suppose another few days or weeks won't make much difference."

"Yeah, but it's a waste of resources." Dash puts his amber away. "Guardians have to be there at all times, making sure people from our side don't interfere with the monument that keeps the hole from getting bigger. And on the other side, they have to make sure it's glamoured and humans don't accidentally walk into it. Anyway, has the scary teacher finished her cigarette yet?"

I peek around the car. "Nope. I don't know how many cigarettes she's planning to smoke, and I don't trust my glamour, so can we open a doorway here on the ground?" I gesture to the space between the two cars.

"Yeah, okay." Dash presses his stylus to the ground.

"Wait, can I try again?" I ask before he writes anything.

"Oh. Yeah, sure. Just don't get frustrated if it still doesn't work." He hands me his stylus while I remove a folded up note from my back pocket. "This stuff takes time to get right."

"Yeah, yeah. Everyone keeps saying that." I hold the paper in one hand and copy the letters onto the ground, speaking the other few words I've now memorized, and trying to imagine magic streaming out of my core, down my arm, and into the stylus. A thrill races through me as the words I've written begin to glow, but when they fade away, nothing happens. "Fine. You do it." I hand the stylus back to Dash.

"You almost got it," he says. "Maybe you just didn't release enough magic through the stylus. That part will become automatic soon, and then this spell will be easy."

"Yeah, whatever. Just open the doorway."

Dash writes the words, and this time, a dark gap into the faerie paths spreads across the ground. "Are you taking us inside the house now?" Dash asks before we climb into the paths. "Remember to focus on exactly the right room if you don't want to land up in front of Chelsea."

"Bedroom. Right. Chelsea will be in her salon all day, so if we stay in my room with the door locked, we should be fine. She always has music playing, so I doubt she'll hear anything."

"With the door locked, huh?" He waggles his eyebrows. "That must be against the rules."

"Idiot," I mutter with a shake of my head. "Chelsea never bothered with rules like that. I doubt she would have cared if I ever had a guy in my bedroom."

"Oh, so you've never—"

"Just get into the faerie paths."

With a snicker, he slips into the darkness, pulling me in after him. I direct all my focus on picturing the inside of my bedroom. The single bed, the desk that used to be a part of Chelsea's salon, the boxes piled up against the wall. When light touches my eyelids, I open them and see the scene I pictured. The darkness melts away as I take a step forward into the room. "Hmm," Dash says, looking around. "It's—"

"Don't."

"I was going to say cozy."

"No you weren't. Okay, these are all the boxes." I gesture to the left side of the room. "It's mostly Chelsea's stuff, but Mom's boxes must be under there somewhere. I don't remember Chelsea ever getting rid of them."

Dash walks to the desk and picks up a photo frame with a picture of Val and me sticking our tongues out at the camera. Val's metal tongue ring is visible, and I've got a heart-shaped candy sitting on my tongue—because my fear of needles meant piercings were *one* thing we would never do together.

"I really miss her," I say quietly. "And I think she's probably seriously mad at me for leaving. Hopefully I'll be able to come back soon and explain things to her. Not the magical things, obviously, but something else. Something I still need to come up with."

"Whatever you eventually tell her," Dash says, returning the frame to the desk, "I'm sure she'll forgive you. She's your best friend."

"Yeah. She's pretty awesome." I start lifting Chelsea's boxes off the top of the collection. "Although she told me she finds you attractive, so her judgement is questionable."

"Interesting." Dash's lips spread into a crooked smile. "You know, she's pretty cute too."

I roll my eyes. "What about Jewel?"

He stands beside me and begins moving boxes with magic from one side of the room onto my bed. "What about her?"

"Don't you have … you know, a thing?"

A box pauses in mid-air. "What thing?"

"Like, you guys are together or something. Or you will be soon."

"What? No, I told you before. We're just friends." The boxes continue their journey across the room. I glance at each one that passes, making sure we're still moving Chelsea's stuff. "She likes this other guy," Dash adds. "Um, Sean something-or-other. He graduated a year ahead of us. I'm sure she used to pine after him."

"She was probably doing that thing girls do where they pretend to like someone else to try and make the guy they're actually interested in jealous."

"Oh. Are you sure? Because normally girls just come out and tell me they like me."

"Of course." I sigh and fold my arms. "I forgot who I was talking to. Oh, wait, stop. I think that's one of Mom's boxes." The box that was about to add itself to my bed, the box with an orange star-shaped sticker on the side, changes direction and lands at our feet instead. "Look for other boxes that have stickers like this," I tell Dash as I move to the desk and grab a pair of scissors from a drawer. I crouch down, slice through the tape, and bend the cardboard flaps back. CDs and DVDs look up at me. Useless entertainment from the past. "Okay, this one looks boring. You can start with that." I move to the second box that just arrived at my side.

"The boring box. Thanks."

I look up. "You pushed me off a cliff."

"Ah, we're back to that, are we?"

"Never gets old."

Two boxes bump into each other, tumble out of the air, and land on Dash's foot. "Aaaaah fffffuzzbuckling hamster balls!"

A loud snort of laughter escapes me. I slap my hand over my mouth before saying, "Are you kidding? You finally feel like swearing and you come up with fuzzbuckling hamster balls?"

"Shut up," he says through gritted teeth.

"Shh." I twist my head around and look toward the bedroom door. Somewhere beyond it, someone is talking. I jump up, move quietly to the door, and lean closer.

"… probably just something in the kitchen," Chelsea is saying. "Like the broom over there. It's always falling over."

I wait, and when I don't hear her voice again, I assume she's gone back into her salon. "All clear," I say to Dash. "Just don't drop any more boxes."

"I think I've found them all." He gestures to the small collection of boxes with colored stickers.

"Great." I sit on the floor beside my second open box, and Dash sits opposite me. "Seriously, though," I say as if the interruption never happened, "Jewel seemed really into you. Maybe you should think about it."

"Uh …" He shuffles through the CDs and DVDs before pushing the box away and pulling another one closer. "Maybe. Maybe not. We grew up together, so I know almost everything about her. We've been through good times and bad. We actually went to our graduation ball together, although just as friends." He removes some books, clothes and an old ice cream container from the second box. I look through Mom's jewelry collection. "In many ways, she probably is perfect for me," he continues. "If we were another two people, maybe we would be. But for me … I just don't think of her like that. She's more like a sister. She's always there, and she's fun to hang out with, and sometimes she's super annoying, but I still love her." He shrugs. "But like a—"

"—sister," I finish, closing the jewelry box, reaching past some old pictures of Mom and me, and moving on to a folder containing a whole bunch of pamphlets. "Right. Just don't tell Jewel that, okay? I mean, you should definitely tell her you don't feel the same way about her, but you should not use the words, 'I think of you as a sister.'"

"Why?"

"It's a cliché. She'll hate it. Just ... use other words."

He nudges my knee with his shoe as a smile grows on his lips. "Look at you being all sympathetic toward someone you don't like. Some might even think you have a heart."

"Of course I have a heart, dumb-ass."

"Yeah, I know," he says quietly, returning the books and clothes to the box. "You wouldn't have hated me so much all these years if you didn't have a heart."

"I'm not sure that makes sense, but okay."

"You know, because of your mom. You hated me because you cared so much about her."

I swallow and look down at all the pamphlets on my lap. They're information and maps for a whole load of different tourist destinations around the country, which is unhelpful, so I shove them back into the folder.

"Looks like she wanted to travel," Dash says, nodding to the folder as he opens the ice cream container. "Oh, what's all this?" He holds up a tiny glass teddy bear clutching a glass heart. Then a miniature china doll and an angel made of dried grass.

"Just ornaments. Mom liked collecting pretty things."

"They're ... kinda ugly."

"Well, yeah, to you and me maybe. But she obviously thought all those little things were pretty."

"To each his own, I guess. Well, her own in this case." He packs the ice cream container away. "Hey, what time is it? Vi was gonna meet us here, wasn't she?"

"Um ..." I look up at the old-fashioned alarm clock beside

the bed. "It's a little after nine."

"Okay. That's about ten at the oasis, I think. Her meeting should be finished soon." He pulls another box forward. "Have I mentioned how nice it is talking to you without the heat of your hatred trying to burn through me? I always wondered what it would be like. You know, just to be friends."

"It is nice, I guess. Kind of a relief, actually. It was tiring always having to be angry around you. And it's nice when you're serious sometimes instead of always joking around."

"Really? You like it when I'm serious? Isn't that … boring?"

"No, not if it's real." I look up at him. "Sometimes, Dash, the situation calls for seriousness. In that case, it really isn't helpful when you joke around."

His gaze moves away from mine, settling on all the boxes on the bed. "I know I joke a lot. But that's because life really sucks sometimes, and joking about it is better than succumbing to dark, depressing thoughts. And joking makes people—most people—laugh, so it's worth it."

"Wait. Did you just say life sucks? Because that I don't believe. Your life is a freaking cakewalk compared to mine."

He leans back on his hands. "Okay firstly, I've never heard of that comparison, but walking on a giant cake sounds amazing, so we should try that sometime. And secondly …" He pauses. "You know what I do for a living, right? I mean, it isn't the safest job in the world."

"Yeah, okay. So?"

"So people have died. People I care about."

I blink, unable to look away from those very green—and suddenly very serious—eyes. "Oh."

"Yeah." He reaches forward and digs into the box in front of him. "We all know, going in, that the life of a guardian is high-risk, but that doesn't stop it from being horrendously shocking and painful when …" He pulls out a file and places it on his lap. "Well, when a classmate or someone who's trained you for years ends up killed."

I press my hands together in my lap. "I'm really sorry."

"It happens," he says lightly. "I'm not the only one. Vi lost her mother when she was very young. Jewel's uncle was killed a few years ago." He flips the file open. "Oh, finally. This looks like something useful."

I crawl around the boxes and sit beside Dash, grateful for the distraction. He pages past old school certificates from the same school I went to before I moved here, medical aid forms, bank account information, and something related to the purchase of a car. "Who's Macy Clarke?" he asks. "I thought your mom's name was Daniela."

"Oh, she was Macy growing up, but she didn't like that name. She changed it to Daniela when I was very young. Legally changed it, I mean. So all these later documents like bank accounts say Daniela, not Macy."

"That's weird."

"I suppose. But none of these pages are useful," I add, my shoulders slumping in disappointment. "What are we hoping to find anyway?"

"I don't know. A birth certificate, or something related to a school or institution from my world, perhaps."

I notice a lump beneath the next page. I reach across Dash and turn the page quickly, but it's just another ornament that tumbles out. A flower made of pink glass or crystal. "These things are everywhere," I grumble, picking it up and dropping it into one of the boxes.

The next page is a photo of two teen girls who, I realize when I take a closer look, are Mom and Chelsea. "Oh my goodness," I whisper. "What if Chelsea and Georgia are just like Mom and me? I didn't think of that until now."

"I'd like to say no because I've never sensed the tiniest hint of magic in either of them, but I'm not sure about anything anymore." He turns to the next page: a lease agreement from fifteen years ago. "What about family?" he asks. "Grandparents? Aunts, uncles, cousins?"

"No grandparents. I think there might be some other cousins. Mom's cousins, I mean, not mine. But I've never met—" My head snaps up as I notice movement near the door. My automatic thought is that Chelsea is somehow opening my locked door, but it's the spreading darkness of a faerie paths doorway that I see. A figure with vibrant purple hair jumps out of the paths and into my bedroom.

"Finally," Aurora says with a smile. "It's about time you showed up here."

CHAPTER TWENTY-SIX

DASH IS ON HIS FEET A SECOND LATER, MAGIC CRACKLING around his fingers. "What are you—" He jerks forward, his eyes slide shut, and he collapses on the floor beside the boxes. Behind him is an unfamiliar young man.

I scramble away until my back hits the edge of the desk before pushing myself up. "Aurora, what the hell is this?"

"We should go," she says to the other faerie. She moves toward me. I launch forward and grab hold of Dash just as something tugs my T-shirt and something else wraps around my arm.

Bright light flares and blinds me, blotting everything out in sudden, brilliant white. When the whiteness fades and I'm able to see again, I find myself in an entirely different place. A garden with flowers and hedges, but the colors are muted and the light is dim. The edges of the scene seem smudged and hazy, like a dream where only a few details are clear. Everywhere I look, I see wisps of black smoke detaching themselves from the environment and disappearing. "Where are we? How did we get here? And what did you do to Dash?"

Aurora looks down at Dash with a disapproving expression. "That's annoying. I was hoping to leave him behind."

"What did you do to him?" I demand.

"Stunner spell," the guy says. Streaks of burgundy color the waves of his black hair. "Don't worry, he'll be fine later. Why don't we sit?" He gestures to a bench behind him.

"Why don't we *sit*? No! I'm not sitting."

"Okay. We'll sit. You can remain standing if you'd prefer that." As if we're stuck inside some ludicrous theatrical work, the two of them sit in unison. "I know that was an unpleasant first impression," he says, "so perhaps we can start again. I'm Roarke. Crown Prince of the Unseelie Court." He gestures to Aurora. "I believe you've met my sister."

Crown Prince.

Unseelie Court.

Sister.

I hear the words, but my brain takes a while to process them. "U-unseelie Court?" I repeat eventually.

"Yes."

"So you …" I look at Aurora. "You're … a princess. Of the Unseelie Court."

"Yes."

I'm standing here with a prince and princess. A magical prince and princess. In a weirdly grayish scene where shadow-like smoke rises continuously from everything. If I hadn't already encountered so much strangeness in the past few days, I'd be convinced this was a dream.

"A member of our court was at that party when you split the earth open," Roarke says. "Who knows how he found his way there, but that's beside the point. He told my father what he saw, and about the words you spoke just before it happened. Dad said it must be a Griffin Ability and that we needed to get you to our court before the Guild found out about it. We didn't realize that this one—" he looks down at Dash "—was a guardian. You ended up at the Guild a whole lot faster than we anticipated. We thought we were too late, but then they sent you to Chevalier House instead."

"And that's where I came in," Aurora says. "I showed up at the Guild, gave them my made-up story, and off to Chevalier House I went."

"Why even bother with all that crap?" I ask, throwing my hands up. "Your father is a *king*. Why couldn't he just storm into Chevalier House and take me himself?"

Roarke sighs. "Emerson, don't you know anything about protective magic?"

"No, I do not. I didn't grow up here, remember?"

"My father did actually visit Chevalier House himself, but he couldn't get onto the property. And he didn't want to upset the Guild by attacking the protective enchantments. He didn't want a whole bunch of guardians descending upon us, demanding we return you. Things would have become messy. So he sent Aurora instead."

I turn my gaze to her. "Poor little Aurora. A slave for a

bunch of witches. Such a traumatizing experience." I let out a bitter laugh. "And all of that was a lie."

"Not *all* of it," she says sheepishly. "My name wasn't a lie. And I do actually have a history with witches. I lived with one when I was very little—before she got tired of me and dumped me at the Unseelie Court. Then Dad decided to adopt me, so that's how I ended up a member of the Unseelie royal family." She smiles at Roarke before her gaze shifts back to me. "But the story about being a slave ... well, Dad said that was a case the Guild dealt with a few years ago. Witches with faerie slaves. It sounded like a good story to me."

"Well it didn't work. So what was your grand plan after I refused to run away with you?"

She crosses one leg neatly over the other and leans back against the bench. "I figured I'd try to get close to you. I thought maybe if you got to know me a little better, you'd trust me. I'm really not as bad as you're probably thinking right now." Her violet eyes sparkle with mirth. Faerie color seems to be the only true color in this oddly muted scene. "I knew I only had a few days to convince you, though. Once the Guild tested you for a Griffin Ability, we'd be out of time."

"I guess you didn't count on me giving away my Griffin Ability all on my own. Sorry to ruin your Plan B."

Aurora shrugs. "I improvised. Went back to the Guild and tried to get you out. Which would have worked, by the way—" she gives me a pointed look "—if you hadn't let those guardians get their hands on me."

"I hope you're not expecting me to apologize."

"No, although you could thank me for helping you escape."

I cross my arms and stare at her. If gratitude is what she wants, she'll be waiting a long time.

"Unfortunately you disappeared after the encounter at the edge of Creepy Hollow," Roarke says, continuing the story, "so we had to make another plan."

"You didn't presume me dead?"

"No, of course not. We know about the Griffin rebels. We assumed they rescued you. We also assumed you'd go back to your hometown at some point, so I've been waiting for you there."

"Well, you guys certainly worked hard to get your hands on me. I guess I should be flattered."

"You're not surprised, are you?" he asks, a crease marring his brow. "Bringing things into being simply by speaking them is an extraordinary power. I don't think anyone's ever been able to do that. Obviously we'd do anything to get you on our side."

"Terrific. Well here I am, so I guess that makes you guys the winners. Congratulations."

Aurora gives me a puzzled look. "We *want* you Emerson. Isn't it nice to be wanted?"

"No! I don't want anyone else to want me." I screw my eyes shut, clench my fists, and reach for my magic. "You don't want me, you don't want me," I repeat over and over, hoping desperately that my Griffin Ability will kick in.

"It's not working," Aurora says, raising her voice a little to speak over me. "We still want you."

I open my eyes, but my hands remain fists. "You want to imprison me, manipulate me, force me to speak horrible, evil things into being. Does that sound about right?"

"Actually, Emerson," Roarke says as he stands. "I'd like to marry you."

An indefinite amount of time passes in silence, with only the sound of my pulse throbbing in my ears. Then I blink. "Say that again."

"I would like to marry you."

I step back, raising my hands. If my eyebrows could climb any higher, I think they'd be in my hair. "You know what? I don't generally use words like this, but I feel they're appropriate in this situation: you're crazy, Roarke. Bonkers. Loony. Completely nuts and one hundred percent unhinged. *I am not marrying you.*"

He tilts his head a fraction to the side. "No one's been able to help your mother yet, have they?"

A shiver that has nothing to do with my Griffin Ability raises the hairs on my arms. "What do you know about my mother?"

"I know her mind is sick. And I know that your friends can't help her."

"You don't know that. Maybe they can help her."

He shakes his head. "They don't know what made her the way she is."

"And you do?"

His lips stretch slowly into a smile. "I do. And I know the magic required to heal her."

"I assume you're not going to tell me."

"Not unless you marry me, no."

"I'm not marrying you!" I yell. "It's—I don't even know

where to begin with how utterly insane that is. It's not happening."

"It isn't insane. It makes a lot of sense, actually. In the history of your world—the human world—royal marriages were often used to solidify alliances between countries. This is a similar concept. We would like to ally ourselves with a source of great power, so—"

"So you want to marry it. Wow. That has got to be the least romantic proposal anyone in either world has ever been presented with."

His mouth quirks in amusement. "Nobody said this was about romance, Emerson."

"I'm not marrying you! You could be, like, five hundred years old."

"I'm twenty-one."

"It's still not happening."

"Then your mother will never be healed."

I shake my head. "I don't believe you. I don't think you know what's wrong with her. You'd say anything to get me to do what you want. To get me to stay here in this creepy Unseelie Court."

Aurora speaks up. "Oh, this isn't the Unseelie Court."

"Then where are we?"

"Agree to marry me," Roarke says, "and you'll find out."

"NO!"

A quiet mumble catches my attention. I look down at Dash. His hand twitches, his leg moves a little, and he mumbles again. "That can't have been a very strong stunner spell, Roarke," Aurora says. She rises and moves to stand beside him.

"We should take him back. I don't want him waking up here."

"We can take them both back," Roarke says. "I think this conversation is over. For now, at least."

I look back and forth between the two of them. "Wait. Am I missing something? You're not forcing me to go with you to … I don't know, your palace or wherever?"

"No."

"But … I don't understand. You said your father wants my Griffin Ability."

"He does," Roarke says. "And so do I. But he and I have slightly different views on how, exactly, to possess that power. He's happy to force you into doing his will. To keep you as a prisoner. I, on the other hand, would prefer it if you willingly became a member of our court. Our family."

I wonder again if this guy is genuinely insane. "Why would I ever come willingly?"

As if it's the simplest answer in the world, he says, "To save your mother."

"Come on, Roarke," Aurora says. "Let's go."

"I'd like you to keep this, Emerson," Roarke says, holding out the smallest mirror I've ever seen. It's round and would fit easily into the palm of my hand. "A simple touch of magic, and it will contact me. If you change your mind, you can let me know."

I stare at the mirror without taking it. "I won't be changing my mind."

"Well, if you won't take it …" He steps closer, grips my shoulder so I can't move away, and slips the mirror into the left front pocket of my jeans. He's so close now. So close and so damn sure of himself. He'll have no idea what's hit him when I bring my knee right up into his—

"What's going on?" Dash asks. He sits up, blinks, then jumps quickly to his feet.

"It's okay." I hurry to his side before he can attack anyone. I wouldn't mind seeing Roarke flat on the ground, but right now it's probably more important to get out of here. "These friendly people were just about to let us go," I say to Dash. "I'll explain everything when we get back."

"Roarke? Aurora?" a deep voice calls from beyond the hedge on our right.

"Dammit," Roarke mutters. "Go that way," he says to us, pointing in the other direction. "Hide."

I don't need to be told twice. I grab Dash's arm, and together we run. Past hedges and rose bushes and through the rising wisps of smoke. The garden is endless, with the same features repeating over and over and the edges of my vision remaining hazy. Eventually, Dash tugs me to a stop. Shadow-black smoke dances and curls around us. He swats at it. "You have a *lot* of explaining to do, Em," he pants. "But let's get the hell out of here first." He pats his jacket, finds his stylus, and bends down to write on the ground.

Nothing happens.

"What the fffffudge-pixie? Why isn't it working?"

"What the *what*? Okay, when we're done panicking, we're going to have a serious conversation about your extremely weird curse words."

"Em! Why can't I open the faerie paths?"

"I—I don't know. We didn't actually get here through the

faerie paths. There was a bright flash, and then we arrived."

"That's very strange." Dash turns slowly, looking around. "I don't even know if we're in our world."

Something moves against one of the hedges. An unnatural shape, twisting and stretching and pulling away from the leaves. "Dash." Sick terror coalesces in my stomach. I reach for his hand and grip it tightly. "What is that?"

I hear his intake of breath the moment he sees it. "What the ..." His hand tightens around mine. He pulls me closer against his side. The ghostly shape—a being so black it could be made of the darkness of the faerie paths—billows and shifts and dives toward us.

Dash's hand flies up. Bright sparks shoot away from him, heading straight for the shadow creature. Unfortunately, the magic passes right through the shifting darkness and out the other side, as if this being is made of nothing.

"Run!" We take off again, faster than before, weaving and dodging through this endless, smoke-mist garden. I throw a look over my shoulder, and the creature is high in the air, bigger and closer. Then it swoops down, becoming a twisting snake-like thing gliding over the grass in pursuit of us. "Crap oh crap oh crap," I gasp, looking forward and forcing my legs to move faster. "Wait, is that a door?" Off to the left, in the center of another hedge, I see an open arched doorway and light beyond it.

"Yes." Dash swerves toward it. "Dammit, this place makes no sense."

"I know, just run!" My feet slam the grass. My arms pump against the air. We're almost there when an icy coldness slithers over my shoulder. I jerk away as a desperate scream breaks free from my throat. We hurtle through the doorway and Dash swings his arm around, slamming the door shut with a burst of magic and bringing us to a skidding halt on a polished wooden floor.

I spin around, facing the door while backing away from it. My chest heaves as I catch my breath. My heart slams repeatedly against the inside of my ribcage. "Are you okay?" Dash pants. My hand is still clamped tightly around his, and there's no chance in hell of me letting go right now. He feels like my only anchor in this nightmarish world that could lift me up and whip me away at any moment.

"I ... I think so. Are you okay?"

"I don't know," he says. "I'm starting to wonder if I'm still unconscious and stuck in a dream."

"A nightmare is more like it." When the door remains firmly closed, I risk moving my eyes away from it. I look up, but there's nothing above us. At least, if there is a ceiling, it's so high up I can't see it. The wooden floor and the wall on either side of the arched door extend forever on both sides. I turn to look behind me—and realize there's a large opening in the air. "Dash." I point to the piece of land and the ocean beyond it. "Do you see that?"

Dash steps around me, not letting go of my hand. He leans forward, staring intently. "That's ... Holy shizmonkey. That's Velazar Island. The part with the monument. You can see the monument at the bottom edge there. Em, this ..." His eyes trace around the whole of the opening. "This is the tear in the veil."

It makes no sense to me at all that we've ended up here, but if that's our world on the other side of this hole, then ... "Can we get through it?"

"I hope so." He pulls me forward. We reach the opening, and when nothing holds us back, we keep going. One foot onto the monument. Then another. I let go of Dash's hand as he jumps down. I quickly follow him.

With two feet safely on the ground in a world of genuine color and bright, midday sun, I look out at the ocean. Vast and magnificent. Waves surging forward. More powerful and awe-inspiring than I could have imagined.

"Okay *that* makes no sense," Dash says.

I look back to see what he's talking about. On the other side of the gaping hole in the air, instead of an arched door and a polished floor, I see a field and blue sky. "But ... that isn't where we just came from."

"No," Dash murmurs. "We were somewhere else entirely. Somewhere ... I don't know. In between here and there?"

"Hey! What are you doing here?" A spark of magic whizzes past us. Two guardians come running out from behind the monument. I duck down and twist out of the way as Dash opens a doorway to the faerie paths. I dive into it with him, clearing my mind and trusting him to take us somewhere safe.

CHAPTER TWENTY-SEVEN

"WHY ARE WE IN CHELSEA'S BACKYARD?" I ASK THE MOMENT the darkness clears and I find myself on crunchy, half-dead grass.

"We need that last box," Dash says. "The one with the files. We might still find something useful in there. We can take it back to the oasis and *then*—" he runs a hand through his hair "—then we can try to figure out what the heck we just ran from and where we were."

"And what an Unseelie prince and princess have to do with any of it."

Dash's mouth drops open. "Did you say—"

"I did."

"Wow. So that's why she tried to help you escape from the Guild. She wanted to take you to the Unseelies. Wait, but why did they let you go so easily now?"

I sigh. "I'll explain later."

"Hey, there you guys are," a familiar voice says. Violet walks around the side of the house toward us. "I got here a few minutes ago and found a bit of a mess in the bedroom with all those boxes. I tried to find both of you, and for some reason my Griffin Ability came up with nothing, which was a little alarming. So I'm glad to see you're safe."

"You couldn't find us?" Dash asks. He looks at me. "We can add that to the list of seriously weird things about that creepy garden."

Violet stops in front of us. "What are you talking about? Where were you?"

"We can explain back at the oasis," I tell her. "We just want to get one of those boxes from inside and take it with us."

"Okay," she says slowly. Concern tightens her features, but then she breathes in, appearing to shake it off. "Em, look what I've got." She holds up a vial with a cork stopper. "Ana gave it to me this morning. Ready to start testing that Griffin Ability?"

A flare of excitement lights up inside me. "Yes. Definitely."

Dash steps away. "I'll go get the—" He stops, frowning as he looks around at the fence. Something rustles beyond it, followed by the muted sound of footsteps on grass. "Was someone watching us?" he asks. He walks past me, pulls himself up into the spindly tree in the corner of the garden, and looks over the fence. "Well, if someone was watching us, they're gone now."

"We're glamoured anyway," Violet says as Dash jumps down, "so it doesn't matter."

"You guys might be," I say, "but I'm probably not. I doubt my glamour's working. I probably look like I'm standing here talking to myself." Which, I realize, will convince anyone watching me that I've finally gone off the deep end just like everyone in Stanmeade thought I would.

"Let's get that box," Violet says. "We can go inside through the paths. I think your aunt is in the kitchen making coffee or tea or something."

"Ah, lovely, you're still here."

I whip back around at the sound of the voice. It's her, the woman in the silver cloak, hurrying out of the faerie paths and into Chelsea's backyard. The vial of elixir slips from Violet's fingers as she sweeps her hands up and around. A slight ripple in the air confirms that a shield has formed around us. "Who are you?" she asks. Beside her, Dash reaches into the air. A glittering sword appears in one hand, and a whip in the other.

The woman lowers her hood, revealing a black mask covering most of her face. All I see are her lips and eyes. "You can call me Ada," she says. "And then you can hand Em over."

"Not happening," Violet says.

Then, as if this situation needed an additional complication, the back door swings open and Chelsea comes running out. "Emerson, where the hell have you been?" she shouts. Her narrowed eyes stare only at me, which confirms my suspicion that I'm the only one here without a glamour. Then abruptly, her expression changes. Her eyes widen, watching me with a mixture of fear and confusion. As if she knows she's supposed to be afraid of me now but can't remember why. She takes a few careful steps back. Her eyes dart down to the phone in her hand as she begins tapping the screen. "Just … stay calm, okay? I don't want any trouble."

"Oh, what a waste of time," Ada says. In a few quick strides, she's in front of Chelsea. She touches her shoulder—

"No!" Violet shouts. She drops the shield.

—and Chelsea becomes a statue of glass. A bow and arrow blaze into existence in Violet's outstretched arms. Ada raises her leg and kicks Chelsea. Then she twists out of the way, the arrow zooms past her, and Chelsea strikes the ground, shattering into countless glass shards.

I gasp and push both hands into my hair. "That didn't just happen," I whisper.

The back door bangs again, and this time it's Georgia running out. "Mom!" she screams.

"Stop!" Violet yells as Ada turns to Georgia. Violet lunges forward just as Dash's whip lashes out. The whip encircles Ada's wrist and Violet leaps onto her back. The two of them tumble to the ground, but it's too late. Glass rushes up Georgia's body, solidifying her into a statue almost instantly.

"Vi, watch out!" Dash yells, running to Violet's aid. Violet rolls away from Ada and jumps to her feet. Ada swings her leg around, knocking Georgia to the ground. She shatters apart just like her mother.

I tug at my hair, swearing repeatedly, guilt and terror threatening to consume me, because I know *this is all happening because of me.* Ada dodges Violet and Dash's magic and spins around. Her fingertips graze Violet's arm before flashing out and striking Dash's hand.

"No, no, NO!" I yell, but again, it's too late. Glass consumes them, turning them to motionless, faceted statues. Ada raises her leg. "Stop! Just stop! I'll do whatever you want!"

She pauses. Lowers her foot to the ground. "You know it's too late for them, right? There's no coming back from this."

I drop onto my knees, my shaking legs no longer able to hold me up. "What do you want? My Griffin Ability? That's fine. I'll go with you. I—I don't know how to make it work, but I'll try. Just please, don't kill them."

She barks out a laugh. "I think they're dead already, Em."

"Tell me what you want from me," I beg.

Ada steps away from Violet and Dash, which leaves me almost wilting with relief. *It's hard to kill a faerie,* Violet told me. *Our magic can help us survive a great many things that would kill a human.* I can still see her and Dash. They're solid glass, but they're still there. As long as they aren't shattered into a million pieces, there's hope for them.

"You know," Ada says, facing me with her hands on her hips, "I always wondered if you might have a Griffin Ability hiding within you. And if you did, I wondered if it might ever make itself known, or if it would remain blocked forever, along with the rest of your magic." She tilts her head to the side, examining me. "You don't know how to use it though, do you. You would have stopped me already if you did."

It takes a few moments for the full meaning of her words to sink in. "You ... wait. You know who I am?"

"I've known you almost as long as you've been alive, Em. That's why I was here a few days ago, checking in with someone. The someone who's been watching you for me.

Imagine if I'd come a few hours later," she adds with a wicked grin. "That someone would have had a *far* more interesting update for me."

This is getting freakier by the second. "Someone's been— Who? Was it that man you killed? The one I saw you turn to glass?"

"No, no. That was just someone who followed me here. Someone who thought he could ambush and kill me." She chuckles. "It didn't take much effort to get rid of him."

I shudder at how easily she speaks about killing people. "Then who? And how do you know me? Who—*what* am I? And what the hell do you want from me?"

She gives me a pitying smile as she moves closer. "I know all this attention has probably gone to your head, so it might come as a surprise to hear that I don't actually want *you*."

"Y-you don't?"

"No. At least not yet. I want your mother."

Your mother.

A chill races across my skin. I swallow past the nausea rising up my throat. "Why? That makes no sense."

"It doesn't have to make sense to you, Em. Just tell me where she is."

I slowly shake my head. "You can't have her."

Ada crouches down in front of me. "Would you prefer to watch this town become consumed by broken glass? Would you like to watch your friends fracture and shatter and die?"

"Of course I don't want that."

"Then you simply need to tell me where your mother is.

I'm not going to hurt her. Well, perhaps I should rephrase that. I'm not going to *kill* her. I'm just going to do something a little bit ... irreversible."

My face is wet with all the tears I don't usually allow to fall. "I can't."

"Yes you can."

"I can't, I can't," I wail, covering my face with my hands. "How can you ask me to do this? She's my *mother*. I love her more than anything."

"Then you have left me no choice."

I lower my hands to see her leaning forward. She presses her fingers into the earth. "What are you doing?"

She doesn't answer. Where her fingers meet the earth, glass begins spreading slowly outwards. Blades of grass harden, fracture, and break apart. I jump up and back away from the encroaching splinters. Meanwhile, Ada has moved to the side of the house. She flattens her palm against the wall, and glass spreads out around her hand.

"Wait, please stop. You don't have to do this."

"You're forcing me to do this, Em. As long as you don't tell me what I want to know, this magic will keep spreading, and it will fracture everything in its path. This town will soon be nothing but shattered glass."

I look desperately around. The glass inches closer to Violet and Dash. If it reaches them, they'll shatter apart. I won't get a chance to see if they're still alive beneath their hardened glass shells. I let out a wordless cry, covering my face again. This all comes down to one impossible choice: who do I save? Mom? Or Violet, Dash and the rest of Stanmeade? "Don't make me choose," I moan. I peek through my fingers. The glass shards have almost reached Violet. They're barely a foot away from the edge of her boot.

Inching closer.

And closer.

And I can't give up my own mother, but what about *all these people who are going to die*?

"Okay stop! I'll tell you." Misery and self-loathing crack my heart open. "She's at White Cedars. Just make it stop, please!"

"White Cedars," Ada repeats. "Thank you, dear Em." She walks past me to the fence and opens a doorway to the faerie paths.

"Wait. You need to stop the glass."

"To be honest, Em, I've never liked this town. I always felt a little sorry for you having to live here."

"What? No! Are you seriously going to destroy an entire town and everyone in it?"

"I don't know. I guess we'll see how far the magic gets." She walks into the paths and looks back over her shoulder. "You can run and save yourself, or sit here and let the glass crack you apart like everyone else. It's your choice. Personally, I'd prefer it if you save yourself. I might one day have a use for you if you get that ability under control." She laughs. "And how deliciously ironic it would be if you were the one who helped me see the revenge plan through."

With a burst of anger, I launch myself after her. If I can get into the paths—if I can get to Mom before Ada does—

But the darkness closes up. The fence reappears, and I crash into it. Pain flares through my shoulder, my arm, and I slide down to the ground, groaning out loud. I clutch my shoulder while thoughts of how utterly useless I am beat against the inside of my head. I possess a power that people would kill to get their hands on, but I can't—

The vial.

The elixir that will stimulate my Griffin Ability.

I jump up, leap across the patches of glass, and search for the vial Violet dropped. It must be on the grass somewhere. And once I've taken this elixir, my ability will *stay* on, right? Then I can yell out more than one command.

The creaking, screeching sound of the house beginning to fall apart startles me. I look across at Violet. The glass has almost reached her boot. "No," I whisper. My eyes return to their desperate search of the ground as my brain plays through all the things I need to shout out.

Daniela Clarke, you are invisible. No one can find you or hurt you or kill you.

Glass, reverse your magic. Stop moving, stop shattering, stop killing.

Violet and Dash, you are not made of glass. Return to your original forms.

Finally, I spot the vial. It's near the base of the tree Dash climbed, pieces of glass just about touching it. I jump over more glass, race toward it, drop down, reach for it—but Ada's magic has touched it. Shards stab into it, splintering and crushing it, and I dare not touch it for fear that her magic will spread into me.

The elixir is gone.

A great sob rips through my chest. I stand and step back,

watching the unstoppable glass magic. It's reached Violet's boot now, splintering along the front edge. I can't save her, and I can't save Mom. As more tears course down my cheeks, I squeeze my eyes shut. I open my mouth and pour all the pain from the last five years into one aching scream. I scream until I can't breathe anymore.

And then—hope.

I sense that shiver, that brief pulse of power rushing through me, and I have a split second to decide: save Mom—or save everyone here. My words come tumbling out in a desperate rush. "Glass magic, you have no power! Reverse, vanish, return everything and everyone to the way they were before and restore all—" The deep reverberation in my voice is gone by the time I reach the word 'restore,' but I think I uttered enough of the command.

I look around, holding my breath, waiting for my power to take effect.

The glass stops moving. Slowly, it sinks into the ground, leaving the lawn as it was before. Pieces of Chelsea and Georgia rush back together and, as utterly impossible as it seems, my aunt and cousin begin moving, groaning, sitting up. The broken side of the house pieces itself back together like a demolition scene in reverse. And Violet and Dash—

They gasp for air, sucking in great deep breaths of it as the glass vanishes from around their bodies. "Oh thank goodness." I rush across the yard toward them.

"What just—"

"Take me to White Cedars! Please, it's urgent. Ada went there to get Mom."

Violet turns swiftly to the wall and writes against it. "Dash, get back to the oasis. Tell Ryn and Chase what's happened. I'll take Em." I grasp her hand and rush into the darkness with her.

We're still running when we come out the other side on the lawn in front of White Cedars Healing Institute.

"I know where her room is," I say as we race past the reception area, healers shouting after us. Along the corridor, turn, another corridor. I run into her room, past a pile of glass on the floor, and tug the curtain back. "She's still here," I say, relief flooding my body. "She's here, but ..." I look at the floor, at the sharp glass pieces. "But Ada was here too. Mom?" I turn back to her and shake her arm. "Mom, wake up." But she doesn't stir, and I can't help hearing Ada's voice in my head: *I'm just going to do something a little bit ... irreversible.*

Healers rush in then, and we're forced to wait outside. They confirm that Mom's still alive, but that's all they say before they shut Mom's door and one of them leads us back to the waiting area. Last night, I found the gentle lighting, soft chairs and herbal scents comforting, but none of it helps today. Nothing can comfort me when I'm convinced there's something terribly wrong with Mom.

"Tell me what happened after Dash and I were turned to glass," Violet says gently. Her words remind me abruptly that just minutes ago she was essentially dead. She was a non-moving, non-breathing statue, all because she got involved with me and my mother. But instead of freaking out about it, she's now comforting *me.*

I push my guilt down and tell her everything. The glass

spreading everywhere, the vial of elixir breaking, Ada forcing me to choose between Mom and everyone else. "I failed," I whisper to her when I'm done.

She wraps both arms around me and hugs me tightly, which only intensifies my guilt. "You saved a whole town full of people, Em." She pulls back and looks intently at me. "Your cousin and aunt should be—*were*—dead. Your magic saved them. That isn't a failure. That's ..."

A scary kind of power, I think to myself. Out loud, I say, "But I failed my mother."

Violet, of course, tries to convince me otherwise, but I know the truth. I gave my own mother up to a magical being who wanted to hurt her in some way. After all my promises that I'd make a better life for the two of us. And that means I failed her.

Finally, one of the healers returns to the waiting area. "Is she alive?" I ask immediately, jumping to my feet.

"Yes." The healer, a petite woman with a long braid hanging over one shoulder, gestures for me to sit. "But she appears to be in a deep state of unconsciousness."

"How? Why? What happened to her?"

"We're not certain. The healer who was in the room at the time was attacked and ..." She takes a deep breath. "Well, we've all read about the glass faerie in the news. And you saw what was on the floor."

I nod, realizing that this woman obviously knew the healer Ada killed. "I know. I'm sorry. But isn't there any way you can figure out what happened to her? What would put her into a coma so quickly?"

"There are several possibilities. We've tested for all of them and have ruled them all out."

"Okay, so?" I prompt. "Now what?"

"Well …" The healer looks from me to Violet and back again. "Since there isn't anything else we can do for her at the moment, we'd like to suggest that she might be more comfortable—and safer—if she stayed at home. If she ever wakes up, you can bring her back."

"*If* she ever wakes up? Did you just say *if?*"

"Thank you," Violet rushes to say before the healer can respond. "That sounds like a good idea. I think it would be safer for her to stay with us than to remain here."

The healer nods and stands. "I'll organize the paperwork."

Once she's left the room, Violet says, "Em, we will fix this. You can try using your Griffin Ability and tell her to wake up. If that doesn't work, we'll find something else. I don't know how, but we will. We'll do all the research we can, and when we eventually discover the spell that put her into a coma, we'll be able to get her out of it."

"And if her mind is still sick when she wakes up?"

"Then we'll figure that out too." Her fingers wrap around my hand and squeeze it. She smiles. "Everything will be okay in the end."

I manage to return the smile, because I've realized there is another way for Mom to be okay in the end. A backup plan. A plan Violet would never approve of …

CHAPTER TWENTY-EIGHT

SEVERAL HOURS LATER, I FINISH TUCKING MOM INTO BED in a room of her own at the oasis. I smooth her dark hair back off her forehead, then sit in the chair beside the bed for a while, thinking of all the questions I haven't been able to ask her yet. And all the new questions that have been added to my mental list since this morning. Who is Ada, and how does she know Mom? Why did she want to put Mom into a permanent coma?

Something a little bit ... irreversible.

I push the memory of Ada's words away. I don't want to accept that Mom will never wake up, but it's hard to ignore the facts: Ana prepared more elixir for me this afternoon, and it stimulated my Griffin Ability long enough to tell Mom to wake up—but she didn't respond. It seems that my magical, resonating voice, which had the power to piece two people back together and bring them to life today, somehow cannot wake my mother.

Something a little bit ... irreversible.

If the healers don't know what kind of magic has put Mom into a permanent sleep, then it must be something completely different. Something more sinister. Something that those who ignore laws and play around with dark magic might know about.

And that's where the backup plan comes in.

I stand and walk to the box in the corner of the room. The box Dash went back for while I was at the healing institute with Mom. I was hopeful it might still contain something useful, but a quick look earlier through the remaining files revealed nothing.

I open the box, push my hand down past the files, and feel for the pink crystal flower I dropped in here. After finding it, I cross the room and leave it on the bedside table. It's so small it looks ridiculous sitting there on its own, but I know Mom would like the fact that it's there.

After watching her a little while longer, I kiss her cheek and leave the room, closing the door gently behind me.

* * *

"Come see, come see!" Jack grabs my hand as I head downstairs. "Merrick and Junie added more stuff inside the dome while you were gone." He tugs me all the way down to the bottom of the tree.

"Ah, there she is," Dash says as I step onto the grass. "How are you doing?"

I shrug. "Okay, I guess. You?"

"Feeling better now that I'm no longer a glass statue."

"You know," I say to him, "glass statues are far quieter and less annoying than certain people."

"Ah, come on, you would have missed me if I hadn't made it."

I allow myself a smile. "Maybe."

"Well, anyway, I think you're going to like the latest addition to the oasis."

"Don't tell her!" Jack says. "She has to see first otherwise it ruins the surprise."

The three of us walk together, the conversation remaining light as Jack tells us what he's currently learning at school. I notice Dash sneaking the occasional glance my way, probably trying to figure out if I really am okay.

"Okay, wait," Jack says. "Stop here." We're almost past the orchard, which is illuminated this evening with tiny golden glow-bugs and pink-orange light. "We should blindfold her."

I raise an eyebrow. "Did you blindfold everyone who's come to see this new addition?"

"Yes. Okay, not everyone," Jack admits. "But some people."

"How about if I just close my eyes?"

Jack tilts his head to the side. "Will you promise not to open them?"

"Yes. But you have to promise not to let me trip over anything."

"Yes, of course." He loops his arm through mine, and I close my eyes.

"No peeking," Dash says.

After another minute or so of walking, Jack brings me to a halt. I can smell and hear something that makes me suspicious, but I can't possibly be right. "Okay, you ready?" Jack says. "Open your eyes."

So I do. Goosebumps race across my skin at the sight of the pale stretch of sand and the gentle sunset-colored waves tumbling onto it.

"Isn't it awesome?" Jack says. "We have a beach!"

I blink against the sheen of moisture forming over my eyes. "It's amazing." He takes off across the sand, leaps into the shallow waves, and kicks water into the air.

Dash pushes his hands into his pockets. "Merrick was talking a few days ago about what to add next, and I remembered you looking out the window at the halfway house and asking about the ocean. So I told him it would be cool to have a beach and a little piece of the ocean here."

I bite my lip to get my silly emotions under control, then say, "Today was the first time I saw it in real life. On the island. And that was only for a moment, so it's amazing to have it right here."

"Oh. Really?" Dash faces me. "So that's why you were asking about it that day. We should go see the real thing then. I can take you right now, if you want. Just gotta make sure we aren't ambushed by anyone else who wants to get their evil talons into you."

"No," I say with a smile. "This is perfect for now."

"Hey," a voice calls behind us. Ryn walks onto the sand, followed by Violet and a floating basket. "What do you think of our little bit of the sea?"

"I love it," I tell him.

"We thought we'd have a beach picnic for dinner," Violet says, gesturing to the floating basket. It lands neatly on the sand, and the folded blanket on top rises and spreads itself out beside the basket. We sit while Violet unpacks the food and Jack continues jumping and splashing in the water. Calla and Chase join us a few minutes later, spreading their own blanket next to ours.

We eat our picnic dinner as the sun slowly disappears. At some point, Bandit and Filigree crawl out of the picnic basket in mouse form and wait patiently for some food. Well, Filigree waits patiently; Bandit does a lot of jumping around in between his waiting.

When it's almost too dark to see, floating lanterns appear all the way along the beach. Though I notice each of the adults watching me at some point throughout the evening, no one asks any questions about earlier or proposes any wild theories about Mom or the mysterious glass faerie Ada. It's as if there's an unspoken agreement that tonight isn't for rehashing the day's events. Tonight is for enjoying the beach, appreciating delicious fruits and snacks I've never tasted before, chasing Jack along the sand, and coming up with ideas for what to add next to the oasis.

I soak it all in, knowing this evening is both a first and a last for me.

"Em!" Jack drops down beside me some time after our

meal. "Did I tell you about the new dance we learned this morning?"

"Um, I think you told me about everything else you learned today. I'm not sure you mentioned a dance. Do you have regular dance classes here?"

"We all learn the traditional faerie dances when we're in junior school," Dash explains. "Vi and Ryn didn't want the kids who live here to miss out, so dancing is included in the lessons."

"Can I teach you?" Jack asks me. "Then you can practice with me."

"Oh. Um, okay." Dancing isn't my thing, but I suppose I'll give it a go if it'll make Jack happy. I walk with him a few paces away from the blankets, then face him and take hold of his hands.

"Okay, so you step forward like this. Yes, with that foot first. And then you step back. And our hands come together like this."

"Okay."

"So we repeat that four times, and then we turn around each other like this."

Somewhere behind me, music begins playing. Curious to know where it's coming from, I look over my shoulder and see Ryn urging a glass ball into the air. Colorful lights inside the ball flicker in time to the music, which tells me that's where the music must be coming from. "Amazing," I murmur. "What is that?"

"Em, you're not concentrating," Jack complains.

"Right, sorry."

He demonstrates the next move for me, but I'm finding it hard to keep up. "You know, I hate to say it, Jack, but I think the kind of dancing we do in the human world—where we just sway from side to side—is a whole lot easier. See, you put your arms around my waist—" I move his arms into place "—and I put my arms around your shoulders, and we sway."

"That's super boring. And you're too tall."

"True, but I'm too tall for your dance too."

"You just need a taller partner," Dash says, moving to my side and holding his hand out toward me.

"Oh. No. Thank you. I'm not really into dancing. And … um … I was going to go to bed now anyway."

"So early?" he asks. "Come on, just until the end of the song. We can do your boring swaying thing." He gives me his charming smile, and I see a hint of the Dash all those girls fall over themselves for.

"Fine. Just don't stand on my toes."

"With boring swaying, my dear Emerson, I doubt that will be a problem."

I put my hands around his neck. His arms slide around my waist and pull me closer. I rest my chin on his shoulder, which feels a bit strange, but also kinda nice. We step slowly from side to side, a little more than just a swaying motion, but way simpler than whatever Jack was trying to teach me.

"Em," Dash says quietly. "Emmy. I'm really sorry. About your mom. But at least she's here now. And we'll find a way to heal her. We will. I've been looking out for you ever since I screwed up all those years ago, and I won't stop now. Whatever I can do to help, I'll do it. She'll get better, and you can both

291

stay here, and the two of you will finally have the life you've always promised her."

My eyes travel across the scene, and my heart breaks as I realize that everything I've ever wanted is right here—and that I will never have it. Tears prick my eyes, my throat aches, and suddenly I can't speak. I bite my lip, harder and harder until the tears recede and I can breathe again.

When the song is over, I don't leave immediately. I sit with everyone for a while longer. I laugh at Dash's terrible jokes and smile at Jack's antics. Then I head back to the giant trees along with everyone else. I cheerfully say goodnight and climb up to my room as if nothing is different. As if my chest isn't aching. As if I haven't just said goodbye.

CHAPTER TWENTY-NINE

I OPEN THE WARDROBE, AND INSTEAD OF REACHING FOR pajamas, I pull out the warmest jacket I can find. I don't know how cold it is where I'm going, so it's best to be prepared. "Sorry, Bandit," I say to the wolf cub sleeping on the chair in the corner, "but you won't be coming with me this time. It's safer for you to stay here."

I remove my T-shirt and grab a clean one off the top of the pile—just as I hear footsteps outside my door. "Hey, Em." It's Calla's voice. The door clicks open. "I wanted to ask you if— Oh, I'm sorry."

"No, it's fine," I say with a nervous laugh, turning away as I fumble with the T-shirt.

"I'm sorry, I should have knocked."

"No, no. It's my fault for getting changed without closing the door properly. I didn't think." I pull the T-shirt over my head before turning to face her. But instead of a smile, I find her staring at me, her face devoid of color. "What's wrong? Are you okay?" She can't possibly know what I'm about to do, can she?

"I …" Her hand grasps the doorframe, and she grips it tightly, as if it's the only thing keeping her upright.

"Calla?" I take an uncertain step toward her.

She closes her eyes, shakes her head, and lets out a faint laugh. "I'm sorry." She opens her eyes, blinks, and gives me a half-smile. "I must have had more to drink than I thought. Just a dizzy moment. That's all."

"Um, okay."

"Anyway." She clears her throat. "I just, uh, came up here to ask you if you want to go running around the edge of the oasis with us early in the morning."

"Oh. Actually, I think I'd rather sleep in tomorrow. It's been, you know … quite a day."

She nods, still looking at me a little oddly. "Yeah. Definitely."

"Um, okay. Well, goodnight."

"Night. Hey, Em?" I look up. "That's a pretty tattoo on your shoulder. I didn't notice it before."

"Oh, it isn't a tattoo. Needles freak me out." I reach up and touch my left shoulder. "It's actually a birthmark. My clothes usually cover it, so that's probably why you haven't seen it before."

She nods, gripping the door again, and I start to wonder if

whatever she's drunk tonight might have had its origin in the human realm. "How interesting," she says faintly. "It looks just like a flower."

"Yes, it does." I frown. "Are you sure you're okay?"

"Definitely." She smiles. "Sleep tight, okay?"

I nod, feeling guilty for lying to her. "You too."

She closes the door. Bandit, watching curiously from the chair, lowers his head and watches me through half-closed eyes. Once I'm sure Calla's gone, I slip my hand into my left front pocket and take out the mirror.

* * *

I feel bad for stealing a stylus from Ryn and Vi's kitchen, but I don't have much of a choice since I don't have my own. I don't pass anyone on my way down the stairs, or when I'm walking across the grass. It's almost too easy to slip through the dome layer and into the desert.

I write the faerie paths spell into the sand several times without it working. I don't lose my patience, though. Seeing the words glow this morning gave me confidence that I'm almost there with this faerie paths thing. I try yet again—and excitement races through me at the sight of a dark space opening up. I slide into it, whispering the name I was given.

I'm greeted on the other side by the scene I was told to expect: a natural rock pool in a forest clearing with beams of afternoon light shining through the nearby trees.

"Emerson," a voice says from behind me. "I was a little surprised to hear back from you so soon. You seemed adamant you wouldn't be changing your mind."

I turn to face Roarke. "Circumstances change. I've decided I might be willing to believe that you can help my mother."

He folds his arms across his chest. "Interesting."

"There's just one thing. I'm going to require proof before I accept your proposal. Proof that you know what's wrong with my mother and can fix her."

"That might be difficult," he says, "considering I won't be telling you anything until after we're married."

"But she needs help now. I'll … sign a contract or something. A contract saying that I agree to marry you if you can first heal her."

"A contract?" He laughs. "The kind of contract you're referring to doesn't mean much in this world. What if I heal your mother, and then you decide not to follow through?"

"What if I marry you and then you decide not to heal my mother?"

A hint of amusement touches his lips. "I suppose one of us is going to have to learn to trust the other."

"Well then. I look forward to earning your trust." Because I certainly don't plan to marry this Unseelie Prince without first seeing my mother healthy. "Did you bring the magical device you spoke about?"

"Yes." Roarke reaches inside his long coat and produces a small coin-shaped item. He steps closer and brushes aside the hair behind my ear. It's unsettling having him stand so close, but I pretend it doesn't bother me. He presses the coin to the skin behind my ear, and when he pulls his hand away, the coin remains. I raise my fingers and gently touch it, making sure it doesn't move. "You're certain no one will be able to find me while I'm wearing this? I don't want anyone … interfering with our arrangement."

"Completely certain. The Unseelie Court has been making use of items like this for a very long time."

I let out a slow breath. "Okay then. I guess I'm ready to go with you."

LOOK OUT FOR THE
NEXT BOOK IN THE
CREEPY HOLLOW SERIES!

FIND MORE CREEPY HOLLOW
CONTENT ONLINE
www.creepyhollowbooks.com

ACKNOWLEDGEMENTS

THANK YOU …

To God, for every blessing, and for getting me to the end of another book.

To Jo Mundell, for your proofreading eyes.

To those who read early copies and take the time to write reviews (and for your extra proofreading eyes!).

To all the Creepy Hollow fans out there who look forward with great enthusiasm to every new book in this series.

And to Kyle, for your unending support and encouragement.

Rachel Morgan spent a good deal of her childhood living
in a fantasy land of her own making, crafting endless stories of
make-believe and occasionally writing some of them down.
After completing a degree in genetics and discovering
she still wasn't grown-up enough for a 'real' job, she decided
to return to those story worlds still spinning around her
imagination. These days she spends much of her time
immersed in fantasy land once more, writing fiction
for young adults and those young at heart.

Rachel lives in Cape Town with her husband and
three miniature dachshunds. She is the author of the
bestselling Creepy Hollow series and the sweet
contemporary romance Trouble series.

www.rachel-morgan.com

r

Made in the USA
Columbia, SC
01 May 2020

95287867R00183